I read a book primarily for it
novel does not disappoint. . .
her deliberate language, pulling one weft of story on top of
another, threading back and forth through time in ways that
are heartbreaking, hope offering, and real. In the end, you hold
a colorful orb of story that is crafted with deliberate attention to
the female story, told through the lens of a poet.

—Ashley Mae Hoiland,
author of *A New Constellation* and
One Hundred Birds Taught Me to Fly

In the tradition of the finest literary fiction of the American
West, Twila Newey weaves together the frailty and warmth of
family ties with the mountain landscape's casual cruelty and
transcendent beauty. Four bereaved sisters face the limits and
comforts of their faith in one another and in their religious community, and in the process illuminate the frank humor, dangers,
and graces of Utah women's lives in ways that will delight and
haunt readers long afterward.

—Therese Doucet,
author of *Prisoner of the Castle of Enlightenment*

Sylvia is a masterpiece. It is warm and real and breathes with
life in its complexity and beauty. I have rarely encountered an
author with such an ability to paint the human heart as well as
she paints the landscape of the Wasatch Mountains near Provo,

Utah. Newey shows us the intertangled roots of families that grow like aspens in their connectedness and their majesty on the mountainside. Twila's writing is full of possibility, richness, and a grace that embraces the reader and gives us all a sense of hope amidst the messiness of our lives.

—Steve Evans,
founder of ByCommonConsent.com

Twila Newey's writing is as delicate as dreaming and as enduring as myth. In *Sylvia*, she reveals a family's shifting landscape as its sisters, daughters, and mothers strive to see and accept one another through the lens of grief. With an ear for language and a subtle understanding of the grace and plenitude of loss, Newey is a writer to watch.

—Andrea Bobotis,
author of *The Last List of Miss Judith Kratt*

sylvia

BY COMMON CONSENT PRESS is a non-profit publisher dedicated to producing affordable, high-quality books that help define and shape the Latter-day Saint experience. BCC Press publishes books that address all aspects of Mormon life. Our mission includes finding manuscripts that will contribute to the lives of thoughtful Latter-day Saints, mentoring authors and nurturing projects to completion, and distributing important books to the Mormon audience at the lowest possible cost.

sylvia

TWILA NEWEY

BCC
PRESS

For information contact
By Common Consent Press
4062 S. Evelyn Dr.
Salt Lake City, UT 84124-2250

Cover design: D Christian Harrison
Book design: Andrew Heiss

www.bccpress.org
ISBN-13: 978-1-948218-33-4

10 9 8 7 6 5 4 3 2 1

For
My mother, Janice Dyer Newey, for all the bedtime novels
she read me, one chapter at a time, and my sisters,
Von, Jeanie, Melody, and Syl, who've cared for,
and saved me more times than I can count.

Prologue: Eden

They watched her from the large back seat. She laid one bare arm on the edge of the car window and spread the other across the front seat of the station wagon until her fingertips touched his shoulder. His smile in the rear-view mirror. The side of her face, the slide of her nose and line of her jaw, the bandanna she wore to hold back her hair, fluttered in the breeze. Their eight hands moved toward the two available windows. Small and determined they turned and turned the silver cranks until their faces felt the rush of cool air and they smelled the melting snow. They knelt by the doors on either side and leaned into the wind, felt it catch their hair. Long branches flew past, covered in green buds. The branches stretched over the full stream.

The road followed the stream, curved snakelike past Sundance, past the larger cabins that were just beginning to pop up along the road like looming wooden skeletons. It climbed beyond the granite wall and moved away from the rush of water into silent groves of aspen, wide blue sky in relief behind the still bare branches. The station wagon turned left off the main road onto a flat dirt drive. In the summer, when the air was hot and the heat became visible vibrations that slithered across the asphalt, when the grass beneath the aspen had turned to brittle gold, they would have to roll up the windows because of the dust. But it wasn't summer. The ground was still wet.

Her girls saw the familiar face of the two-story A-frame, mostly large windows, what little wooden shake there was painted gray to hide inevitable weathering. The door she repainted every year to match the color of new aspen leaves, green with light. The car stopped in front of the porch and a tangle of small girl limbs tumbled from the back doors straightening into four individual bodies, stretching into a moving line as they ran toward a narrow trail that led into the grove. They knew it was useless. This was an annual dance. A ritual. Every year they ran for the trail, and every year he yelled,

"Stop! Work before play."

She rubbed the top of their heads as they walked back to the car, their shoulders slumped. They stood in a line. She handed them each a paper bag full of food, toilet paper, clean linens. They grumbled as they carried them into the cabin. The work of preparing the cabin for summer when they would sleep and play here, barefoot with un-brushed hair and sunburnt knees. In the summer it would be mostly them and her, exploring trails or playing in the meadow, the tremulous shade of the aspen along the edges of everything. He came and joined them on weekends, Friday evening through Monday morning. He would muss their hair and plant himself in his large chair in the living room with his books full of equations laid open across his lap. More sat stacked next to him on the floor. Every now and then he would glance up to stare out the wall of windows looking past them.

They were a Mormon family, and when Sunday came they climbed into the station wagon for three hours of church. Sacrament Meeting was quiet coloring through the weekly talks. Members of the ward were assigned spiritual topics to speak on by the bishopric, the three men called to lead them. In Sunday school class they learned the Mormon versions of Bible stories, more stories from the Book of Mormon, and stories about Joseph Smith and other prophets. Primary, a meeting of all the young children, was mostly singing songs about Jesus or the seasons. He would leave again on Monday morning, before any of them were awake, to teach Mathematics at Brigham Young University. Leave them to pause with her as she pointed to the small white flowers like tiny cups made to hold a single dew drop. When she reminded them to feel the grass brush against their bare calves. When they listened to her sing old primary songs about purple pansies and generous streams while she dug around the roots of aspen trees.

"To let them breathe," she said.

They smelled citrus in her hair when she bent close to help them identify flowers from the book with the worn red leather cover. She helped them put the flowers they collected between two pieces of parchment and closed them between the pages. They stacked other books on top for weight. These books, filled with pressed flowers, were their regular summer dinner guests and sat at the end of the table where the Taylor girls ate thick ham sandwiches on homemade, generous, buttered wheat bread.

Each year it was early afternoon by the time they finished stretching the linens over bare mattresses and pulling their quilts from the cedar chests at the bottom of the beds. Each year they found her standing on the porch. She wore blue denim gauchos and one of his old dress shirts with the sleeves rolled up. These were her gardening clothes, her spring and summer wardrobe. She leaned against the broom, her chin resting on the top of her hands, and stared into the trees. When she heard them she did not turn. She said, "I'm watching the light. It's changing again."

Her eyes were gray and widely spaced, like large almond-shaped ponds. They thought their mother was the most beautiful with the sun on her face and fine wisps of hair falling along the edges of her face and curling at her neck. She turned, smiled, and flicked them with the broom.

"Run!"

She laughed as they flew off the porch. Looking back at her over their shoulders, waving their hands, her hand shading her eyes as she watched them disappear down the narrow path between the aspen.

Each year dark eyes of the aspen trunks watched their legs stretch and run down the trail. They knew it wasn't far until the trees opened up into a small meadow, their meadow, where the sun called them together, where their voices could mingle with the early summer stream, loud with melting snow, where they could gather fallen branches and feel soft summer grass beginning to thicken.

This is how they remember her.

And there was evening and there was morning, the first day.

Eve

Her hands were in the soil, her fingers digging around the roots of small weeds. She'd woken early from the dream, the warmth of the small fingers fading from her hand and walked out into the back yard. The smell of citrus hung in the air and she thought of early fall mornings in her mother's garden. Her mom's hair held back by a blue bandanna, turning, smiling, standing barefoot in the cool wet grass. The image hung in the dawn light, between sight and memory, as her mind struggled through the thick heat of the Indian summer morning. The air felt wrong. By late September, mornings should have already begun to turn cool, the air thin and crisp, an intake of breath sufficient to clear out the mists of sleep. Instead it was still heavy with summer fever. The hinges squeaked as the screen door opened. She brushed her dark hair out of her eye with the back of her hand and turned to see who was stepping out with the sunrise.

Just Mo, she thought, *talking to someone on the phone.*

His form was shadow, the rising sun a flash behind him in her eyes. The low murmur of his voice mixed with the buzz of bees at their everyday work. Her eyes followed the small dark dots of their bodies as they visited one plant and then the next. She watched attentively as they burrowed into the tiny flowers.

He touched her on the shoulder. She turned her head back toward him, shading her eyes. He was still a shadow, the sun spilling around his edges.

"It's Roxcy. Evie, your mom—"

She reached out and took the phone from him without listening, waving him off. He didn't move.

"Morning, Rox."

She heard an intake of breath, a shudder.

"Mom was in a car accident, Evie, this morning driving home from California—"

The roar of her own blood pumping in her ears. She looked up at Mo again, the wisteria behind him, fading along the cedar trellis. He was crying, his hand rubbing his forehead. She heard the sound of a car start and pull out of a driveway, a siren somewhere far off. The glasses from last night's dinner sat on the table beneath the green shade umbrella. When he moved to sit beside her, she saw all the grief the sunrise had blocked. She tried to listen to her sister, locate her sister's reliable cheerfulness, but it had vanished. She spit words in Eve's ear.

"The memorial is this coming week. Friday."

"Friday?"

"Yes, I booked you a flight. I sent an email with the link. You can print out your ticket."

"An email," Eve repeated.

"I sent it this morning, early. We all left messages on your phone. I hadn't heard back from you. We'll stay at the cabin together, that way we can go through everything. Evie, she asked to be cremated. She wants us to scatter her ashes somewhere near Timp. o funeral. Mary's already been through her will. We've been up since early three in the morning. She already identified mom's body." Silence "Eve, are you still there?"

"I'm here."

"We have to at least have a memorial service, right? What about all mom's old friends from the Fourth Ward. She lived there for so long. We all did. Eve?"

"Yes?"

"I can't keep her ashes on my mantel." Roxcy let go an incomprehensible torrent of words, something about the Church Handbook, because of the resurrection. She wasn't clear on the particulars. Of course, she'd never actually read the Church handbook. George would know. She'd ask George, but she was fairly certain cremation was discouraged. She didn't know anyone who'd been cremated.

"I don't understand," Eve said quietly. She felt Mo's arm around her.

"I don't either. Why would she ask us to do that? I have to go, mom's bishop is calling. We're all coming to pick you up at the airport. You land at eleven-thirty tonight. I'm sorry. I know it's late. It was the best I could do for a same-day flight. She heard her sister's voice catch.

"What'll we do without her?"

"I don't know."

"I have to go. I'm glad you're coming tonight. I love you."

"Love you too."

7

The sun felt hot on the back of Eve's neck. Her dark hair pulled back from her olive face. Her gray eyes blurred. Mo lifted the phone from her hand. She thought she should try and stand, do something, but she couldn't move. She curled herself inward wrapped her arms around her legs, bent her neck down until her forehead rested on her knees. Folded. Mo moved behind her. His arms wrapped around her, the solidness of his body holding her together. More than a year now of him having to hold her together. She knew Mo and her mom had been watching her now for signs of another fissure, trying to mend any hint of a crack. Eve could smell citrus, see her mother's image hovering in the garden. She wanted to tell Mo this was the work of the spirit, this small familiar comfort in the unfamiliar heat. But he didn't believe in anything but her, so she kept it to herself.

"I'm sorry, Eve, so sorry," his breath in her ear.

"This past year, Mo—"

He held her closer.

"Do you want me to come with you?"

"No . . . No, finish the conference." She shook her head back and forth then rested against his arm. "Fly out in a few days, for the service. We'll need time alone. Just the four of us."

He sat with her for the next hour as grief came in sets, like waves that tossed her, the strong current threatening to pull her back out to sea. Her long arms held her knees to close to her chest, curled in. His arm around her shaking shoulders. He walked her inside when the temperature hit 90 on the thermostat, telling her she should lay down, try and rest. He pulled down a shade.

"You'll be Ok here alone?"

"Yes, I'm ok, really. Go work on your lecture. I'll try and rest. I should try to rest."

She opened the door to the small bathroom and flipped the switch. Bright white tile glared in the canned light. Eve caught her reflection, her gray eyes the same color as her mother's. Her thick, dark eyebrows pulled together. She thought of the stains she'd left in the grout in the downstairs bathroom as she gathered her soap, her moisturizer, mascara, and toothbrush placing them into a plastic baggie. The reassurance of touching everyday things. She packed as though she was going to Utah for a visit. Her warm coat hung in their hall closet, along with her winter sweaters and boots, all the things she would need for September nights up Provo Canyon. September marked the beginning of unpredictable weather in the Wasatch Mountains, where the evidence of her mom's life waited in the small cabin. It filled the little, manageable, rooms where Eve had been allowed to hide quietly, more than a year ago, for the whole spring. Where she had been allowed time and space to recover. Where she'd wake, remember, begin to cry and feel her mom's familiar arms gather her in, hold and rock her, as if she were still small.

How much loss can one body carry without breaking? She thought, and folded a skirt and shirt she'd laid out for the evening, a dinner she and Mo were supposed to attend with the dean. She put it in her suitcase, zipping the edges closed. Tired, she climbed into the unmade bed. Her phone lay on the nightstand. It was her habit to turn it off each night before bed. She reached for it and pressed the on switch. Her sister's names appeared in her voicemail. She put the phone back down. Mo was right. She needed to close her eyes for just a minute, just for a minute. As soon as she closed her eyes to rest she felt like a child waiting for her mother to tell her a story—her name story.

—

At night, when the house went still, Eve knew her mama would come and lie next to her, the familiar rhythms of her voice in her ear as she fell asleep, the same story repeated each night. About Eve, the mother of all living. That was something she had heard in a Primary lesson, at church and silently added to how she thought of herself. She smiled, closed her eyes, and waited. When her mom walked over from laying baby Anna in her crib, Eve smelled the garden on her pillow. She held Eve's hand and began, her voice low and quiet.

The sky is covered in dark clouds.

I can't remember a single day of gray until recently, she thought.

She felt annoyed with the sun, refusing to come out and interrupt her rest. Her whole life had shifted and with or without its light, she would get up and face the day; no hysteric fits, no tears.

"Did you eat anything?"

"Yes," he said.

"I'm going for a walk then."

"All right."

And she walked out. She felt him watching her, wanting her to turn back and smile at him, but it took energy to reassure Adam all the time and she was tired.

She walked for a long time. The path was wide and empty.

How was she supposed to feel—happy, sad, free? She wondered, unable to settle on just one. So different from the beginning. In the beginning things were simple. She stood in front of him and smiled. He smiled back.

"Hello," he had said.

"Hello," she had said.

And from there everything went down hill for her. Living the same day from sleep to waking wore on her. It didn't seem to phase him. She wanted to see clearly, to know, but the shalls and shall nots complicated things. She ran through it one more time, trying to sort it out.

"God, Father and Mother, had said no."

But Eve also knew they wouldn't be surprised when she plucked it and bit in. She could see this when she looked at them. They had long talks about all the plants, always beneath that tree, overlooking their reflections in the stream, while Adam wandered off to count things. He thought of everything in categories. Eve preferred, nuance, complication, and conversations to Adam's daily reports. And as sunny and pleasant as everything was, she explained how she wanted—badly wanted—something more than reflections and colors that never changed. The Mother looked at her. Eve saw herself in the familiar face and smiled.

Yearning. The Mother gave her the word, said it was part of being human. And again, there was something of herself that Eve heard and felt in the sound of that voice. The way they smiled at her made her think it must be right to try. So, when that serpent-like man slithered in and said it was the only way, Eve asked only once. *There is no other way?* And her teeth broke through the skin and her tongue savored the sweetness. She let the juice run down her chin.

God said no, but they knew that Eve would, even should, and now everyone was acting shocked and angry—gray skies, worried querying looks from Adam.

Well, you can't please everyone all of the time. She knew that now. Adam didn't even consider before he said *No*. He was so sure.

"I suppose surety has its appeal," Eve thought as she watched the shadows of dancing aspen. She looked up into the color of the leaves, felt the way the light shifted. "How can I explain that particular color of green, the hints of yellow beneath, the way it changes when the light passes through? When he sees in black and white."

It took a lot of explaining, over and over, coaxing him toward understanding. In the end she had to put it in the simplest terms: she'd taken the fruit' and if he wanted to be with her, he'd have to try it too. He had finally agreed to take a bite, to try and understand. He couldn't deny that it was delicious, not after he pressed the liquid out and let the sweetness fill his mouth.

She chose Adam, now, even if it had not really been her choice in the beginning, and ultimately, he chose her. It was clear in his quiet efforts to be near her, the surety of his touch. Despite the gulf of difference between them, she knew that he loved her, soul and body.

She reached the familiar stream and knelt on the bank to take one last look at the woman in the water. Eve was alone except for the rampant pink blossoms on the tree. The large dark eyes that looked up from her reflection were open. She touched

her finger to the water, watched the ensuing circles ripple across
the surface of the small pond, her image disrupted, spreading
into blossom.

"It's a beginning," she said aloud and turned to walk back
toward Adam.

—

Eve turned over and blinked out of memory into the present, caught in another wave of grief, feeling the palpable emptiness inside of her body. She could count the absences: five. The emptiness less threatening now. The pull that almost took her the day Mo had lifted her from the couch. He must have carried her. She had never asked him why he came home early that day. When she closed her eyes she could still see the thin rivers of blood running bright between the tile. And in the weeks afterward: when she had held out her hands and they seemed to float, wholly unconnected to her, when her sorrow rose like an enormous wave, breaking over her, the churning crush keeping her down until she had let go, let it engulf her. When the sadness seemed like the only real thing left her mom came and took her home. Drove her all the way to the cabin to rest.

—

It was late spring. The family house on Oak had just sold. On the porch, saying goodbye to him, she felt the weight of his body, felt his need for her, inhaled the smell of him beneath lemon scented soap, and it stirred nothing. Her mom went inside to get a few things and left them there alone. He breathed, in and out, in her ear. He made her promise him again and again that she'd be all right, that she'd come back home soon. His palms warm on her cool cheek, her face in his big hands as his voice shook. She looked at his furrowed brow. She watched his lips move. She could not look at his eyes.

"I promise. I promise," she said, not feeling sure of anything.

Her mom walked up then and put a hand on his shoulder.

"It's just for a little while, Mo. Let me take care of her for a bit. You need some time to take care of yourself. It's been too much for both of you, everything will to be all right. You'll talk on the phone. You can come get her in a couple of months, like we talked about. You trust me, don't you?" Her mouth smiled at him, but her eyes did not. They held onto his.

"I do. I trust you, Sylvia. Thank you."

"Walk us to the car then. Here, take her bag will you? Come on, Evie."

Eve let him hold her hand, thread her fingers through his in the familiar way. She stepped into the car. He bent down. She leaned out of the window. They kissed each other and then she watched him watch them drive away. They turned the corner and he was gone. Another goodbye. She did not know if this one was final. She did not trust her own words, her inept body. Her mom handed her a pillow. She insisted Eve lower the seat and rest. Eve slept across I-70, over Vail Pass and through the roaring curves of Glenwood Canyon, missing the towering outcropping of honey-colored rock, the slits of blue sky. When she awoke, Colorado's Western Slope was three hours behind them. This was the valley of her childhood. The setting sun melted on the Western horizon, a soft golden light over the dying lake. It was April, and spring spread across the face of the mountains like a green continent, a wandering map. Snow still covered the top edge of Mount Timpanogos. The sky stretched out above the ridges of the mountain top, pervasive and blue. Eve pressed her forehead to the car window and stared out, the colors passing, the images a blur. The glass felt cool on her forehead. She waited for the ache, somewhere between elation and pain, that usually attended her first glimpse of these familiar peaks. But it was lost with their almost baby. She couldn't feel anything now. She laid back down and closed her eyes. They pulled onto the dirt driveway to the cabin just after the sunset. Her mom turned off the car.

"Open your eyes Evie, we're here."

She saw the open wall of windows. The gray shake. The bright green door. Crocus bloomed in still sleeping grass.

—

Eve opened her eyes in the dark room. She had not rested. Her mind, untethered, had wandered backwards, away from the present. The morning heat, the sound of buzzing bees like a far-off ringing in her ears. Her mom had saved her life. She'd driven 500 miles to pick her up and 500 miles to take her to the cabin. She wrapped her in a thin soft quilt, sat her next to the fire, and fed her soup and homemade bread. Sat next to her reading about ferns. Slowly coaxing her outside to watch the aspen leaves unfurl. Eve's trees, the only children she could seem to grow and nourish. They watched the light and shade mingle in the grass.

Her mom asked her questions about the grove. What did she know about the relationship between the ferns and the aspen? She had been curious about this grass, did Eve know why it was different, gold at the edges? They walked down the old paths to the meadow. She never asked her to talk, but Eve told her everything while the crocus bloomed and faded, then the tulips, then the wild iris. Trusting her mother to keep this last blight between the two of them, not worry her sisters with her gloom. Her mom had listened, held space for her sorrow, and that space gave Eve back her life, Mo, her work, herself. And now she was gone?

Roxcy

Two bees circled the chandeliers, moving lazily around the hundreds of tear-drop crystals.

Was there a door open somewhere? How had they come in?

Roxcy watched the small black dots. Her gaze shifted to the fine layer of dust on the surface of each crystal. She felt the impulse to get up and find the ladder, take off her slippers, climb up barefoot—the cool metal against her skin—and begin the careful removal of each small piece of glass. To gently drop them into a large bowl of soapy water and then another bowl, clear and warm for rinsing. To pull out a pile of soft white cloths and shine them dry. The thought of the warm water against her hands, the motion of rubbing each one until the light passed through and split into sparkle, seemed like a miracle she could use. This was how she could stay the grief. This was always how she dealt with every difficulty, filling her time with unnecessary work. Her way to avoid choking on sadness, the constant threat rising up into her throat, to spoil her face, leaving the rims of her eyes red and raw. The bees buzzed round and round. As Roxcy watched the light pass through the crystals of the chandelier, watched it split and scatter, she wondered if George had heard the bees or noticed the dust. She hoped not. If he'd noticed it would worry him. Maria, their cleaning lady, had come twice a week when the kids were still at home. Once a week now that Peter, her youngest, was the only one left. But Roxcy was the only one who touched the chandelier. She squinted her eyes; the dust was fine and just becoming noticeable. The buzzing was only noticeable because of the deep quiet of the empty house. Maybe Peter's struggle had to do with this sudden emptiness too. Their house had been so busy, so full, for so long. His four siblings all gone to college, living in the dorms, or apartments. A couple of them married now, thinking about starting their own families. She didn't know how George would react if he knew the way Peter had slipped, had crossed such a clear line—not once, but three times.

She knew it would change the way her friends saw her; they would think that she'd failed somehow. And they would see Peter as wayward, a person to avoid, a possible danger to their own teenage children. If people found out about the drinking, he would be labeled as a bad influence, and the good kids would be discouraged from associating with him. Just like the Crawford's girl who had pulled him down with her. To get some guidance or at least assurance that Pete would be all right. Roxcy had planned to talk to her mom about the problem when she got back from California. Instead, she was planning her memorial service.

She blinked and felt the way her body ached, the weight of interrupted rest. She'd been up since 3:00, since Anna's phone call. Roxcy had left messages on her kid's phones, "Call me as soon as possible." She'd talked to Mary and called Eve just as the sun rose. She had let George sleep. He was working too hard, her sweet George, her constant. He was up now, walking toward her in a dark navy suit and a red tie. He set his briefcase down and kissed her on the cheek. She poured him a glass of orange juice, stood up to fry him an egg and make some toast, handed it to him, and told him to sit down, to eat. She waited until he finished to repeat the words *"Mom was in a fatal car accident this morning."* He held her hand as she went through the details, his eyes full of concern, her eyes filling to the brink. She knew she couldn't look at him directly, or she'd sob in an unattractive way. *Too much to do,* she thought. *No time to fall apart,* and poured herself a glass of lemon water from the other pitcher.

"I couldn't be more sorry, Rox. It's just, well, such a shock. Do you need me to take the day off?"

"Could you?"

"Of course. I'll have to call and have my secretary reschedule meetings, especially the one on the Florida case. That's starting to blow up, but I'm sure one day away—"

"Go in, George. I have a million things to do anyway. But can you be home for dinner? I leave for the cabin late tonight. I don't want to leave Pete on his own. He needs you. Especially now."

"Oh, Pete'll be ok. He's a good boy, but I can't imagine they wouldn't understand me leaving a bit early given the circumstances."

"George, he just lost his Grandma. He loved her. I don't want to leave him alone and I have to pick up Evie and head to the cabin. Promise me—"

"You're right. I wasn't thinking. I can't imagine it, you know? Sylvia gone—doesn't seem possible. I'll be here no later than nine p.m. but I'll try to make it home by six for dinner. I love you, Roxcy." He pulled her to him. "It's awful, I know it's awful, but at least we know she's with her Heavenly Father and in the Savior's care. Reunited with your dad too. I imagine that's a happy reunion."

She looked up at him. He was still tall but his hair had darkened. It was going gray around the temples. She touched the silver strands with her finger.

"Yes."

These were the words for loss. She'd used them herself when her friends or people in her ward had lost grandparents, parents, even children. She felt guilty that the words felt empty. *They should help.* She thought, *like a sounding brass, a tinkling cymbal.* Her mind struggled to connect eternity to the present reality that her mom was forever absent from the here and now.

"I'd better be off. I'm already running a little late and I have a meeting, but only if you're sure you'll be alright?"

"I'll be fine, George. But you'll make the arrangements for the building? I want the one on Ninth East where she spent so many years, where we grew up. It's important to me. And get some people to help with set up, will you? We'll need tables and chairs in the cultural hall for the lunch. I've left a message with her current bishop. And come home for dinner if you can, spend the evening with me and Pete. I don't want him to be here alone tonight."

"Ok. I'll be here. And I'll take care of all the building and set up arrangements. I'll leave the office early? I'll be here so we can all have dinner together."

"Thank you." She reached out and touched his shoulder. "I'm sorry. Really sorry. Your mom was such a light."

He held her for a moment, quickly kissed her cheek, grabbed his briefcase, and was off. Light spread into the kitchen through the large glass doors, through the windows of the living and dining rooms. Her mom had never liked George the way she had Wayne. Wayne, how odd. It had been years since she'd thought of him. He wouldn't have left her for work. He would have insisted that she pause, take a walk, that she feel all of it. She heard the garage door open and close. She didn't want to pause. She didn't want to feel any of it. She refilled her large glass with water and walked back across the house to the library. It was a small room, the only carpeted room in the house, large windows, everything soft, illuminated. She sat down at her desk. The surface was neat and ordered. Roxcy took out a pencil with the tip neatly sharpened and sat up straight, as if preparing to take a test.

Memorial Service
- ☐ Call Mom's Bishop
- ☐ Finalize the day and time of the memorial (Friday 10:00 a.m.)
- ☐ Ask George if Anna can participate in dressing without a current temple recommend
- ☐ Dress mom's body in her temple clothes
- ☐ Cremation
- ☐ Find out how quickly we'll have her remains

- [ ] Choose an urn
- [ ] Create program for memorial service
- [ ] Coordinate with Mom's Bishop, send out invites, write obituary
- [ ] Sit down with my own family this evening
- [ ] Get a photo of mom framed for each of my children
- [ ] Call my sisters with assignments
  Assignments:
- [ ] Mary—pick up programs from printer
- [ ] Eve—choose flowers (I'll place the order)
- [ ] Anna—memorial photos (have back up in case Anna doesn't follow through)

She marked off the things she'd already done. She would make the appointment for dressing her mother's body and talk to the crematorium as soon as they opened. Three hours until 10:00 a.m. She had formatted the invitations, including the file from her mom's contacts and an old address book, addressing and shipping them off. Two hours, 9:00 a.m. She checked each small circle again. There was something, some error, but her sluggish mind could not find it.

She looked out of the tall arched windows into the back yard, a full acre of lawn, still as green as early spring despite being mid-September in a drought year. Everything else was brown, the mountain sides parched and brittle looking. The older Hispanic man George had recently hired knelt over the flower beds, leaning slightly forward. The posture of prayer, the same posture her mom held for all those years—weeding, planting, shaping and reshaping her beds on Oak Lane. Jose?

Jeffe? She couldn't recall his name. A man the missionaries were working with. Jesus? No, she would have remembered that. Why would anyone name a child Jesus? Impossible to live up to. But he kept the lawn green the way George liked it, lush and full. He'd needed a job. Maybe he'd left the back door open when he came into use the bathroom. Sometimes he did that. Maybe that's how the bees had come in. Bees like the ones that hid in thick grass along the edge of flower beds when she was small.

⌒

They were pretending to be fairies when Roxcy stepped toward the long purple branch and felt a sharp pain on the ball of her small foot. When Mary heard her scream she ran toward her, but their mom yelled, "Stop! Grab Anna please. Evie, go put on your sandals, Ok?" Mary obeyed and hoisted Anna onto her hip, just as their mom lifted Roxcy into a hug.

"Make the hurting stop, mama."

"We'll fix you up."

She carried Roxcy inside, pushing aside the billowing white curtain. She sat her on the edge of the counter and opened the drawer where the band aids, pens, nail clippers, and scraps of paper lived. She lifted her foot carefully. Roxcy felt the small flat edges of cold metal touch against the hot ache and flinched. She held the tweezers out to show Roxcy the short, fine thread of black with a tiny white ball at the end.

"How about something sweet from a bee to make up for the sting? Honey and butter and on wheat bread?"

"Yes, please."

"I think you should forgive the bee, Rox, because even though they say the symbol of the beehive was Brigham Young's idea, sounds more like Eliza Roxcy Snow's idea to me. Bees are always busy like she was, like you are.

"Will you tell me my story, mama?"

"If you promise to keep the crumbs on your plate."

"I promise."

Her mom pulled Roxcy onto her lap and kissed the top of her head. This was a rare thing, just the two of them together. She had to share her mama's attention with Mary and Evie and now Anna, the baby. She loved the pleasant, familiar weight of her mom's arm around her. She heard her mama's voice quiet, beginning the taste of honey on her tongue.

Eliza Roxcy Snow stood over the tired oxen and felt a momentary urge to lie down next to them and give up. The days on the trail were long. She looked into the animals' eyes, glazed over with exhaustion, watery, pleading for rest and caught her own disheveled reflection: a worn-out woman, dusty and defeated. She thought of Joseph, her husband, the prophet, gone on to his heavenly home and wished he were there to speak in his powerful way and renew her strength. A small hand tugged on her skirt.

"Are they sick?"

The girl's face was dirty beneath the brim of her faded bonnet. Roxcy took the edge of her own apron and wiped the little face as best she could.

"No, overworked, I think."

"Oh."

And so am I, Roxcy thought.

Brigham Young himself left these women and children in her care, trusted in her to bring them safely to the valley. He took the other men ahead to forge the trail. Her only job right now was to keep her little company headed in the right direction.

"Everything will be alright," she said.

"How?"

"God always provides."

She crouched down and looked right in the little girl's eyes.

"You run and tell everyone to reload the wagon and get ready to walk."

She watched the little girl turn and run toward the people, and Eliza Roxcy Snow knelt beside the tired oxen. She placed one hand on each of their heads and felt heat pulsing from her palms onto their rough foreheads. She'd healed people, why not oxen?

"Dear Heavenly Father." Roxcy prayed aloud. "We need these Oxen to get us where you've told us to go. Put thy power into the bodies of these humble beasts and give us, your servants, strength to carry on. In the name of Jesus Christ and by his power, Amen."

Low groans came from the animals as they began to shift slowly, to lift their heavy bodies from the dusty ground.

"Thank you." She said aloud, smiling up at the wide sky. She felt her spirit breathe in the vast space.

The women and children stood watching her, some mouths open, some heads bowed in prayer, but Roxcy stood with her hands on her hips and scowled into the disheveled wagon bed. The contents were thrown in so that the provisions were unreachable, large chests piled precariously on top of smaller ones.

"Do I need to remind you that God's house is a house of order? Are we not God's people?"

She managed the unloading and reloading of every item. The older boys listened and lifted. The heavy chests made benches where mothers could nurse and there was a nice space in the middle for when the littlest walkers got tired and had to rest. She laid out several blankets and directed the nursing mothers to climb in with their babies.

"Can I trust you'll take care of these children better than you did the cargo?"

"Yes, Sister Roxcy. Thank you, Sister Roxcy."

All right then.

She felt a new surge of energy as the wheels creaked into motion. She felt like herself again, saw her life as a string of miracles, allowing her to follow the Lord wherever He might require.

———

Sitting there in the library at her desk the full fatigue hit Roxcy. Waking at 3 a.m. to Anna's sobbing voice. The constant worry in the back of her mind for Pete. Holding all her emotions in to get through the things that must be taken care of and the feeling she had missed something important.

What she wanted was to close her eyes and wake up a year ago, or three years ago, or twenty, when her oldest were still babies. When everything had felt like a blessing: the velvet baby skin, the small dimples at the elbow. She would do a few things differently. Carpet the whole house, make it more welcoming and warm like their home on Oak. Make every room more like this little library. The soft carpet, the walls of books, the light, bright and warm. Not hardwood and marble, cold linen, and shade.

There was no marble or hardwood in their house on Oak Lane. No echoes. The plush brown carpet had been soft under her feet. The rooms were small, safe, neat and full of activity. They used to spend hours on rainy days building cities by stacking the books off of the family room shelves into many-colored towers. The blue, red, green, yellow and black spines like buildings she'd never seen. She remembered the care it took to navigate the strange metropolis, moving intentionally so she would not accidentally topple the precarious civilization. As her sisters lost interest—when the rain stopped and they disappeared into the yard or found a Nancy Drew and laid on the sofa for the rest of the afternoon—she would begin the unbuilding, the restacking, and remaking of the bookshelf. The forms were fluid. Sometimes she blocked them by color, other times by size. Sometimes she created waves of tall to short repeating across the wall of shelves.

That time was gone, her own children nearly grown. Her mom had sold the house on Oak and with it, all of Roxcy's memories. She felt another wave of exhaustion, stood up, and walked into the warm rectangular light. She laid down on the library carpet, closed her eyes and felt the sun on her face.

Roxcy had just come in from her Thursday morning tennis match, something she never could've managed when the kids were small. Now three were grown and gone, with the last two in high school. Football season had ended for Pete in the fall. Her daughter's play had finished in February, and she would graduate in five weeks, move into the dorms at BYU, and then only Peter would be left at home. The normal end of the school year ruckus had grown more and more quiet. Roxcy walked into the library and laid down on the carpet in the patch of sun that came through windows.

The sun felt warm on her bare legs. She closed her eyes. An unwelcome amount of silence had crept into her life. She might go hours now without bumping into someone in her hall or kitchen. She'd finished all the laundry, done the dishes, left the beds, the bathrooms and floors for Maria, gone to brunch with her girlfriends, played tennis, and heard the echo of her own steps through her house when she came home in the afternoon.

A shadow passed over her body, and Roxcy turned on her side to look out the window. Dark clouds covered the sun. She sat up, walked back through the echoes, grabbed her keys and almost tripped down the steps on her way out the door into the garage. She pulled her car out into an afternoon thunderstorm, heavy drops loud against her windshield, the clean smell blowing into the car through the vents. Without thinking she drove toward home, toward Oak Lane. Her mom would tell her she was a good mother, a good woman, that it would get easier to be alone, that everything would be all right. The Creamery was on the way, where the old Carson's market had been. As children they occasionally stopped after school for Marathon Bars, Big Hunks or went across the street to the Texaco for forbidden cans of caffeinated soda—Mr. Pibb, Pepsi, or Coke—that had clanked from the vending machine. She pulled in and ran through the rain to grab a pint of her mom's favorite ice cream.

Cold sheets of rain fell and splashed off the gray pavement. The deep gutters turned into narrow, concrete streams. Her windshield wipers barely kept up as she drove up Birch, past the house that looked like a long rectangular palace of some sort, covered in gold filigree. She felt the relief of familiarity as Birch Street turned into Oak Lane and she pulled into their driveway just past the stop sign. In the second the window cleared she saw the sign stuck in her mom's lawn: *For Sale By Owner*. She blinked. She stepped out of the car and held her hand up to shield her eyes from the rain. Her mother's phone number written in permanent black ink across the bottom of the sign was their home phone number for as long as she could remember. The bottom of the paper bag that held the ice cream gave way and she grabbed for the small white pint, catching it in her left hand. The branches of the white birch wept, a small stream trickled down the left side of wide concrete steps that rounded the house to the front door. Ivy that climbed up the side of the house dripped steadily under the roof line. She ran up the stairs, automatically adjusting for the width and slope, and found the front door open.

"Mom?"

"In here. Oh, Roxcy! Good, come on in. Don't you love the smell of a spring thunderstorm?"

"What's going on?" She stood dripping on the carpet, the small pint of ice cream in her left hand, the soaked broken bag in her right. In the room several boxes stood open, filled with books. The shelves were nearly empty."

"Oh! You're soaked. Let me get you a towel."

"The sign out front—"

"I have an offer on the house!"

"What?" Roxcy felt dizzy. She sat down on the arm of the sofa. Her mom wrapped a large bath towel around her.

"It sold in three days. I was going to call you girls later this week so you could come and choose a few things—anything that's important to you. I'm getting rid of most of it. They want to move in in two weeks."

"Since when are you selling the house?"

"Roxcy! We talked about this at dinner, right after dad's funeral and again the last time we were all at the cabin. Is that ice cream? You knew."

Roxcy nodded, "Blackberry Brickle."

"My favorite!"

"I know."

She heard her mom walk toward the kitchen, heard the freezer open and close.

"The house is too big for me. Your dad's been gone for a year now. It was really too big for the two of us but, you know, your dad didn't like change."

Roxcy watched as her mother scooted a pile of books over. She grabbed a blanket and put her arm around her and rubbed her shoulder to try and warm her up.

"Where on earth will you go?" Roxcy said.

"You really didn't know? Oh, Rox, I'm sorry. I honestly don't understand how this happened."

"I'm the one who doesn't understand, mom."

"I'm moving to the cabin. Winter's a little long, but I don't mind. I start school summer semester. I told everyone over dinner at your place last month."

"I was probably in the kitchen. I hardly sit down to eat when I'm cooking. You know that."

"Well, Rox, you can understand. You have lives of your own and have for a long time. I'm going to have a new adventure. And the cabin is a better size for me, less to keep up."

Roxcy stood up, her eyebrows knit together like a poorly mended seam.

"Get your hands off of your hips, Rox. I can see you're upset. Please sit back down. I'm not sure how this happened, but try to see things from my perspective."

"What about your grandchildren? Don't you want to see them graduate and, and . . ."

"And what, sweetie? I'm not moving to Africa. Although, I might travel there at some point. I'd like to see the savanna before I die, And the rainforests. Can you imagine the undergrowth, the size of the ferns?!?"

"This is coming out of nowhere, Mom."

"It's not sweetie. This has been coming for a very long time. Anyway, you love the cabin!"

Roxcy's eyes clouded. Her mom tucked a loose piece of wet hair behind her ear. She looked into her eyes and pulled her in close, hugging her for a long time. When she pulled back, she held Roxcy's face in her hands for a minute and then kissed her forehead.

"I'm right here, Roxcy. It's about the same distance whether I'm here or at the cabin from your place. I'm not going anywhere."

—

The sun felt hot on Roxcy's cheeks. She didn't open her eyes. She told herself it was lack of sleep, as her loud sobs filled the small library. To lose her mom, without warning. Wasn't she allowed to cry when she was alone, when she wasn't requiring anyone else to hold the tight, round ball of grief in her stomach? She could have called her a month ago, the first time Pete had come home drunk. But she hadn't called. She'd kept her distance, nourished her hurt like an angry child. And now? Roxcy covered her face with her hands, a wave of nausea moved through her. The Howards. She'd sent an invitation to Aunt Violet from dad's old address book. They hadn't had any contact with that family since the night Anna was born. That was the mistake. That was it. Her phone rang again on the desk. She ignored it. She had to call the printer before they were sent out but couldn't seem to find the energy to move. There was a knock on the glass door and she sat up wiping the tears beneath her eyes with the pad of her thumb, quickly smoothing her skirt. The gardener stood there looking in, his arms full of daisies.

Mary

She scratched the dog's back end and moved her hand up the coarse white fur of his spine.

"Well, she's not answering Fred. She's probably busy making arrangements for mom's memorial."

Mary talked to Fred this way, as if he understood and might answer back, more often now that her only son had gone away for college. She'd taken the day off of work, a mistake, she now realized. Her mane of curls was pulled back into an unruly ponytail. She still wore the sweatpants and t-shirt she'd slept in and no makeup. She wore hardly any makeup anyway. Her large hazel eyes had become more striking with age. She looked 10 years younger than she was, and her wide shoulders matched her hips-a perfect hourglass. But today Mary could have used her morning routine. Her routine kept her mind from going down the proverbial rabbit hole. Every time one of her loved one's left, she had to fight an uneasy feeling of dread. An intruder might get in in their absence, their plane would crash, their car would go off the road. As it turned out the feeling had been a reliable harbinger three times in her life, her mother's death being the third.

A rigid schedule saved her from imagining the possibility of disaster implicit in every day. With Hank so far away in Chicago, with Eve flying in this evening, and given the worst had already happened, she should have kept to her normal schedule: wake, eat a small breakfast, take Fred for his walk, shower, walk to her office, and spend the day balancing the numbers that made up other people's lives.

The empty hours loomed ahead before they all left for the airport to pick up Eve. Fred looked over his shoulder at her and snuffled, his jaw protruding. Her Old English Bulldog, shared his name with Mary's late husband, the Marine, who had died twenty years ago. She had chosen the dog's name without thinking. Now it seemed right to her. Mary looked back at Fred. The warmth of afternoon light filled the room. She could still take Fred out for his walk and then shower. It would be good for both of them.

"You want to go for a walk?"

He jumped off the couch and picked up his leash with his mouth. He brought it back to her, whining and dancing, his nails clicking on the hardwood. They made their way down the steps.

She and Hank had lived in this condo since he was a toddler. Teaching him to navigate the steep staircase had nearly killed her with worry. They'd moved shortly after losing Hank's father, her husband Fred. She had immediately child proofed everything: a permanent gate at the top of the stairs, plug covers, child locks on all the cupboards. Her hot water never set above 100° to avoid accidental scalding. Hank used to press his little face on the glass of the huge west-facing window that looked out onto the large maple in the backyard. She had to remind herself it did not open. It was double paned. He would not fall out. The living room was open to the kitchen with high ceilings that made the condo feel larger than it was. There were two good sized bedrooms, each with its own bath.

Now Hank's room was empty. She left his room as he had left it, neat and spare. He was in the engineering program at The University of Chicago. She was surprised by how easily she'd adjusted to his absence. She'd spent Hank's entire life, eighteen years, worried about the day he would leave. So, it felt strange to experience him being elsewhere, in any measure, as relief. Strange to feel the sudden lightness—not being responsible for knowing his whereabouts, or the worry when he was five or ten minutes late. It was nice to shop for only herself, to not have the temptation of junk food in the cupboards and the worry of the carcinogens they contained. She discovered how much she looked forward to walking into the quiet house at the end of the day. Of course at night, when she closed her eyes, she knew that his heartbeat was too far from hers and the mother-worries came. Was he getting enough to eat? Was he finding a good group of friends? Was he finding time to rest? This disturbing ambivalence, the odd manageability of his sudden absence, was not dissimilar to what she'd felt when she'd been informed that his father had died, a surprising lightness edged by soft grief entangled with hazy guilt. Thinking about the parallel made her uncomfortable.

For as long as she could remember she'd been responsible for caring for someone, beginning with her younger sisters. She'd been helping some child get ready for church every Sunday for her entire life. Now her Sabbath was silence without rush or urgency. She'd wake, take Fred for a walk, shower, and dress, knowing that she had plenty of time before she had to be in the pews. She enjoyed watching the families file in, some looking neatly perfect, others harried and tired. Mary invited those less-than-perfect families to sit with her. She kept butter-rum life-savers in her bag and handed out Hank's little felt quiet books. She wasn't responsible for these children's safety or education, so she could just relax and enjoy them. The weekly taking of the sacrament had always been a grounding ritual for her. Now, with no child to teach, she could fall fully into contemplation. The repeated prayer, the bread and water, the five minutes every week to anchor herself in the love of God, was an unexpected gift.

Her mom's death was entirely different: all weight. Mary had awakened the night before the accident with her heart racing in her chest. It was 3:30 a.m. The old nightmare always came at this hour, so she had ignored the feeling that she ought to call her mom and tell her to stay in California. Thinking it was only the dream that had left her feeling unsettled. And now the desperate regret that she had not picked up the phone and told her not to get in the car, to wait.

She struggled with the continued feeling of desperation as she and Fred walked past the quiet houses, beneath the generous limbs of the old sycamores. They walked past the building that had once been the city library, converted into an office building, past the mediocre Mexican restaurant, the trendy bistro, the sandwich shop that kept changing ownership and names. Occasional voices floated from inside the restaurants as doors opened. People walked to their cars, talking and laughing. The sound of traffic came in waves. When they came to University Avenue, they stopped at the city building with its large Greek columns and the well-manicured grass gone yellow at the edges. It had been a hot, dry summer. Fred struggled up the slippery marble steps, huffing and panting until they reached the top and she leaned on a column to observe the progress of construction across the street. A fire had almost destroyed the Provo Tabernacle. The gigantic frame of the old brick building sat suspended above an enormous hole beneath, supported by a series of crossing I-beams. The church was restoring the historic building by turning it into a temple. Mary looked forward to having that liminal space, where this existence and the next bumped against each other, within walking distance. She would more often be able to move through those odd and beautiful rituals that gave her a concrete way to connect with the idea of eternity—rituals that drew her to God, to everyone past and present, and now, particularly, to her mother. But she did worry that the round white temple where she'd received her endowment, where she and Fred had married, would be neglected. People here preferred older styles of buildings. They liked tradition, and the round temple was an odd, modern looking thing. She loved it. Built in the 1960's, the steeple had been like a series of golden waterfalls until President Hinckley had it white washed. It was one of the landmarks of her childhood, and she felt sorry for it next to the old-fashioned beauty and appeal this restored building would have.

A car honked and Mary looked right toward the stop light. A new restaurant sat where the old Walgreens used to be, the windows hung with white drapes and small flickering candles on each table. Many of the buildings were the same as they had been when she was a child, but the businesses had changed. She loved the familiar street, remembering summer hours in the hot sun when she, her mom, and her sisters walked block after block during the summer sidewalk sales buying new school clothes for the coming year. They would walk up to Provo Bakery afterwards for a donut or a roll. The cool bakery air was always a relief after the hot walk, the jingle of the bell, the smell of yeast in the air. She and her mom had kept up the tradition, increased the frequency. Every summer since Mary had lived on Center, they walked there together once a week, usually on Saturday mornings. The marquee of the University Theater, where she'd slept out for tickets to see the first Indiana Jones, was long gone. The building had been converted into just another office building. It was the building where she went to work each day for her accounting firm. After twenty years they'd finally made her a partner. It was only last week that she met her mom outside the glass doors to walk to the bakery, because she wouldn't be there the next Saturday. She'd be in California.

—

The early morning dry heat of late August felt like walking into something solid. It started early and ended well after sunset.

"Morning, Mary!"

"Looks like you've been working in the garden, mom."

"Just a little around the cabin. I'm trying some California ferns in our grove. I stopped by your house. What are you doing at work on a Saturday?"

"One of my clients needed to meet. When do you head back there anyway?

"In a couple of weeks. How's our Hank doing these days?"

Mary understood this as a courtesy. She knew Hank called his Nana every Sunday after he talked to her, and he'd only been gone a couple of weeks.

"He sounds happy. He's already talking to the Registrar about taking time off for his mission next year."

"I swear that one came out a grown up. Not that you didn't do a good job."

"Couldn't have done it without you. Speaking of which, how's it going with Anna and the girls?" Mary asked.

"She's plugging along. Those girls of hers are busy, busy. They always have a little project going with scraps they pull from Anna's fabric pile."

They both squinted into the bright sun. Bees buzzed from one dandelion to the next along the narrow stretches of grass in between sidewalk and curb. A tiny bell rang as they opened the door into the familiar cool air of the bakery and the smell of yeast. Trays of donuts, muffins, and rolls filled the slanted glass cases. They made their choices and reluctantly walked back out to sit on a bench in the shade. Her mom pulled the cinnamon butterflake roll from the white paper bag. She held it with a small piece of parchment paper. Mary used her piece of pastry paper to remove some of the chocolate from the top of her éclair.

"Do you still have the nightmares, Mary?"

Mary glanced at her mom and then examined the éclair. She put the chocolate covered paper back into the white paper bag.

"That's out of the blue."

"I guess it is. But there's this woman in my ward, she's one of those who probably shares too much, you know, but she'd been abused by her older brother as a child. I never asked you exactly—"

"It was so long ago. I never—I mean—aside from the occasional bad dream, I don't even think about it."

Mary took a bite of her éclair and looked down.

"She said counseling has made a big difference for her. I was just wondering if you've ever thought of talking to someone?"

"No. I—I don't know. I mean, that was so many years ago. We're adults now."

"We? Mary saw her mother's face drop like a sinkhole. "Roxcy. Oh. I didn't know what to do back then and Anna was just an infant. I wasn't getting enough sleep, trying to care for all of you. I knew something had happened because you were coming in almost every night. And I did refuse to go to their house again. I just stopped talking to your Aunt Violet; it was awkward, but I knew she wouldn't push. Your father's family hates any kind of conflict. They kept inviting us, and he kept making up excuses until they just stopped. The whole situation was such a mess, so strained. And I never asked you, did I? I meant to and then the nightmares seemed to get less frequent. I never circled back to talk through it and figure out what to do."

"Mom, it's fine. We're fine now. It was a blip."

"You were constantly following your little sisters to make sure they were all right. And the truth is, I needed that. I may have had a little postpartum depression. It took me a long time to feel like myself."

"I had no idea, mom."

"None of that makes it okay. I've had years. I'm so sorry, Mary. I'm so, so sorry. I—"

"Do you know where they are now?"

"I think they moved up to Salt Lake somewhere. Dad kept in touch. Who was it? Your uncle?"

"No, the oldest boy, Paul."

Her mom sat very still. Mary could see the anger behind her eyes, in her clenched jaw.

"By the time I was back to myself, your dad also insisted that we let sleeping dogs lie. He didn't

want to make the situation more uncomfortable than it already was. I should have pushed. I should've insisted."

"She was his sister, mom."

"It doesn't matter. I should have—"

"You have nothing to be sorry for, mom. One difficult thing in an otherwise really great childhood, you know? Everyone has one or two." Mary paused. There were details that still haunted her, but they belonged to her now. She could share other things with her mom, but it was too late for this. She didn't want to unearth this particular fear, the anger and sadness. It seemed to belong to the darkness and the past. Not a conversation for the bright sunlight. "Can we drop it?"

"Okay. But please know that if I had to do anything over—"

"Please, mom, I really don't want to talk about this."

"All right, Mary. You know I love you."

"I do."

"I can tell you about my ferns!"

Mary smiled and felt relief as she listened to the rise and fall of her mom's voice talking about something she loved: how she was driving so she could bring home samples. She thought one of the varieties was once native to Utah and might grow nicely beneath the steps up to the condo. She'd bring enough to plant there. She also wanted to compare them to the Brackens that grew around the cabin. Mary had the thought that she shouldn't drive. Statistically speaking driving was much more dangerous than flying. All she said was,

"How long will you be gone this trip?

"Just a couple of weeks. Check in on Anna for me while I'm gone, will you? You remember how crazy the beginning of the school year can be."

Mary took the last bite of her éclair. She licked the custard and chocolate off of her fingers. They stood and crossed the street on the way back, following the deepest shade. She felt the uneasiness come loose somewhere inside her and spread out across her chest, fall into her stomach. Her mom held her hand and they talked about Fred the dog, who would be offended that they'd left him behind. Her mom suggested a quick stop by the bagel shop to pick up a doggie biscuit, so they turned west on center and walked a little further. Mary chose not to think about the snow storm, the car ride, the night Anna was born. She tucked the first night that her fears had been an actual premonition back into the dark where it belonged.

—

Mary looked down at her dog, Fred, and he looked up at her. His tongue hung out to one side panting.

"Shall we go home?" Mary said.

He didn't answer or move. She reached into her pocket, and he immediately stood. She held the treat in her hand, just out of reach until they arrived back at her front door. Mary allowed Fred to snuffle the treat from her hand when they reached the bottom of the stairs up to their condo. She pulled another out to get him to make the final climb. She unlocked her door, threw the keys on the table and walked through the small open kitchen to lay down on her large, brown sectional sofa. The tears came as they always did, heavy and silent. They felt like relief in the strangeness of that haunting, the strangeness her mom's sudden death. Fred laid by her feet, unwilling or unable to make the jump up after his last exertion. She picked up her laptop, and Fred shifted until he was on top of her left foot and leaned into her leg. She leaned over and patted his head. She turned on her computer and accessed the files she'd been working on that morning. Numbers were reasonable. Two plus two always equaled four. Like church every week, they repeated in predictable patterns. Taking the sacrament as a reminder that you and God had made an agreement. A reminder that the promises you made to God would make you kinder, keep you free from addiction, give every action and interaction greater meaning and depth. If you read your scriptures daily, prayed daily, attended church each Sunday, then there was a sure rhythm to life, and it was in this rhythm that Mary felt held and loved. Her mind began to calm, her breath becoming steady and even. She knew, from long experience, that when difficulty came there was also comfort in these repetitions. Math and the gospel were the safe worlds in which she preferred to live. Unlike people, unlike death, they were predictable.

The sun had moved directly behind the Maple tree, the dappled, fading light fell, rose- colored, across the room. Mary closed her laptop and her eyes. She listened for a knock on her door, her mom's face there, the familiar rise and fall of her voice. There was no knock, no face, but her mom's voice reverberated across memory—a comforting echo spanning the years of Mary's childhood. The bedtime story, her name story, repeated every night, almost like a chant.

~

She was counting the seeds when the angel appeared. She looked up and thought,

I suppose I should feel startled.

She did not feel startled. She noticed that his feet hovered just above the ground. He wore a long loose robe, as most men did in those days, and stood there quietly, slightly elevated and observing her work. Perhaps his silence was what set her at ease. He emitted a lot of light, which made it difficult to make out the shape of his nose, or see the color of his eyes. She shielded her eyes as she would from the sun and said.

"Can I help you?"

"I see you're planting," he said

"Yes, I am . . . and counting."

"Your method shows great care."

"I like order," she said.

"That is why you don't scatter and then thin out?"

"It seems wasteful and much harder to keep track of."

"Interesting." He stepped down and bent to examine the rows *more closely.*

"I like to know the number. To know each plant," she said.

"I see."

"Were you a farmer?"

"Oh, I farmed a little in my day. Mostly I taught," he said.

"That's good work too," she said.

The light dimmed as he stepped to the ground. She could see him more clearly. His eyes and hair were brown. His eyebrows were bushy, dark. They reminded her of the hairy caterpillars that sometimes chewed holes in her leaves. She liked his nose, which was a little long for his round face and slightly crooked.

"I'm here to ask a favor of you," he said.

"Oh?" *She looked at him.*

And It all seemed perfectly reasonable to Mary. She knew it might be complicated, trying to explain things to Joseph, but the angel reassured her that he would come around. The only thing that scared her was the unpredictability of birth.

"I'm a little worried," she said.

"Go on."

"It's just that I'd like to know when exactly the baby will come. But, I suppose, that is not possible here."

"No, it's not possible. You'll have to have faith. You'll have to—"

"All right then, I'll do my best." She said cutting him off and standing up.

It took a long time for her choice to show. Long enough that she and Joseph were well into married life. He had been understandably upset at first, when Mary explained, even threatened to call off their marriage, so Mary practiced patience. Eventually, the angel appeared to him too and, as promised, Joseph came around.

It was spring when they had to make the journey to Bethlehem. She felt sad to leave her garden. The shoots, so carefully counted, were coming up through the dry earth. Her belly sprouted with them. The baby inside was active and often felt as if he were crowded, reaching for more room. The new roundness threw her body off balance.

It was a very hot day when Joseph brought the donkey round. She was giving her counted rows one last drink of water. A neighbor girl promised to tend them in her absence.

"Mary, we're ready," Joseph said impatiently.

"I'm almost finished," she sighed.

Mary brushed the dust off her hands and picked up the bucket. The water pooled on the dry ground, then bubbled and sank. She watched the earth grow dark around the edges of her green plants and felt satisfied.

"Mary, it's time."

"I'm coming."

She walked slowly, one hand on her low back, feeling her bones groan under the extra weight. Joseph held out his hand.

"Do you have the ledgers?" She asked.

"Yes."

"I worked very hard to line up all the numbers, Joseph."

"I have everything," he said.

"All right then, I'd like to walk a little ways,"

"But Mary—"

"A donkey, even as sweet as this one is, is not comfortable at the moment, Joseph."

"You are very slow, Mary."

"I am very big, Joseph."

She looked at him steadily and he nodded his head. As they walked she counted her steps, finding peace as the numbers grew. Then she counted the number of people they passed.

"Hello, Shalom," she said and silently, to herself: Twenty-one.

She saw Joseph trying to not to smile. He was not good at hiding anything. But she kept things close and pondered them in her heart.

—

Mary closed her eyes and sat for a moment, trying to hold onto the particular rhythm of her memory. The thought of a world without her mom had never occurred to her . It should have. Her mother was aging. She'd watched her hair turn from blond to brown, watched the gray streaks thicken and spread. People don't stay here forever. Death is a part of life. Death is a part of God's eternal plan. Her father had died, but they all knew his heart was weak, and there was time to prepare. And her father was only a presence on the edges of her life. He was evenings and weekends. Her mom was all day, every day. How was it possible that Mary wouldn't ever see her stoop to run her fingers along a line of moss that bloomed between the cracks in the sidewalk?

In Mary's mind her mom should have, somehow, been exempt from the rules that governed other bodies. She should have lived as long as her grove of aspens and the ferns, she so loved, that grew beneath them. She hadn't cried when Anna called simply because she couldn't believe it. It seemed like someone must have made a mistake. She opened her eyes when she felt Fred's hot rank breath on her face. He'd jumped up onto the couch, and his paws were on top of her thighs, his scrunched face close to hers in concern. She stroked Fred's fat back. Why had she named him Fred? After that boy she married and had never been able to fully love. That man who only lived long enough to make her a mother, to give her her sweet Hank. Irrationally, it felt like she'd found an awful way to balance a complicated equation.

Her phone clanged. She told Fred to sit, and he ignored her. She reached around, leaning toward the coffee table and picked it up. A text from Roxcy asking her to check in with Anna about changing the sheets. Mary thought it likely that Roxcy had already texted Anna herself about the sheets. She wondered if she should text Anna or Roxcy? Why didn't Roxcy just send group messages? The blue light from the phone lit the room like a small rectangular flashlight, and Mary realized she was sitting in the dark. The sun had set.

Anna

Anna breathed in the smell of her two small daughters—a mix of sweat, peanut butter, and apple juice. Tonight, no baths. Tonight she'd do what her mom would do. They all lay down in her mom's bed.

"I miss Grandma."

"Me too, Honey."

"Who will make us dinner?" Honey began to wail.

"Shh, shh, I will. And your Aunties are coming to stay and help sort through Nana's things."

"You can't cook. When are they coming?"

"Well, you'll be at your dad's most of the time, but they'll be at Nana's memorial. We'll make sure we have dinner with all of them before Evie goes home."

"I don't want to go to Dad's house. I want to see Auntie Evie." Lula said, folding her arms across her chest with six-year-old certainty. She had dark curls and her sister light. The difference in color signified nothing about their temperaments which, like their mother's, tended toward freedom seeking and having things their own way.

"You will. It's not for long, just five sleeps."

"I'm sad." Honey wiped the tears with the back of her hand and scratched her nose. Anna noticed her nails needed trimming and thought—*tomorrow*.

"Is she in the Celestial Kingdom?"

"She's with God," Anna said, kissing the top of her head.

Lula narrowed her eyes and looked at her. "How do you know, mom?"

"I can feel it in my bones," Anna said.

"Daddy says that's the Holy Ghost," Lula said.

"Yes, that's what he says," and thought, *that's what he says at the moment, because it's convenient.* Anna was careful. She made a conscious effort to leave the animosity she felt towards Matt out of her relationship with her daughters. She also wanted to leave the church out of her relationship with her daughters, which was more difficult. As part of their divorce agreement, he'd insisted that the girls continue attending church, which meant they would go with him, and she'd have little control over the nonsense they ingested. Her mother had been taking them with her, as a compromise, but now . . .

"My primary teacher, says so too. She says it's a warm feeling."

Honey asked if her bones felt warm. Anna lied and said they felt peaceful, like knitting a soft blanket, like listening to Nana tell her a bedtime story when she was small. So the girls begged her for the story, for Nana's story about her name. When she said she was too tired tonight, they answered she was always too tired, which was true. She always felt tired. The small heads leaned into her shoulders. She ran her fingers across Honey's curls and nuzzled the top of Lula's head.

She knew she should move them to their own beds before she started. A good mother would maintain a regular routine. Roxcy would maintain a regular routine. But Matt would be here to pick them up soon. So, she began, talking low, trying to remember, trying to mimic the cadence of her mom's voice. And the words came easily from some old fold in her mind, as if her mom was speaking them through her, like grace.

Anna felt the wool move against her worn hands, lifting the thread back and through, her body falling into the familiar rhythm as she reached for the wooden weaving sword to blend the single thread with the group. She chose a rich purple and blue, the color of a summer sky. She had spun this thread, for the small blanket, from the soft wool of a lamb.

Something of his own to drag on the ground. Some little comfort for a tiny king who will hold the world's sorrow, she thought.

Her mother taught her to work the loom when she was a child, the way to rest the thread on her fingers, using the tension of the vertical to anchor the horizontal, how to ease the thread upward with the long wooden weaving sword, the warp and the weft, the rhythm of creation.

At seven she stood in front of her first loom, her small fingers awkwardly working, noticing when the wool moved over her skin-created heat. The repetitive movement opened a window in her mind, and she heard God's voice in the whisper of thread saying,

Watch.

Anna looked over at her mother, who worked on a larger loom just a few steps away, to see if she'd also heard. Her mother wove undisturbed. She moved the thread easily, quickly wielding the sword to form her near-perfect fabric.

Anna said nothing. She continued with the work, looking at her mother's hands, willing her fingers to move more smoothly.

She returned to the loom each morning, quiet, waiting, until her hands also began to move easily, her body swaying slightly with the motion. The individual threads of color began to glisten as dappled light formed an image of a very young mother and her baby boy. Her hands kept moving, but it felt as if she stepped out of her body and into the image. Then it was only his eyes, as deep as a well and just opening. They were dark brown, full of light. They saw everything. She stopped weaving and her hands dropped to her sides. She stood still in front of the loom.

Her mother looked from her own loom toward her daughter, her hands not pausing from their work.

"What's the matter, Anna? Why have you stopped?"

"I saw The Messiah, Mama. A tiny baby."

Her mother's sword clattered to the ground as she stepped toward Anna. She bent down low to look into her eyes. She felt her forehead for fever, her fingers still warm with friction. She stood up tall, put both of her hands on her hips and tapped her foot.

"Where, Anna"

"In my loom, Mama."

Her mother examined the threads.

Well, be quiet about it, child. She picked up the wooden instrument, placed it in her daughter's hand and turned back to her own loom. Without looking at Anna she said,

"If you see anything else, you must tell me."

"Yes, Mama."

A month later, Anna stood quietly in the doorway to the kitchen. Her mother knelt scrubbing the tile floor, her light gray robe dark with water, her sleeves pulled up. Anna noticed the way the muscle shifted beneath the skin of her forearm as she moved the rag in wide circles across the floor. When she stepped into the room, her mother did not pause to look at her.

"What is it?"

"It was his whole face this time, Mama. He was a grown man, but the same eyes."

As she scrubbed, her mother looked up at her and smiled. She began to hum. She did not tell Anna to be quiet. She finished the floor, changed her robe, took Anna's hand and walked her down the dusty road to the temple. The men stood on the steps talking low, their voices like the hum around a hive of bees.

"My daughter saw The Messiah in her loom."

The white beards turned, their watery eyes fixed on Anna. Some of them turned away, back to their arguments. One of them moved toward her and touched her softly on the shoulder. His eyes were foggy with age. His breath smelled of dust.

"Tell me."

She spoke and he listened, nodding his tired-looking head. Soon she couldn't leave the house without people whispering as she passed them in the street. This was the little girl who saw visions in her loom.

As she grew, so did the light. Sonorous scenes flashed across the threads of her loom, overlapping violence and beauty, thread and wood, sinew and bone. Scenes that would have left her bereft and fearful but for the accompaniment of the light, which was love infinitely wide, unfathomably deep. When the butcher smiled *as he handed her some lamb, there it was. When she picked up the little one who fell and scraped her knee, there it was. The old woman stooped and worn; the man with the wide, square shoulders that pulled the carts; the old rabbi at prayer; the young seamstress working her needle up and down.*

She had watched and waited for seventy years. Now, finally, Anna walked into the temple with the small blanket carefully folded in her hands. The men parted to make way for her. The young girl stood before her, looking a bit bewildered and holding a small bundle in her arms. Anna smiled. She touched the young mother on the crown of her head. Her old fingers and felt the familiar heat rise to the tips, as though she were working the threads. She took them from the girl's head, kissed them and touched the baby's forehead, pausing for a long moment to fall into the depths of those dark pools.

Perfect. Anna handed Mary the small blanket. "To keep him warm. To give him comfort when the path is hard."

"Shalom, Nevi'ah."

The women looked at each other for a moment before Anna turned toward home. It was time to put away her yarns, to oil the loom in preparation for its next owner, time to lay down her sword.

They were asleep, their breath smooth and deep, the weight of their small, warm bodies leaning into her. Anna sat for a moment, her eyelids heavy, a blink that lasted five seconds, then ten. And then she roused herself, carefully shifting Lula to one side. Honey wrapped around her like a monkey, wiry limbs clinging, but she unwound them and slipped free. This was when she missed him, at the end of the day. He was a piece of shit. She knew it, so the weakness of her longing, the loneliness she felt for him to touch her sometimes, made her hate herself. He would be here in an hour and a half to pick up the girls. Mary said she'd come a little early so she wouldn't have to see him alone, or at all if she preferred. Her mom had been the buffer since she left him. She had done everything she could to fill the void, to mend the torn seam of Anna's life.

—

She felt the weight of the day in her shoulders as she balanced the small box of thread on one arm and opened the door to the cabin. Anna walked into the quiet, the sound of running water in the kitchen, the lights turned low.

Then the girls are already in bed, she thought.

She'd missed laying them down again. She used to look forward to nights off, when she got a break from bedtime routines, from reading the same story a hundred times. She'd hoped to sort the yarn and smell the day in Lula's and Honey's hair but the shop was busy, and she'd extended the hours. Women came to purchase materials to make their wares for the bi-annual Beehive Bazzar, often with two, three, or four small children—some in strollers, others hanging onto the bottom of handmade skirts. All day the hum of conversation, the whine of tired children, the sound of stroller wheels on the wood floor of her shop. Most were young, in their early twenties, looking for a socially acceptable creative outlet and maybe some additional income for their ever-growing families.

Anna set the small box down and dropped her purse onto the child-sized bench in the entry that blocked the eight bright handprints made when she and her sisters had been small, when life had been predictable and happy. Her mom's books lay spread across the table beside a pile of papers with a pen sitting on top. Her mom stood over the sink. The dishes clinked softly in the dishwasher.

"I'm so sorry, Mom."

"For what?"

"For being late again. Thanks for picking the girls up. I don't know how I would do this without you. I can finish the dishes." She kissed her mom on the cheek.

"Busy is good, and the dishes are done. You look tired. Go sit down."

Anna obeyed, She picked up a book off the coffee table, a picture of a green fern on the cover.

"And I'm sorry for interrupting all your plans."

"Life is a series of interrupted plans, my dear. Anyone who doesn't accept that is going to be pretty miserable most of the time. I'll warm up some pasta in the fridge, nothing fancy. You go sit down."

She walked over into the living room and plopped on the sofa, watching the moonlight spread through the dining room windows, watching the aspens, spare and blue in the light. The weather was changing, no big spring storm in the forecast, good news for her business which, to be really successful, required women from Provo to drive up the canyon. When she finished, she opened the dishwasher, put her bowl in the top rack, put the soap in the dispenser, and pressed start. She walked back over to the couch and let herself stop.

She was tired of talking, pulling fabrics that would lie nicely across shoulders, tired of explaining the way the color would compliment someone's eyes, blue, green, or brown. Tired of interacting with this flow of young women whose lives seemed to be following a neat plan, whose marriages were still intact, whose faces were unendingly cheerful. Her body felt heavy, and when she closed her eyes she saw swirling blues, greens, pinks and oranges. She felt her mom sit on the sofa next to her, put the warm bowl in her hands, her aching feet being lifted up.

"Long day, huh?"

"Yes." Anna felt her eyes burn, her body pulsed with emotion. She missed Matt. The prick. "There's no way I could do this without you," she repeated. "I'd be back with him. I never want to be back with him."

"I'm here, sweetie."

Her mom put her arm around her, stroked her hair and Anna relaxed then drifted.

—

The girls' bags were packed, ready. She'd almost called Matt this morning in her grief. Instead she had called Jake. She'd been so careful to keep him separate from her real life. He was only that blessed half an hour, sometimes forty minutes, every Thursday morning. But in her sadness she'd crossed the thick black line of separation she'd drawn in her mind. Jake had driven up the canyon in the dark of pre-dawn, before the girls were awake. He'd sat next to her on the porch and stroked her hair while she fell apart and then, while she slept on the couch, quietly did her dishes, and changed the sheets in the main floor bedrooms. He'd wiped down the bathroom too. He was gone before the sun rose and woke her.

Anna quietly closed the bedroom door behind her, leaving the girls in her bed. The cabin was lit up. She'd turned every light on. She walked into the living room and sat down on the couch. There was a picture on the coffee table, her mom coming through the sliding door on Oak, her arms full of purple iris. She'd bent low and told Anna to stroke the soft petal, feel the fuzzy yellow line. Anna stood and pulled one of the large glass jars off the shelf. She rummaged through the rainbow of yarn to the fine silk, a fuzzy thread of purple. In the bright light she sat again, picking up two small needles and began to knit. She forgot that the sheets needed changing on the girls' beds in the loft.

And there was evening and there was morning, the second day.

They waited at the baggage claim, watching the suitcases circle on the slowly rotating steel plates, a hopeless merry-go-round. One blue, two black, evidence of someone's mistake, the owners of the bags waiting somewhere else in another airport. She saw them before they saw her. Mary with her wild hair twirling out from her ponytail, her straight broad shoulders and alert gaze scanning the crowd. Roxcy, as blond as she had been as a child, wearing neatly pressed trousers and a navy blue cardigan. And Anna looking like she'd rolled out of bed, knitting needles holding a messy bun on the back of her head, loose linen pants and a sleeveless t-shirt. Eve smiled and sighed. She walked up to Mary and touched her shoulder.

"Evie!" Mary wrapped her in a short strong squeeze. She smelled a little of dog, a little of some vanilla perfume or lotion.

"The flight was all right?"

"Yes, fine."

Roxcy patted her shoulder as she hugged her. All their voices unnaturally low. The back of a finger quickly swiping beneath an eye. The quiver of a chin or lower lip. When Anna stepped forward, she held onto her sister for a long time saying nothing. Eve answered each embrace. Her thin arms ached with the relief of them, the chorus of their voices a balm.

"So glad you're here."

"How is Mo?"

"Let me take your bag."

"This way, we're on the first floor, just out these doors."

They walked together toward short-term parking. They walked in silence, not wanting to shout their private sorrow over car engines, the laughter of a family meeting their missionary coming home, the sound of airplanes taking off and landing, the air heavy with exhaust. Mary loaded Eve's small bag into the trunk while the others climbed into the white SUV, sliding themselves onto the cool leather seats. Roxcy drove. Mary sat next to her in the front. Eve and Anna on either end in the back, four seat belt clicks, amidst the rustle of settling bodies. Eve looked out the window and said

"How did it happen?"

"I told you when I called yesterday—" Roxcy made eye contact with Eve in the rear view mirror.

"That was only this morning, Rox. A car crash. No details."

"It's been a long day. I'm sorry. Can someone else? Mary?"

"She was on the way home from Tahoe—"

"Right, her fern babies," Eve said.

Anna unlatched her seat belt and scooted to the middle seat so she was next to her, their knees touched.

"Yes, it was early in the morning, 2:30 am. They said it looked like she fell asleep. The car went off the road and hit a telephone pole. She died instantly. Head trauma."

"I wish she'd never gone back to school." Roxcy leaned forward over the steering wheel, her eyes straight on the road ahead.

"She put it off for us, then again when dad's heart started to fail." Anna said.

"I just didn't see the urgency. She had plenty to live on."

"Not everything is about money, Roxcy. She wanted—"
Eve felt Anna tense. She interrupted:

"A car accident . . . that doesn't seem right, does it?"

"I didn't think she could die." Mary laughed softly. "I know it's irrational, but I never entertained the possibility of a world without her."

If this were a normal ride from the airport, their mom would be driving. The car would be full of their voices, laughter, the air filled with details—children, work, husbands. They were not the Mormon sisters who called each other every day to express frustration about what one or the other had done. They called here and there. They called whenever they had good news to share. Their mom tried to get them all together at the cabin at least once a year, but there had been gaps in recent years when they were too busy with kids, work, or church to find the time.

Their children, the cousins, were friendly and enjoyed each other's company, but not to the exclusion of people outside their extended family circle. They were not the Mormon family that gathered in generations each Sunday for family dinner at Grandma and Grandpa's house. That sat at the foot of the old patriarch to read scriptures or watch short inspirational films about the power of the priesthood, about prayer or honesty. But every few years, when they were all together, the Taylor girls talked, over each other, all at once and then taking turns. They cooked together and ate together and settled back into the roles they had as kids. They remembered their 2 Nephi 2:25: *Adam fell that men might be and men are that they might have joy.* And filled their shared time and space, mostly, with the unbroken pieces of their lives. All the good things. Joy, they had learned through years of scripture study, in Sunday School and Seminary, was the central purpose of creation.

In recent years Anna's situation had complicated the usually upbeat exchange. Her sadness and anger occasionally spilled over the accepted familial boundaries. But, without saying it, they all agreed that, given what Matt had done, it was understandable. Too much, too public for just their mom to hold. They tried to be compassionate and offer support, but it felt thin and weak as atrophied muscle. Sadness was inescapable, of course, but it was something they had learned to keep to themselves and share only with her. With her it was safe from judgment about failure, weakness, or self-indulgence. They knew she would bring softness, rest and also, somehow, the pliable strength they needed to carry on. She noticed, could see, when something troubled one of them, and she opened up space for one-on-one time: a quiet walk somewhere, along a trail near the cabin, or a drive to the store with her to pick up some ice cream, or even a moment alone in the kitchen or hallway. But what to do with this shared and plumb-less grief? Her sudden absence had rolled like an earthquake shifting the family landscape leaving a deep chasm without a clear path across.

It was dark as they drove the long stretch on I-15. The lights from houses dotted the foothills. Every few miles there was a stretch lit up in neon strip-malls or large theater complexes showing Mormon movies: *Napoleon Dynamite*, *Sons of Provo*, *The Work and The Glory*. They passed the Utah State Prison, flooded with light and left to the desert. An absence of lawn or tree, coils of barbed wire running along the top of the tall fence like sharp tumbleweed. On the other side, they knew, sat the Point of the Mountain, the halfway mark between Salt Lake and Provo. As children they'd pressed their noses to the window looking for the bright blue, green, and yellow gliders, sometimes low enough to see a tiny person holding the bar, a trapeze artist without a net. That was back when the tall, sandy hill was still large enough to look like the beginning or ending of a mountain range. Over the years, gravel trucks had loaded the earth into their huge beds, had literally moved the mountain, flattened it, one truck load at a time.

The relentless billboards shuffled past, shiny white teeth, headless torsos with breast implants, smiling families in crisp white shirts and modest dresses. The car turned off the exit onto 8th North, a thoroughfare lined with more strip malls, gas stations, grocery stores, and strings of restaurants, past State Street where dim porch lights replaced the glaring neon, and over the curved pass where Provo Canyon opened, wide, dark, and quiet. They made weak attempts at conversation a couple of times. How is so and so? Fine. And work, home? Fine, busy, always busy. But the details of their lives seemed inconsequential. They couldn't locate any happiness in the shared silence, only the shock of finding themselves motherless and in, or nearing, midlife. It made each of them feel like a child again. They could not speak about tomorrow. Tomorrow they would go together to dress their mother's body in her temple clothes. To acknowledge tomorrow would be to accept that she was really gone.

When they turned off the wide canyon road and started the familiar wind-up toward Sundance, Eve rolled down her window, and her sisters followed. The air smelled of fall and water. The noise of the running stream mingled with the hum of the engine, and they felt the relief of sound, the familiar rushing water, settle around them. They passed the Sundance parking lot, passed the large cabins, whose lights peered through aspen until the road turned dark and they knew they were almost there. The car turned onto the dirt drive, dusty from a dry summer, and they rolled up their windows. They saw the circle of porch light spread across the bright green door. It was after midnight, a new day.

Mary

After almost thirty years she still woke up catching her breath, her pillow damp. Mary rarely cried in her real life, but when she was asleep, still a child in her mind, she hadn't yet found the lever to manage her emotions. She counted five deep breaths and felt for Fred nudging him with her foot. He rolled onto his back offering his belly for a rub. She scooted toward the bottom of the bed and obliged.

"It's Ok. Ok. . . . Thank you, Fred." She said aloud.

Mary needed to hear her own voice as a sliver of dim light slid through the thin gap in the curtains. She wrapped the old quilt from her mom's bed around her shoulders, gray and gold, strips of well-worn cotton, sewn vertically, soft against her neck. It still smelled of her mom's citrusy lotions and shampoo. She walked to the window and pulled open the drapes and checked the lock. Her old habit. The moon, perfectly round, covered the grove in blue light. The tall, tremulous shadows of the aspens stretched across the bedroom floor.

There must be a breeze, she thought.

She could guess the time. The dream came like clock-work: 3:30 a.m. It came more frequently in the fall, which made sense. This was the 123rd time. She reminded herself again that everything was fine. Said aloud

"Everything is fine."

Except it wasn't. She was in her mom's room, and her mom was gone. Mary got out of bed again, walked to the door and quietly turned the doorknob. She checked the lock on the front door, the door to the garage. Mary had the thought the whole house might be empty. She couldn't shake the feeling of some nebulous horror, the worry that all her sisters were gone too. She moved carefully up the narrow stairs to the loft and saw Eve and Anna asleep in their beds. One, Two ... She turned the doorknob of Roxcy's room and walked quietly to the window. It was locked. Roxcy's breath, soft, deep and even. Three. Mary slipped back into her own bed leaving the door to her room open. She could hear better that way. Her feet were cold, and she eased them beneath Fred and lay back down and counted her breaths, one, two, three, four, five—in, one, two, three, four, five—out. She breathed in and out, in and out.

—

Mary tried to breathe in and out very slowly. Tomorrow she'd turn eleven, old enough to do what her mom had taught her to do when the nightmare came.

Breathe in and out, then come tell me.

She wiped away the tears on the back of her hand. Their father found the bunk beds second hand. There wasn't a ladder. She carefully climbed over the side of the top bunk. Her foot felt for the flat edge of the frame. Another blind step backwards and her toes felt the silent, deep carpet beneath them. She let go and stepped down.

Mary moved her hands along the edge of the mattress on the bottom bunk and knelt close, waiting for her eyes to adjust to the darkness. She quieted her own breathing to hear Roxcy's. She was asleep, safe. The large, rectangular bedroom window was big enough to climb out if there were a fire, which meant it was big enough for someone to climb in through the dark. She pushed open the thick green drapes. Mary checked the lock on the window. The moon shone bright for a moment, a blue light, and then went dark.

There must be clouds, she thought.

She left the drapes open just a crack, climbed down, and felt her way to the door. She moved her hand along the wood-paneled walls in the hallway, her fingers feeling for each seam. Bright blue light spread across the carpet, bounced off the narrow walls, illuminated the path to her parents' room. She thought,

Now the clouds have parted.

She moved quickly and quietly. Her mom slept on the right-hand side of a large king-sized bed, which took up most of the room. Her mom had explained that their father was a light sleeper. If he woke, he often couldn't quiet his mind enough to return to sleep. His head was full of important equations. If they needed her in the night, if there was a bad dream, if they were sick, they should come in very quietly. Mary listened and obeyed. She moved carefully. She could see the outline of her father on his side. She tiptoed around the foot of the bed, knelt on the floor on the right side of the bed and reached to find her mother's hand. When her fingers touched their warmth, her mother immediately slipped out of bed, as if she'd been awake waiting for her. She knelt and hugged her for a minute before taking her hand walking Mary back down the long moonlit hallway to her bedroom.

She whispered in her ear. "You're a good big sister, Mary. You're safe. Roxcy's safe. Evie and Anna are safe. I'm right here. I'll always be right here."

Mary cried silently. The tears running over her smooth cheeks. Her mom knelt down and looked into her eyes before she held her close again. She stroked her hair and wiped the tears away with the soft pad of her finger. She opened the drapes wide and let the moonlight into the room. Mary scaled back up the frame of the bunk bed.

"Would you like me to stay?"

"I'll be alright, Mama." This is what she had called her mother when she was very young. She still felt very young when she woke from the dream even though she was almost eleven.

"I know you will. Would you like me to stay?"

"Yes, please."

She leaned over the edge and watched as her mom pulled a thin mat from beneath the bed and a blanket from the closet shelf. When she closed her eyes and listened for her mama's breathing to match hers to the familiar rhythm. She fell asleep, aware of blue moonlight on her eyelids, listening to the in and out of her mother's breath.

~

Mary pulled the covers up around her and Fred, the dog, burrowed his way to the top of the bed. He lay down heavily next to her licking her nose, his breath musty and thick. She reminded herself that she was a grown woman, that it was only a bad dream. She closed her eyes and breathed in and out, slow deep breaths. One at a time the images disappeared.

The blue pool.

The tall thin shadow.

Her little sisters behind her.

The anger rising.

The full force of it in her arms.

The push.

The man falling backwards.

The ripple over the submerged body.

The face of her dead husband staring blankly up at her.

The surface of the water, unmoving, clear.

Eve

She mistook the blue light of the moon for the early morning light of years earlier, thought she'd heard her mom whisper in her ear, thought she heard the barely perceptible slide of the glass door. But that was the house on Oak. There were no sliding doors at the cabin. Eve turned on her side, blinked, saw Anna's long form stir beneath the covers on the other bed and shift back into stillness. She blinked again and looked up at the white-washed A-line of the roof, moon-illuminated, pale blue above her head, thought of the morning sky when the sun was a light yellow line stretched across the muted horizon.

⁓

Open your eyes, Evie. Come out to the garden.
Pre-dawn light fingered the edges of the lavender curtains. Baby Anna shifted in her crib. Eve felt the comfort

of her own warmth in the bed for a moment and blinked. She saw her mom slip out the door, leaving it open just a crack, the almost-morning light a line across the carpet. She listened for the slide of the glass door, like the rustle of a breeze. Smiling, she slipped quietly from beneath the covers and felt her bare feet sink into the thick shag carpet. Eve ran her hand along the wood-paneled hallway, feeling the grooves with her fingertips. The pale light from the skylights lay in long rectangular blocks along the floor. She loved spring and summer, when days began to lengthen and this was her every morning. The gray-blue-just-before-sunrise light passed through the folding French doors that separated the entry from the living room. The ones she dusted every week, wrapping a butter knife in a soft cloth and moving it back and forth between each angled slat. The neat living room, two magazines on the kidney shaped coffee table—a funny name for their house, coffee table. There was never coffee. Mormons didn't drink coffee, or tea or alcohol. They didn't smoke cigarettes. Mormon mothers had babies, clean houses. Their hands were always full. Mormon fathers went to work, had church meetings on Sunday all day and Wednesday nights. Families read scriptures and prayed together. They attended their Sunday meetings, canned tomatoes, peaches, and green beans from their gardens. Eve knew that their house followed those rules too, except her mom grew flowers instead of food. All the surfaces in the room were clear, every book placed carefully back on the built-in shelves on either side of the fireplace. Her father's leather chair in the left corner, the long moss-colored couch facing the fireplace in the center of the room, and the clean off-white curtains to the right that billowed out filling with the early spring air. A place for everything, and everything in its place.

The quiet music of wind chimes blew in. A few songbirds practiced their morning vocal warm-ups. The breeze caught the hem of her nightgown and raised the hair on her legs. It was a little short for her now, a hand-me-down from Mary to Roxcy to her. Another inch and it would be Anna's. She would be seven in a few months, and then eight, and then nine. Eve stepped out onto the patio, felt the shock of cold concrete on her feet, and ran across the damp grass. The crocus spread through the lawn. Their little cups gathered tiny pools of morning dew. Her mom knelt over a flower bed, hands working the soil, her hair pulled back into a haphazard bun. Eve stood close silently observing the way her mother's hands moved through the soil, like a prayer. Her bare fingers slid into a green clump and gently worked the roots free, spread them out, attending to each plant that needed to be divided. She never wore gardening gloves. So, there was often the thin line of dirt beneath her mom's nails. When Eve looked up her mom's eyes looked back at her. They were gray, like hers, today.

"Good morning, Evie, my dear. You have some mail on the counter."

Eve smiled and turned. She ran back across the lawn, the soft flannel of the old nightgown brushing against her shins. She paused for just a moment over the heating vent, held out her arms, and allowed the fabric to billow wide. Between the letter from the school and a utility bill, she found a larger brown envelope addressed to Ms. Eve Taylor. Inside were three small packets with pastel illustrations of pink and white cosmos, bright blue stocks of delphinium, warm yellow coreopsis and purple Penstemon. She ran back outside.

"The seeds came!"

"Show me." Her mother put down her gardening tools and reached out to her.

Eve knelt next to her, quiet, and watched her run her fingers over the back of each packet.

"Every plant is a little different, Evie. Like children, each one needs different things. Coreopsis likes lots of sun and a big deep drink now and then. You'll need to keep the soil of the delphinium moist all the time and plant it where it can have a little shade in the afternoon. The Cosmos are easy, just plant them in plenty of sunshine and they'll be happy."

"Alright." Eve said.

"Show me where you think they'll do well."

She held out the packets and Eve took them and walked slowly along the edge of the flower beds. Nothing had bloomed yet, though she could see where the tulips would be, the soft green sprouts full, almost ready. Eve put the delphinium there and looked back at her mom.

"Good."

From mid-spring through summer the garden would be full of flowers, one spilling over onto another until it became a pleasant blur of color. Crowded bunches of yellow and white daffodil, blue Siberian Squill, tulips, pink, purple, creamy yellow and the smell of blooming lilac. By May, fragrant clumps of purple, yellow and white bearded Iris. Followed by daylily, lupine, tall Shasta Daisies that came with the heat and air thick with lavender and lemon verbena. All of it mixed with the scent of fresh-turned earth.

Eve put the coreopsis and penstemon near the spot where the daylilies would come. She placed the cosmos near the lavendar.

"Perfect!" Her mom said, holding out her arms. Eve ran back into a hug.

"You're going to be a good mama someday, Evie. A gardener who knows her plants will know how to care for her little ones too."

Eve smiled.

———

Half asleep Eve's hand moved to her flat stomach, the familiar emptiness. Mornings in the garden belonged to memory, her mom only reachable through these old electric currents in her mind, a twitch in her brain. The dreams of having a child of her own gone too. *Perhaps*, Eve thought, *mom is looking for the little girl who wanders into my dreams with that warmth that I can't seem to keep.* Perhaps she could hold those small fingers in her hand in some other existence without feeling them slip away. She could almost see them together bent over a flower bed, the little girl reaching out, her mom taking the small dimpled hand in hers, looking back at Eve over her shoulder. The image gave her comfort. Eve blinked slowly and rolled back into sleep.

Roxcy

A small round light fell across the page. The words on the edges still in shadow. Roxcy read:

and the suckling child shall play on the hole of the asp, and the weaned child shall put his

hand in the cockatrice's den. They shall not hurt nor destroy in all my holy mountain; for the earth shall be full of the knowledge of the Lord as the waters cover the sea.

The incomprehensible images left her feeling light-headed. Roxcy needed a clear story, Nephi's *I have been born of goodly parents therefore I was taught* or Alma leaving the corrupt priests of Noah, repenting *of his sins and iniquities* and going among the people to preach the word of God, or the two thousand stripling warriors declaring *we do not doubt, our mothers knew it* before going into battle against impossible odds. The Book of Mormon was full of people doing things, following faith-based compasses, being baptized, fighting wars, going on missions. God always clearly guided them. She looked hard for any reassurance that her son Peter would be okay. There were so many stories of promising teenagers falling off the straight and narrow path. Losing their way because of addiction. She searched the words again for any reassurance that this would not happen. Even a tiny line that would quell her fear. She found only a puzzle. In the past weeks she'd looked to her scriptures desperately. Her ward was reading the Book of Mormon in three months. She'd hoped for a miracle that fell within her prescribed reading plan, which she followed religiously in order to meet her reading goal. So, she was stuck in the midst of 2 Nephi, a restatement of Isaiah's confounding poetry. She hated poetry. Roxcy sighed and closed the book. She ran her hand over the soft leather cover. She should get up anyway and start the cracked-wheat cereal. Her mom had made it for them through the late fall and winter, as the days shortened and they walked to early morning seminary before the sunrise in warm coats and scarves. She'd been fourteen the first time she'd read the Book of Mormon on her own. The same age as Joseph Smith—the boy prophet. She'd struggled to stay awake through these same passages as Brother Clark droned on and on about the power of metaphor. She hated metaphors. Why not just say what you mean?

The large pot sat on the counter, pulled out and arranged last night after the long drive up the canyon. After her sisters had settled in and all she heard were the familiar noises of the cabin at night, the scrape of an aspen branch on the roof, the fridge beginning to hum—a pause—and hum again. Roxcy thought of each meal as an offering, her gift to her sisters, the comfort she knew how to give. She filled a large pot with water and turned on the stove—falling into the habit of careful quiet she'd practiced when her children were small. The water began to boil, and she poured in the wheat, cracked yesterday in her grandma's old mill. She stirred it, turned it low, and watched the small bubbles in the center of the pot for a moment before placing a lid on top. She laid the spoon down and stepped away.

Roxcy recreated the picture of the table she'd formed in her mind. She'd found some green placemats for the table, the color of new aspen leaves, another nod to their mom. She executed each step of her design with careful attention. She arranged each mat and stepped back to inspect. The blue porcelain bowls came next, and then pink tulips that waited in a vase on the counter. She reached to clear Anna's centerpiece but paused and turned the cube to look at each photograph. She stopped at the picture of her and her mother—a close up of their faces in profile. Their foreheads touched, both of them laughing about something she was too young at the time to remember now.

Was she three-years-old? How old had she been when her mom first told her her name story?

She remembered when she'd learned it was fictional, her first year at BYU, some girl in her church history class raising her hand to correct the teacher about when polygamy had actually ended. The girl described Eliza Roxcy Snow, her namesake, as self-serving and a disloyal friend. Roxcy had felt her anger rise in response to the girl's lie. But Sheri, her best friend, handed her the book *Mormon Enigma* to read. It was about Emma Smith, Joseph's first wife, who had sacrificed family, security, everything—to marry him. Roxcy learned that Emma had taken Eliza into their home, trusted, and loved her. Eliza Roxcy Snow thanked her by secretly marrying Joseph Smith when he began the practice polygamy behind Emma's back. A betrayal that destroyed their friendship. After Joseph died Eliza became the polygamist wife of the next Mormon prophet, Brigham Young, a man some people claimed, pointedly demonized Emma to secure his position as prophet.

She preferred her mother's, simpler, version of Eliza Roxcy Snow. It focused on different aspects of her character, with little relation to historical accounts. Although she was famous for her organizational skills and responsible for the early primary and youth programs of the church, Roxcy could find no account of her ever healing any tired oxen. There were many accounts of the healing blessings she performed on other women. But these were problematic as well, because women weren't allowed to do that anymore. She didn't really want to think about why that was and, really, had no desire to know more about the past. After all, she lived in a wonderful present. So when she laid *Mormon Enigma* on her nightstand, Roxcy discarded its unsettling facts and kept her mother's version. She loved her church, which had only brought happiness and order to her life and decided then that she wasn't interested in any information that might threaten her relationship with her faith, even if it was true.

The lid on the pot began to clink. Roxcy looked up, saw the steam from the cracked wheat circling the dim light above the stove. She placed the photo cube carefully down where she'd found it and walked over to stir the cereal.

~

The clock read 5:15 a.m. Roxcy had set her alarm early for her first day of early morning seminary. She'd already started memorizing the verses for scripture chase. Mary said they had donuts every Friday. Now that she was 14 and a Freshman, Roxcy would join the small crowd of teenagers who carpooled to the seminary building across the parking lot from Provo High. She'd opted for the early morning class so she could squeeze in an extra class, and because her friends were all doing the same. The steam circled around the light above the stove in a warm haze. She'd measured the cracked wheat, water, and put it on the stove to cook, while her mom set out four bowls. The whole kitchen felt warm and filled with the nutty, comforting smell of the cereal.

"You excited, Rox?"

"Yes!"

"Hand me the butter will you?"

"How much?"

"A cube please."

Her mom never used margarine. Roxcy unwrapped the stick of butter and dropped it into the bubbling cereal.

"I'll stir it, mom."

"I'm all right. Can you grab the brown sugar off the shelf there and set out some bowls and spoons?" She kissed her mom on the cheek.

"Sure. Can we use the blue porcelain?"

"I suppose, it is a special occasion."

Roxcy felt grown-up helping her mom with the breakfast. In less than half an hour she'd be sitting in a room full of other tired teenagers making a sacrifice to wake up early to learn the scriptures. She opened the cupboard and carefully pulled out four bowls the color of an early morning sky; barely blue. They were the perfect size. You could hold them in both hands, your fingers almost touching, and warm your hands.

"Go make sure Mary's up and we'll eat," Her mom said. Her father mussed her hair as she passed him walking through the French doors.

—

Roxcy heard the old pine floorboard creak and turned.

"Do I smell cracked wheat?" Mary whispered.

"You do."

The sun began to rise in a thin bright line of red across the horizon. The whole room blushed.

"Oh, look at that!" Roxcy said.

They watched clouds blossom, deep pink, and golden rays shot out like an annunciation. The two of them sat together absorbed by the strange, raw, light.

"I guess it's a good thing I can't sleep past six anymore. Even when I don't sleep well." Mary's voice was still thick with silence.

"You didn't sleep well?"

"I had a bad dream." She paused. "The one I always have, maybe because Mom brought up the Howards the last time we talked."

"Really? How odd." Roxcy stopped and looked at Mary.

"Do you remember them, going to their house to swim, Dad's sister, Violet? Well, the dream is about the night Anna was born. "

"I remember a little." Roxcy smoothed her apron and then smiled, "I was just thinking about my first day of seminary, how I got up and cooked this with mom. I guess it's normal to have the past all stirred up at times like these."

Mary took the cue and changed the subject.

"Did you sleep all right?" Mary twisted the end of her thick dark braid, noting that Roxcy was already dressed neatly in a simple a-line skirt and cotton, button-down blouse.

"I guess, all things considered," Roxcy said. "Anna's bed is too firm for me, but it was nice of her to give up her room."

"Well, what can I do to help?"

Roxcy handed her the four bowls.

"You could put these on the table. Mary, carefully!"

"I've got them. That sunrise keeps getting better."

"It's gorgeous." Roxcy said and sighed deeply.

Anna

Anna rolled onto her stomach, pulling the pillow on top of her head. The murmur of lowered voices climbed the line of the ceiling and slid into the loft. Familiar echoes wandered pathways of her tired brain.

—

The sweet smell of the cracked wheat woke her. It traveled the length of the hallway to her room. She sat up, yawned, and opened the drapes wide to check the light. Their window faced north, but she was small and did not know the sun rose in the east. The room filled with pink light. She left the drapes open, grabbed her soft blanket and the book off of her nightstand, and walked the rosy hallway, sleep still pulling on her eyelids. Her school started three hours after Mary and now Roxcy left for seminary and Eve one hour later than

Farrer Junior High. She'd heard her older two sisters leave, Eve was probably still sleeping.

Anna could still slide comfortably into a small, secret space she'd discovered between the cupboards and the breakfast bar. She'd kept its existence to herself for games of hide-and-seek. This morning she slid in while her mother's back was turned cooking over the stove. Her hand searched for the flashlight in the corner. She held the light over the book and opened it up. Pictures of quilts, the intricate patterns and colorful fabrics a pleasure for her young eyes: a pinwheel almost in motion on the surface of the blue fabric, the pink and white overlapping rings, the bold squares of red, yellow and green, a line of light purple tulips with pale green leaves. She wanted to feel textures of them, expected them to be slightly raised so she could run her small finger along, feel the stitch line.

She heard footsteps, saw her father's old brown shoes through the thin crack. She paused, put the book down, and leaned forward on her knees. She'd already missed some of the conversation. They spoke in lowered voices. Anna saw the heels of her mom's bare feet. The heels had small, white, cracks in them and stood in the middle of the gold linoleum floor, her ankles splattered with dirt and the fraying hem of her thin denim pants visible through the thin slit in the cupboards.

"It's impractical," her father said.

"My tuition would be free. My mom could help with kids some. She's getting older, but she could be here when they get home from school. This was always the plan, David. I want to finish my B.A. and start my Master's Degree. I told you that before we got married."

"But you got pregnant right away, and the plan changed."

"Yes, I did. Four times, because you wanted a boy. And the girls are finally all in school this year. Besides, what if something happened to you?"

"I have a good policy, Sylvia. I've taken care of you and the girls. You're the most important—you know I've taken care of that."

There was a pause.

"What is this actually about, David?"

Another pause.

"This is going to sound wrong . . . but honestly, it's bad timing. There's still some unresolved tension with all that feminist stuff from a few years ago. It's strained on campus right now. And President Benson has been talking a lot about the importance of women staying home—"

"I know what the Prophet says. I heard his talk. I just happen to disagree."

"Why not wait until the girls are through school?"

"That doesn't make any sense!"

"We have to be flexible."

"I have to be flexible." Her mother raised her voice.

"Shhh! Anna . . ." He whispered. There was a long pause before he continued. "That's not fair, Sylvia".

"That's reality, David. You should go. Professors shouldn't be late. That might be frowned upon."

"Sylvia—"

"Just go."

Anna waited until she heard the front door close and slipped out.

Her mom's back was to her. Anna saw her rub her nose against the sleeve of the old white shirt, something they were told never to do, even if they had a bad cold. Then she leaned on the counter with her face in her hands, sobbing. She knew her mom sometimes cried when she felt the spirit, when she bore her testimony at church. She cried when she was angry, the time they knocked the peonies all over the carpet and broke her favorite vase playing tag in the house. But the only time she'd seen her cry like this was when she told them that grandpa died. Her body shook like aspen leaves in the wind, her shoulders curled in. Her father had put his arm tight around her mom's shoulders then. She ran and grabbed onto her mom's waist from behind.

"Anna!"

"It's ok, mom."

She turned, leaned down and gave Anna an Eskimo kiss. Then she wiped her own tears away with the back of her hand. She took a long, deep breath. Anna reached her arms around and hugged her mama again.

"Thank you, sweetie. I'm ok now. Really."

"Well, I'm hungry," Anna said.

"Grab a bowl." Her mama smiled down at her. They dodged each other, her mom moving toward the stove, Anna going under her arm and opening the cupboard.

She watched her spoon the steaming cereal into a bowl, noticed that her breath still caught and shuddered. Her mother slid a tin of brown sugar toward Anna.

"Get the sugar before you put the spoon in your cereal."

"I know, mom!"

"Ok, you know."

She handed her the teaspoon.

"I'm never getting married," Anna said

"Where did you come from anyway? Did you hear your dad and me talking?"

"Yes, and I'm going to have a quilt shop and a bookshop and sell art." The cereal tasted sweet, felt warm on her tongue.

"Well, I don't see why you can't have all those shops and be married," her mom said.

"You can't be married and have a job."

"Well, I can understand why you would—"

"You know a lot about plants. You know more about plants than anyone. But you don't get to have a plant store because you're married and your a mom."

Her mom walked behind her. She couldn't see her face, but her cheek felt nice against Anna's hair.

"You don't have to choose, Anna. Your life can be full of all your loves: children, quilt shops, bookshops and a kind husband—everything your heart desires. Dad is a kind, good man; he just worries and the worries cloud his thinking. So, I have take things slow."

—

The bright morning light filled the loft. She could almost feel the pressure and warmth of her mother's cheek on her head. Anna lifted off the pillow and the illusion dissipated. Eve's bed was made, and she could hear her sister's talking in low voices downstairs. She sat on the edge of the bed and stretched for a minute before standing, walked to the railing, and leaned over.

"I'm up now. You don't have to whisper," she yelled.

"Come down and eat breakfast before it's cold," said Roxcy

She pulled a robe on over her camisole, twirled her long brown hair back into a knot, and walked down the narrow stairs. She held her hand to her forehead as if saluting, her hazel eyes in a squint.

"I envy your ability to sleep in," Roxcy said. Anna noticed Roxcy's neat, clean outfit, her hair and makeup just so, and felt annoyed.

"What time is it?" Anna yawned.

"7:30."

"I didn't realize that qualified as sleeping in," she laughed

"Well, it is for me, and our appointment is at nine o'clock. It takes about 30 minutes to get there from here."

"Appointment?" Anna looked at Eve.

Roxcy answered. "We're dressing mom's body today, remember?"

Everything went still for a moment.

"That's right, I knew that. I'm sorry," Anna said.

Roxcy continued "The cabin is really homey. All the color and cozy clutter—"

"What does that mean?" Anna laughed.

"I meant it as a compliment. I could never live with it, but it fits you."

Anna smiled and thought, *here we go.* She had neither the money nor the time to decorate and maintain her house the way Roxcy did, neat lines, earth tones everywhere, the best fabrics and fixtures. Anna covered her walls with her girls' art. Spinning mobiles of felted woodland birds hung from the lower ceiling in the dining room and from plant hangers that she'd attached to the taller bookshelves. Baskets stacked with fabrics filled the corners. The books her mother had loved enough to move with her to the cabin shared crowded shelves with glass containers of hand-wound yarn, baskets full of knitting needles and sewing notions. Anna had replaced the old drapes, maroon with mallard ducks, with a bright modern floral print full of movement, pink, yellow, gray and mossy green that picked up the color of the old sectional. They hung from high rods tall enough to cover the wall of windows.

"We should close those drapes tonight. It's so bright in here in the morning," she said.

"I didn't even think of it," Mary said. "And we'd miss the sunrise. It was beautiful this morning."

"Mom always watched the sunrise from the porch," Anna said, watching Roxcy move through the kitchen and dining room as if they belonged to her. She'd rearranged the glasses on the shelves and cleared the counter space of appliances. She even brought the set of blue bowls she'd taken from the house on Oak Lane without asking anyone when their mom had moved. Anna needed a cup of coffee. Where had Roxcy put her coffee maker?

Roxcy picked up a small knitted iris off the table. She rubbed one of the petals between her fingers.

Anna thought *She's always judging me. She hasn't even noticed the pictures, mom in the garden with each of us, blooming iris in every background.*

Anna's irritation rose. She'd spent a lot of time searching through the photo albums for each one. Had spent a long time looking at the one of her on her mother's hip in a white onesie, covered with dirt, laughing. Her mom smiling, one arm supporting Anna and the other full of cut purple Iris. She'd examined the petal, the shape, the textures, choosing a fine silk yarn in deep purple, a fuzzy yellow and lavender. The soft click, the stitches knit together. The rhythm of the needles, like rocking, had been a comfort. And now Roxcy was looking for evidence of her inadequacy again, a dropped stitch, a broken home, too little faith.

"Rox, please put it down."

"Oh, sorry. They're so pretty."

Anna watched her sister's face for any sign of a smirk.

"Did you sleep all right?" She said.

"Yes, thank you for giving up your room. You didn't have to do that," Roxcy said.

"I don't mind sharing with Evie. Just like old times." Anna reached over and squeezed Eve's hand. Eve returned her smile.

"Well, it was very thoughtful. Everything's ready; we should pray," Roxcy said

They sat, bowed their heads, and prayed. When Anna reached for the bowl of brown sugar, her robe slipped open. Her three sisters all saw the low v of the camisole, the bare shoulder—witnessed the proof that she'd taken off her garments. She winced internally. Part of her had believed in those special underclothes that were supposed to represent fidelity and protection. She'd worn them faithfully beneath her knee-length shorts and capped sleeves on hot summer days because she thought they meant something. But ultimately, they'd failed on both counts. No more magic underwear when there was no magic. She took them off the day she and Matt officially separated. And she felt irritated that her sisters looked away as if she'd done something wrong, as if she were responsible.

No one said anything, but the discomfort hovered. Mary mentioned how good the cereal tasted. Eve squeezed Roxcy's hand and thanked her.

Roxcy looked down at her bowl and tried not to feel angry.

It didn't matter that Anna stopped wearing the symbols of her faith, the simple white cloth that covered shoulder and thigh. It didn't matter that the garment was a sacred reminder of the most essential and sacred commitments Anna had made to God. It was enough that Anna had been through the temple. She had been an endowed, active member of the church not long ago. That was the only requirement for her participation. George had checked the leadership handbook for her. There was no mention of current practice, or spiritual worthiness, required to dress the body of a loved one. To dress the dead in the ceremonial clothing of the temple wove worlds together. It was sacred ritual of passage. It didn't matter that Anna had chosen to reject everything they all held sacred. Roxcy felt defensive of her faith with her own sister and defensive that she had to feel defensive. But it did not matter what she personally thought or felt. She didn't want to think. She didn't want to feel angry or scared or sad. She didn't want to think of her mother's body burned to dust when she needed her desperately needed her here. What mattered was that they'd all go together to dress her together.

The off-white brick ranch looked small from the front. A neat lawn and short-trimmed hedge lined the porch. The charcoal door had a brass knocker, a lion's head holding a ring in its mouth. An older couple from Mary's ward ran the small mortuary. The man opened the door, his face deeply wrinkled, like a series of desert canyons. He wore bifocals low on his nose and held each of their hands for a moment as they walked through the door, looking at them through watery blue eyes. His wife came in behind him, resembling all the old women they'd known through the years, her hair curled, like loose, wispy cotton. A slight hump in her back. The skin on her hands veined vellum. She smelled of rose water and old age. She led them down the hallway, talking as she walked across the blue carpet, past a painting of Jesus with the little children.

"Your mother was a beautiful woman. We did our best to cover the injury on her forehead, and we've dressed her in her temple garments and dress." She opened the door to a dim room. "The rest of the clothes are just draped on the chair there. There's an intercom here. Please press this button and call if you need anything. I'm so sorry, girls. Heavenly Father must have needed her back with him for something pretty important, I guess. At least there's the comfort that she's on to a better place. Do you have any questions before I leave you?"

"No."

"Thank you."

"Thank you."

"Thank you."

She smiled at them. The door closed. Anna moved away from the long table and sat in a high-backed chair off to one corner. Eve walked over.

"You all right?"

"I need a minute."

Another painting hung above the body. Lazarus wrapped in cotton strips, the barren background a desert and Jesus in a white robe, one arm touching his friend the other outstretched like a magician. Roxcy walked to the table and looked down at the face. The broad forehead, square jaw and full lips. Their mother's face looked young. All the muscles in her face had relaxed. She moved a strand of the dark hair, streaked with gray, touched it with her fingertips. There was slight, sickening, depression in her forehead. Mary touched her shoulder. She held a simple white pleated robe hung over one arm. Working in silence, they carefully placed the veil on her head, slipped the robe over one shoulder, and tied the green apron around her waist. They dressed her in myth. Mary handed Anna the white slippers. Each of them had seen her dressed this way their first time through the temple. They had all heard her whisper in their ears.

It's strange, but there's beauty here too.

Anna carefully slid the slippers on the inanimate feet. She had been the one to identify the body, to bear the brunt of the first shock.

It was finished, and they stood close to each other, a hand held, an arm around a waist, a head on a shoulder. Together they searched the face for signs of their mom.

"I don't feel her," Roxcy's voice was quiet. "People talk about how the spirit often stays near the body for a while after someone dies."

"Mom wasn't the lingering type though, was she?" Mary smiled her eyes brimming.

Anna let go of Roxcy's hand. She lifted her head from Eve's shoulder and opened the door.

"She's gone," she said and walked out.

Anna walked down the hall and straight out. She did not pause to thank the old woman who was waiting in the entry. Mary, Roxcy, and Eve did. Roxcy apologized for Anna and handed her the small cylinder made from an aspen tree, the wood sanded smooth. The woman talked them through the timing, when they might pick up the ashes-Thursday ten a.m. Mary thanked her. They walked out the door. Eve stood still, staring at a painting that hung along the opposite wall, hidden from the direct light of the front window. She'd not noticed it when they'd come in.

"Salvador Dahli," the woman said.

"Yes," said Eve, surprised.

"I know we're not much for the crucifixion, but I'm partial to modern art and saw it on a trip to New York many years ago . . . there was something about it. My husband doesn't like it, thinks it's gruesome. You see? He's pushed the plant in front of it again." She walked over, bent down and shifted the pot. "But I love it. The whole composition is right somehow, the position of his body, the woman, the way she's leaning back."

"Yes, exactly," Eve said and thought, *a woman of sorrow, acquainted with grief.*

She turned and took hold of the woman's hand, the knotted knuckles warm. The woman put her other hand on Eve's cheek.

"Thank you," Eve said.

And there was the evening and there was the morning, the third day.

The four of them were on the path without her now. They looked back and forth between two trails: one that followed the stream and one that crossed it. The light and shadow of the aspens colluded on the path, shifting in the breeze. They'd been teenagers the last time they hiked the trail together. It had been more than a decade since they'd all hiked the trail with their parents, their father going on to summit while their mom walked the wildflower meadows and soaked her feet in the jewel-like lake. It was late in the season, but they wanted to feel whether or not the wildflower meadows were where they should scatter her ashes next summer when the snow melted. Roxcy pointed to the smaller path that crossed the stream. Anna pointed to the wider, steeper path that followed it. Mary rubbed her forehead. Eve stood silent, two or three steps away. She watched the patterns float on the ground. She looked up, tuned out their voices and studied her sisters. Anna's lips a long dash, insistent, persistent movement. She was all length, neck, arms, fingers, legs. Her limbs, like the aspens branches, seemed to extend just beyond the edge of her. She looked out at the world from their mom's eyes, wide-spaced, large, almond-shaped.

Roxcy stood with her hands on her hips, her lips moving fast, no perceptible breaks for breath. Occasionally she moved her right hand to point, and her head turned. The long neat bob moved with her, sleek and shiny. Her hair still the same bright blond it had been when she was a child. Eve wondered what it cost her to maintain such a perfect illusion. Roxcy's smooth tan face, another piece of their mother twirling down the genetic ladder.

Mary's full lips opened and closed in short, strong bursts. Her dark wavy hair framed her oval face. The sun caught threads, veins of silver, followed a familiar pattern of gray. The shade settled in the deepening creases around her eyes and mouth. The lines of her face making her more and more like their mother over time. Her arm pointed straight, steadily toward the steeper fork.

Eternity, Eve thought.

They continued like this Roxcy then Mary, Anna, Anna, Roxcy, Mary, Anna, Roxcy, Roxcy, Mary, Roxcy . . . It looked like an ancient Celtic dance as she watched their arms, their mouths, the language of gesture. They were repeating themselves, every nuance of movement familiar, the water in the stream an accompaniment, a fluid syncopation.

She rested her hand on one of the many aspens that bordered the path. Her round eyes following their movements and walked along the edge of them unnoticed. She took the map from Anna's hands. She flew here just for this purpose. Anna needed her hands to argue. They all needed Eve's silence.

She thought, *I belong more to the grove.*

She could feel the pull of it, the low thrum of the roots beneath her and the lure of liquid light. She closed her eyes and felt the play of leaf shadow across her face, her shoulder and began the lecture in her mind.

The largest living organism on earth is an aspen grove. The aspen belongs to the family Populus and is the most widespread tree in North America. It ranges from the Atlantic to the Pacific, across Canada and, in the Western U.S., extends to higher and higher altitudes as it travels south through all the great mountain ranges and into Mexico. The trees are known for their resilience and intrusive root systems. Each Aspen tree is not a separate being, but shoots of the same tree dependent on an ever-expanding series of connections, one organism with a shared root system. Aspens are prevalent in the Colorado Rockies and Wasatch Mountain ranges, where we will study them over the course of this semester. They grow in enormous groves. The largest is called Pando, a Latin word meaning "to spread." Consisting of well over 40,000 trees and located in Southwestern Utah near Fish Lake, it covers over 100 acres.

She'd spent the last ten years of her life studying the life of these trees, their entangled mess of connection. Author of twelve papers on the behaviors of connective roots, their strengths and weaknesses, their relationships to other plants, she knew them in a way she might not know her sisters, from the deep underneath to the many-eyed trunks and green fruition. She understood the joys and sorrows of an aspen grove. Eve felt the deep shadow before she saw it, the breeze picked up. She opened her eyes and looked West. A fast, dark bank of clouds moved toward the blue sky above them.

"The map is more recent than that book, Roxcy," Anna said. She didn't notice the map was gone from her hands.

"Turning feels wrong. We shouldn't be turning," Roxcy stood with one hand on her hip.

"Well, maybe—" Mary tried, her eyebrows lifted.

"Could we just make a decision and go!?!" Anna threw up her hands.

Roxcy looked down at her book. "The trail guide says—*'Follow the clearly marked path, across a stream before continuing up the mountain in a series of switchbacks.'* It says we stay straight and cross the stream. If we turn that way, it takes us away from the stream."

Eve watched gray gather and build over their heads.

Mary sat down on a fallen tree close to the path. She wiped the perspiration off her forehead with the back of her forearm. She unzipped a backpack and pulled out a ham sandwich.

"Is anyone else hungry?"

"Oh my God!" Anna said. Roxcy visibly flinched. "We can't even decide on what direction we're supposed to go, and you're eating?"

"Well, we're stopped anyway," said Mary

"All right, give me one of those." Anna walked over and sat next to Mary.

Roxcy finally turned to Eve.

"Evie, which way?"

"We may need to rethink the hike," Eve said. She pointed up and west.

The sky ended all argument. Mary and Anna quickly rewrapped the sandwiches and returned them to the pack. Anna threw the pack over one shoulder and began to run.

"How far have we come?" Mary walked briskly beside Roxcy.

"Not far, maybe fifteen minutes."

The wind picked up. The temperature fell. Without the warning of thunder thick, cold drops of rain started to fall, slowly at first, and then in sheets. It was difficult to see a few feet ahead. They all ran. Anna stood by the car, drenched and laughing. The loud rush of rain hit the pavement.

"I don't have the keys!" She yelled. Her sisters ran through the rain to save her.

The afternoon plan shifted from the outside solace of a shared hike to the inside work of sorting through physical reminders of their mother's sudden absence. Mary crumpled newspapers below dry logs. She watched the flames mingle and grow blue, orange, blue. When the logs were wrapped in generous light, she flipped a small switch, and the fire's heat blew out into the room. They leaned, their heads close together, to read the saved cards, dumped from a shiny red shoebox, each one was addressed to "My Sylvia" and contained feelings they'd never heard their father express aloud:

I'm no good without you.

I hope you know you are everything to me.

All I want is to be with you and the girls.

He'd been an essential background in their home, fading in and out, a distracted, rigid, and kind presence. The sentimental lines seemed incongruous with their lived experience of his uncrossable distance. But here it was, evidence that their father had felt deeply, that she and they had been ever-present for him. They gently placed the cards back in the shoebox, one at a time, handled them like fragile things. The red box went in the "To Keep" pile, only the most essential physical evidence of her life, her immaculate dresses, her favorite books of poetry with notes in the margins: an anthology of The Romantics, and *Song's of Innocence and Experience* by Blake, Yeats, Emerson, Whitman, Dickinson, Frost, Oliver, Merwin, and her most well-worn gardening and wildflower books.

They passed around family picture albums, slipping out the photos they wanted, leaving bright white squares on the yellowing pages. They checked with each other, making sure no one else wanted this particular one, setting some aside in a manila folder to make copies. By the evening, everything felt too close, the small space, the smell of cardboard boxes, the reality of her absence confirmed by this sorting of her life into piles.

The temperature had dropped again. They felt the cold seeping through the wall of windows, watched the sheets of water turn to swirling snow in a blink. An early snow could mean the beginning of winter, or merely an empty threat melted by morning sunlight, leaving behind no evidence but dark, moist ground.

Eve pulled one of the large plush chairs toward the fire and sat with a picture album open on her lap. She watched the flames flash, feeling the cold just outside the circle of heat. It was an early album, her mother, her father, her grandparents, Mary and Roxcy as babies, the color washed out.

Roxcy began stacking boxes marked for Deseret Industries, the Mormon equivalent of Goodwill, moving from the living room to the entry. She sorted through piles of papers, putting any financial documents aside for Mary to look at.

Mary put them aside and announced she needed a break from the overwhelming stacks. She announced that she thought she would take a hot shower and retreated to the bathroom. She handed Anna the picture of their mother she'd been staring at.

She thought, *who will balance our impossible equations, now that she's gone.*

Anna held the picture up, examining the girl, her mom as a teenager: a white button-down shirt tied up around her ribs, high-waisted shorts, her elbows leaning back on the hood of an old white truck. Her own eyes looked back at her frozen in time. She already knew the woman this girl would become, a mother to four daughters, a lover of plants, a mender of ripped seams.

She thought, *Now, who will weave in our loose threads?*

She let her eyes run along the bookshelves lining the tall wall, looking for the right spot to put this in a frame. The shelves surrounded the fireplace, like the shelves in their living room on Oak Lane, they gave the room the feeling of a library. She'd grown up comfortable around books, scanning shelves, running two fingers along the spines and slipping into secret corners with pages of abstract paintings, loving the color and texture, feeling disappointed when she ran her finger over and found it smooth. There were lost hours spent in books filled with old fashioned dresses and her grandma's book of quilts she'd looked through until she wore out the spine and she had to sew it back together with a thick needle and red embroidery floss. The large book of Rodin's sculpture. The first time she saw Le Baiser. She studied it for days, his hand on her thigh, her arm pulling him to her, the heat of desire captured in cold white marble. At twelve she'd stumbled through *Leaves of Grass . . . I am drawn by its breath as if I were no more than a helpless vapor, all falls aside but myself and it . . . mad filaments, ungovernable, Hair, bosom, hips, bend of legs, negligent falling hands all diffused . . . ebb stung by the flow and flow stung by the ebb, love-flesh swelling and deliciously aching, limitless limpid jets of love hot and enormous, quivering . . .* the mystery of it, the words running through her mind like a revelation. At thirteen, these were the lines that ran through her mind the first time she ever touched herself to climax. This comfort with the bodies of books, with small, private spaces and secrets kept only for herself, were pleasures she took with her to college. Her hidden spot at the BYU library. She'd searched for the right corner and found a small table tucked back between the stacks on the third floor. Every afternoon, she laid out her scraps of real fabric, her sketch book, her pencils and went to work with the magnified heat of sunlight on her right cheek and arm. She could tell the time by how the light from the window spread across her books, which she had spread across the table.

—

Anna walked into the library craving her daily solitude. Her morning classes, full of collaborative projects, left her hungry for warm light spread across her table, her chair. When she turned the corner, he was not a pleasant shock, but irritation, his feet up, sipping from a thermos. He didn't look up.

"Excuse me, you're in my seat," she said.

"I was under the impression these seats were for public use."

"Look, you can move or . . ."

"Or what?" His eyes were Paul Newman blue.

In fact, Anna thought, *he looked like him, when he'd been young anyway. In that sad movie she'd watched with her mom, Cool Hand Luke?*

She met his gaze and held it. "What's in your thermos? Hopefully it's empty, because there's a sign right there indicating that food and drink are not allowed in the library."

He looked at her for a minute and slid the thermos toward her.

"I'll share," he said. "You look thirsty."

She saw his wide smile, the way he let his hair curl around his ears. She took the thermos and drank smelling the coffee before the it hit her tongue. The taste too direct, too acrid. She winced. He stood up and offered her the chair.

"Thank you," she said and sat down next to him.

"What'd you think?"

"Too bitter," She said.

Aside from coffee being on the long list of shall nots for Mormons, and therefore in violation of the BYU honor code, an even more rigorous list of shall nots. His hair also straddled the acceptable length line. He ran his hand over the stubble on his cheek. Men were to keep their hair short and be clean-shaven. How was he getting into the testing center? The jawbone, the thick blond hair and dark eyebrows above those eyes.

She pulled a book from her backpack: *Fashion in the First Half of the Twentieth Century* and opened to the picture of an ivory corset. She studied the rib breaking curve of it with her finger, tracing the whalebone, picked up her pencil, and opened her sketchbook. He put his hands behind his head, arms in a rhombus and leaned back on two legs of his chair. Without looking up she said,

"You'll fall, leaning back like that. It's just a matter of time."

"You sound like my mom," he said.

"For such a smart woman, she seems to have produced a fairly stupid child."

He laughed out loud, and she couldn't help smiling down at her book. She still didn't look at him.

"What's your name?" He said, his breath suddenly in her ear.

For the next week, every afternoon Anna found him there, sitting in her private sunlight. He would move to the other chair and slide the thermos toward her without looking up. She would sit down and open one of her books on garment construction, or pull out swatches of fabric for her dressmaking class and take a sip. He'd added cream and a little sugar. She liked it with the additions, the sweet masking the bitter. She'd work until she felt him looking at her, smiling at her. Occasionally, she looked up and returned his smile. They spoke very little. At the end of the week, on a Friday afternoon after the sun had slipped away from the table to the far wall, she stood up and stretched.

"You ready, Matt?"

"For what?"

"I'm guessing I'm not the first girl you've made out with here. Do you have a favorite spot?"

He stood up and took her hand. She followed him through the maze of gray metal shelving, the smell of old paper and ink, of the new industrial carpet. They reached the end of a row. The shelves turned and formed an L. He leaned against the wall and pulled her in. He kissed her neck, her ear, her mouth. Her arms rested on his shoulders, her hand in his hair. It was dark outside when they walked back to the table and put their books into their backpacks. She looked at him and said,

"That was fun."

He smiled.

"See you next week," she said, turned and walked out.

This was how they met. Hours on their feet. Him against the wall. Her against the wall. A shielded corner, his hands moving over her clothes, his tongue in her ear, the exchanged heat of their breath. Her hand moving down his back one leg wrapped around him, his hand moving beneath her shirt, unbuttoning her pants and slipping two fingers down, moving them against her.

From the time she was twelve until she graduated at eighteen from Young Women's, earning her gold medallion, she'd been taught to avoid something her Sunday School teachers called "heavy petting." The term was vague. It came up in chastity lessons, so she knew it had to do with sex. No sex before marriage. Keep yourself pure. Wear modest clothing: no thighs or shoulders exposed. Her body a constant temptation to boys. No one wants to chew previously chewed gum. When you put a nail through a board it leaves a hole. At the Sunday School demonstration of this object lesson, she had mentioned wood filler, her teacher dismissed the solution claiming the board would never be the same. She mentioned knots that occurred naturally that sometimes fell out leaving a hole. They were interesting, beautiful. He talked over her, restating what he said before. So she continued to explore the possibilities silently.

What if you painted it bright green or blue, or sanded and stained it? Wouldn't it be more beautiful, something new, more interesting than before. Or just left a circle there, an opening.

Leaning against the wall in the library, she thought, *This must be heavy petting. His fingers moving against her, wet.* She came, her legs weak, her toes tingled.

He kissed her softly, his face close to hers.

"I can't do this anymore," he said.

"Oh?" She tried to move away but she was pinned. He didn't step back. He looked into her eyes. They were almost the same height.

"Do you have roommates, Anna?"

"What?"

"My legs are tired. We need a couch."

"Oh," she laughed. She kissed him. "I do. They'd report you for your hair length." She kissed him again. "They'd report me for associating with you. Guilt by association, you see. Proper little Honor Code Nazis. Do you have roommates?"

"I do and they're traveling next week. Soccer players."

"Give me your address then. You have a kitchen table?" She said.

He smiled. "You're something."

"For our books, to study," she rolled her eyes.

"Mmmhmm, for our books." He kissed her, his lips parted.

On their way out he pulled her close and slipped a small blue piece of paper into her back pocket.

"See you tomorrow," she said.

"At my place, our regular time?"

"Yeah, but Matt . . ."

"What?"

"I really to have to study," she said.

He turned to walk out looking back at her with a smile.

⌣

The storm picked up outside the cabin windows. White beginning to wipe out all color. Anna stood up and walked to the bookshelf, felt the heat from the fire intensify. She ran her fingers along the spines on the third shelf from the top until she found it. Fashion at the Turn of the Century. An anachronism now. Written in 1979 before the century turned again. She took the book back to the chair and opened it to the picture of the corset. She pulled out the blue slip of paper with that address marking the page.

⌣

Matt opened the door and she stood there for a moment, nervous and determined.

"Come in."

Anna smiled and walked into a living room, spare and clean, a large black leather couch, a big-screened TV and in the adjoining kitchen a small round kitchen table. She set her books on the table.

He took her hand and pulled her toward the couch. She pulled him back toward the hallway.

"Which room is yours?" Feigned confidence. This would be her first time, another secret place, to open a new book.

"The one at the end of the hall," He said.

He reassured her that it wouldn't hurt, that they could kiss for a long time first, that he would touch her until she was ready.

She laughed, nervous. "Have you done this before?"

He didn't answer. He kissed her mouth, her neck, lifted her shirt over her head and kissed her breast. She slid her panties off. She expected to see his garments, was dreading the reminder of what she was choosing to transgress. He'd mentioned that he'd served his mission in Mexico City. He'd mentioned that he'd served as an Assistant to the President. But when he slid out of his jeans, no magic Mormon underwear just plaid boxer shorts.

Matt made sure Anna came, touching her body as if they'd been together for years, before he rolled her on top of him and eased himself in. She felt a slight sting and then he began to move beneath her, slowly, holding her hips in his hands, looking straight up into her eyes.

When she stood to pull on her underwear a thin string of blood trickled down her leg. He handed her a tissue and she thought,

Maybe this is it. He's gotten what he wants and now he won't want me anymore.

It was the chorus of Sunday School and Young Women's teachers over the years more than her own thought.

"I love you, Anna. I've never met anyone like you."

"Oh yeah?" She smiled.

"Yeah."

She climbed back into the bed next to him and laid her head in the curve of his shoulder.

The guilt was surprisingly manageable, just twinges here and there. Mostly when she lied to her mom. But Anna reminded herself that they loved each other. They were planning to get married. She wasn't sleeping with random boys, just Matt. And it was really no one else's business, including her bishop's. She was an adult, not a child. She told her parents she needed more room to lay out her designs, to store her fabric, that her roommates always complained about the mess in their space, which was true. They helped her get her own place. She was a junior after all and had her first job as a T.A. to help cover rent. She and Matt had been together for six months. No one suspected anything.

Anna and her mom cleared away the Sunday dinner dishes rinsing them at the sink, the sound of running water, the clink of plates and glasses, the dim light of dusk through the windows. Matthew normally helped, but he had a broken wrist. Anna watched the way he approached each of her sisters. He touched Roxcy's hand and told her she looked gorgeous, as always. She laughed and thanked him. Asked him how his mother was doing. He always told Roxcy about his mom's selflessness, about the way she'd made their home such a beautiful space. He asked her about her own kids, knew all their names. Matt never touched Mary, other than a firm handshake. How did he know she was uncomfortable with affection, except within her immediate family? He asked for tax advice, gave her management of the trust that he came into when he finished his doctorate. Recommended her accounting firm to his father. On the few occasions he met Eve, he talked to her about trees. He sat next to her, close enough that she didn't have to raise her voice. Were there different types of aspen? He had heard that their root systems were connected, how did that work? What kinds of other plants thrive in aspen groves? It was just after a miscarriage that no one talked about. Anna could see the relief it gave Eve, the break from her own thoughts, and she loved him for it, the way he found what they needed and provided, created a fast sense of intimacy.

When they asked how he'd broken his wrist, Anna strained to hear the newest version.

He talked in a low voice. It was hard to hear him over the clatter of dishes, the running water.

"My friend and I were climbing Devil's Kitchen last weekend. I was near the top when I realized Jonny's knot was no good, saw it slipping. Everything slowed down and sped up at the same time. I was falling, nothing to grab for. Luckily, I was able to spin myself around so that, even from almost thirty feet, I landed on my feet. But off-balance. The impact was so hard it threw me forward. I caught myself with my right hand and felt the bone snap. I actually heard it." He showed them the gruesome yellowish wound on his right palm where he'd stopped his fall. They all leaned in to look. Anna had heard his friend's version, which was quite different, less exciting, 15 feet and just some loose shale, Matt had slipped and pulled out the anchor. But exaggeration was part of his charm. He knew how to work a room.

She smiled and glanced over at her mom, who was staring into the living room, her eyebrows knit together, an expression unnatural to her normally serene face.

"Mom, you ok?"

Her mom looked back to the dishes. Turned the faucet off. "Hmm?"

"What's wrong?"

"Nothing."

"It's something," Anna said, laughed a little.

"Oh, I don't know. It's probably silly but ... How well do you know him, Anna?"

"Um, pretty well, I think," she laughed. "We've been dating for almost a year."

"Right. It's probably nothing then."

"No, say what you're thinking."

"Well ... do you feel like he's performing sometimes?" Her mom looked at her then, held her gaze a little too directly.

Anna looked down and thought. *He's always performing.* She looked over at him. Matt ran his fingers through his hair, moving it out of his eyes, still engaging the small room with the rise and fall of his voice. He winked at her, never breaking the flow of his story.

"It is a show, sometimes. But he's different with me."

"Of course. I shouldn't have said anything." She looked away and placed the plate on the counter to dry.

Anna looked at him again. He stood up and walked over.

"What are you two talking about over here?"

"You," Anna said and kissed him.

They spent nearly every night together at her apartment, had sex every night, sometimes twice, woke up together, showered, dressed and went to class. She was on the pill. On Sundays, they attended church together. She spent that year of sacrament meetings distracted, his hand on her thigh or arm around her shoulders, the memory of the pleasant weight of him on top of her, while she chewed the bread and sipped the tiny cup of water.

"My God," she thought, "My God."

Any initial guilt had gone gray for her. She began to notice how green the June grass looked, felt the cool pleasure of it beneath her feet, noticed the feeling of a silk skirt brushing against her thigh, the hot sun on her cheek, him moving beneath the weight of her, felt all of it as part of the same gift, distinct but connected expressions of the divine.

Sometimes, as she searched for the right cloth for her school projects: a dress, a blouse, a jacket, she took along a magnifying glass to examine the different colors of threads used to create the fabric. She could see the tiny individual strands woven so intimately together they created oneness. This is how Anna began to think of human beings, as thin strands of light and color woven together. They created one vibrant cloth. Fixity, she thought, is a lie. It's a denial of grace, a denial of God. The binary doctrine and practice of Mormonism became suddenly and blatantly wrong in her mind. 1950's gender roles: men are to provide, women to nurture children, limited both women and men. The one true church: Mormons have the only valid ordinances, God only extends His authority to our baptisms, our priesthood offices, and only to boys and men. Mormon marriages are the only truly eternal marriage. The literal interpretations of the doctrines and the narrow way the doctrines were practiced stripped away the vibrancy of human experience, dulled the complex and intricate fabric of existence. All of it suddenly struck her as absurd, given the breadth of humanity, the incalculable strands of individual religious experience. If all things were present to God, the linear progression from preexistence to earthly testing to a neat sorting into kingdoms of glory, judgment based on a tally of good or bad behavior, seemed juvenile. Life was kinetic, messy, layered. So were people. The Mormon worldview didn't seem divine at all but a very human hierarchy obsessed with control and based in fear. Something shifted in her mind. The religion of her childhood no longer had room for the God she experienced as an adult, the grace extant within the everyday, the sensual as spiritual.

Matt led her to believe that he agreed with her, that he also experienced Mormonism as limited. Or perhaps, she assumed he saw things the same way, because he held her in their bed, unmarried after they'd had sex and whispered that she was perfection. Assumed because he wanted to marry her even though she was now impure. He asked her to come with him to Stanford, where he would get his M.S. and then a Ph.D. in Psychology. They both agreed to stop having sex long enough to answer the temple recommend interview honestly. It would make things simpler with their families. They did and were married in the Salt Lake Temple six months later, where her father and mother and his father and mother had been married before them. She never talked to him directly about her ideas. She assumed he was with her in the slow slide into private heresy, so she was wholly unprepared for him to slide into the orthodoxy.

Anna walked into the familiar chapel alone, late as usual, exhausted from wrestling Lulu and the lost battle to brush out Honey's hair. It was the chapel her mom had brought her to as a child. It looked like most Mormon buildings. Inside the chapels, the walls were off-white and free from art. The rooms sat in the center of the building, hallways on either side. There were no windows. Giant brass organ pipes rose up to an A behind the elevated stand. Five steps up to the podium, the leaders sat across the stand. All men. All dressed in suits wearing white shirts and blue, red, or green ties, sometimes striped, sometimes solid. Just as her father had when she was small, Matt sat up there with them now. He'd been called as second counselor in the bishopric when she was still pregnant with Lula. It all felt familiar, as if she'd accidentally fallen into her mother's life rather than her own. Matt was on the tenure track in the Psychology department at BYU and had plans to open his own practice. She and the girls were at home during the week and sitting in one of the shorter pews that lined each wall on Sundays. The soft green velvet of her childhood had been replaced by a durable burgundy weave, rough against her skin.

She looked up at the large, round, brass-rimmed light fixtures hung from the ceiling that reminded her of flying saucers, like a weird signifier that the whole Mormon world had become alien. She made her way down the aisle wrestling Lula on her hip and being pulled by Honey into an almost run. Matt smiled down on her. Anna hated him a little. She knew the part she was supposed to play. She'd watched her mother prepare each week, bath time Saturday night, best dresses, tights, and shoes laid out carefully for the morning. Hair brushed or curled, held back with a barrette, or pulled into a neat ponytail. Walk alone with her children to the building. Help them sit quietly through the first hour and ten minutes of sacrament meeting. As a child, she'd always struggled to sit still. Her mom had traced letters on her back, the light touch of her finger calm, the concentration required to guess occupying Anna's busy mind. She remembered the way her mother's hands had disappeared quietly into the large bag and found the one butterscotch at the bottom, quietly slipping it into Anna's desperate hand.

She wasn't able to fit the role but tried to adapt it to fit her, to make room for herself. Honey and Lula wore comfortable knit dresses and flip-flops. They giggled loudly if someone cried when they bore their testimony, and she put her finger to her mouth, trying to suppress the smile twitching at the edges of her own mouth. They climbed over her and under the benches. People raised their eyebrows. Anna stopped herself from raising her middle finger in response.

Anna watched Honey whenever her little face seemed focused on the stand, the row of men in suits up above them. She noticed her eyes followed the young men in their carefully ironed white shirts and ties as they brought the sacrament to their row. Anna fumbled in the bag, pulled a coloring book out and whispered,

"Do you want to color?"

"Mama, the sacrament."

Anna handed her the tray, and Honey took two pieces of bread and shoved them in her mouth.

"I have snacks," she whispered, taking one piece of bread for herself and putting another in Lula's open waiting mouth.

"Did you bring the clay?"

"Shhh, Honey whisper." Anna pulled the balls of modeling clay from her bag.

"Panda!" Lula shouted.

Sister Smith, who sat in front of her, shot the girls a disapproving look and put her finger to pursed lips. Sister Smith's girls sat perfectly still, their bright blond hair combed and parted into two submissive braids per head. Anna pulled Lula onto her lap, irritated.

"Shhh, whisper. Remember, quietly," she hugged Lula protectively and kissed her cheek until Lula giggled.

"Where are the treats?" Honey said, squeezing between the bench and Anna's legs to get to the bag.

"Honey, sit down. I'll get them."

"How much longer, Mama?"

Her girls seemed unable to speak quietly. Anna looked up at Matthew. He winked at her. She felt her irritation bloom into anger. They were only fifteen minutes into the meeting. They still had the water, three speakers, a closing song, and a prayer to get through. By the time the third speaker started, it was clear the meeting would go long again. Anna took her girls by their hands, left the activities spread across the bench and walked out to the lobby. She told them as long as they were quiet, they were free to move around. Lula laid across the couch, her head in Anna's lap, and sucked her thumb to sleep. It was close to nap time, to lunch time.

Honey did cartwheels to the drinking fountain and cart-wheels back, her dress falling up around her ears with each rotation.

"I want to color," she said, landing in front of Anna, her small cheeks flushed.

"I left everything inside, Honey, why don't you look at the paintings. You like that."

They listened for the closing song and prayer. As the people poured from the chapel her girls ran down the hall toward the primary room. Anna hustled along behind to make sure Lula made it to nursery and then sat for a minute, catching her breath.

"Busy girls," one woman said, smiling kindly at Anna.

"Yes," Anna said and smiled back gratefully.

After the lobby cleared, she walked back into the chapel to gather up the detritus of another failed Sunday effort. A few of the men were still on the stand, including Matt. They shook hands, talking in lowered, deep voices their quiet laughter resonated to the back of the room.

The ultimate boys club; the forever unbreakable glass ceiling—ordained by The Father God, of course.

Anna rolled her eyes. She tossed colored pencils and modeling clay into the open bag. She had been eight when she turned to her mom and said, so loudly that people had turned and looked, "Why don't you ever sit on the stand, mom?" And then when they were home, "And why are all the stories in primary about boys?"

At twelve, Anna wanted to know why she didn't get to pass the sacrament. To her mom's credit she answered that she really didn't know and told her they were good questions to ask. However, in Anna's experience, her mom was the only one who considered these questions good. They were decidedly bad questions for a grown, married Mormon woman with two small daughters. They were worse if your husband taught at BYU and served in the bishopric. And in Provo her girl's friends were all LDS. It was easier, safer, to keep her thoughts to herself, or they might be socially excluded by the nice families. Families who would quietly and efficiently punish them for any deviance from the norm.

Matt touched her on the shoulder.

"Tough day, huh?"

"I hate Sundays." Anna didn't meet his gaze.

"I have a meeting after, Anna. I'm sorry. I'll get home as fast as I can."

"Whatever," she said, shrugging his hand off her shoulder.

She walked toward the door, needed out. She could come back in two hours to get the girls. The girls would tell her what they learned and, depending on their answer, she might make it through another few weeks. She hoped they'd share the beautiful stories about how Jesus healed a woman who no one else cared for and how we should also try and be kind to people who don't have many friends. About how Jesus appeared to Mary, very first, before any of the apostles, and they didn't believe her. And then Anna would feel all right. Less like a pretender. The sun was hot, unrelenting and she followed the shade the few blocks to her house. She dropped the Sunday bag on their living-room couch. The evidence of the rushed morning lay across the house, breakfast dishes still on the counter, a rejected pile of dresses Honey had decided were too itchy strewn down the hallway, a half-finished picture and markers on the table. She sat down on the couch. The cool damp of the swamp-cooler a relief in the dry summer heat. Honey had finally chosen her favorite play dress: cool, soft, blue, and yellow cotton knit shift dress—no waist, no sleeves. She'd run-skipped all the way to the meeting house, her fuzzy blond curls looking like a dandelion gone to seed. Anna ignored the mess and reached for her knitting needles, the clicking rhythm acted like a balm.

Two quiet hours seemed to evaporate, and before she was ready, Anna found herself back at the church following her running girls out the front doors. She held their small, cool hands, and they swung her arms back and forth as they made their way through the wall of heat.

"Sister Smith said what?" Anna held Honey's hand as she skipped beside her.

"That part of following Jesus is dressing modestly."

"And she thought your dress was immodest?" She let go of her hand, and Honey moved out ahead.

"She said my shoulders should be covered."

"Huh. Well, I think your shoulders are beautiful, and it's hot today. You're dress is just right for a hot day."

"Too hot." Lula said. "I too hot."

"I have an idea! Why don't we turn on the sprinklers?"

The two-year-old and four-year-old began jumping up and down. Yes! They wanted to run through the sprinklers. They walked up the sidewalk to their porch.

"Take off your dresses so they don't get wet, OK?"

"OK!" The girls squealed with delight and left their sundresses in piles on the front porch.

She got two towels and laid them over the railing. In her Sunday best, she pulled the hose into the front yard, beads of sweat running down her face. Sister Smith lived three doors down with her, well-coiffed, tow-headed brigade of girls, six in all. Anna had heard her say how much they still longed for a little boy. She turned on the water, and her girls began to laugh loudly, squealing and stripping off their underwear. Cars passed, families on their way home from church. Anna smiled wide and waved. Her small girls romped, completely naked, in and out of the sprinkling water.

"You two are so beautiful! Bodies are wonderful!!" She yelled as Matt walked up the sidewalk, loosening his tie. "Sister Smith told the girls that they were not good followers of Jesus today because they're showing their shoulders."

"Hello to you too," he said, putting his arm around her waist and kissing her. "It's been a long day."

"Yeah, I know. I got the girls ready for and to church *all by myself* and home *all by myself*. Just like I do every damn week, dear. Sunday is always a really long day."

"Do you think this is the best idea?" He leaned in close and said this very quietly. "Maybe we should move the party to the back yard. It's Sunday—"

"Who in the hell are you?"

"Anna," he smiled at her. "I'm on your side, but we have to play the game, right? You're not going to change Sister Smith. She homeschools her kids so they won't be exposed to the evil world here in Provo." He laughed and pulled her to him.

"Honey is four years old, Matthew. Lula is two. Their shoulders are not sexual. Nothing about their bodies is sexual. They, literally, cannot be immodest."

"You're right. You're completely right."

She ignored him.

He kissed her on the neck just below her ear. "I want to get out of these clothes. If we moved the sprinkler to the back, you could come help me?"

Her body relaxed. She whispered in his ear, "If you'll go invite Sister Smith to join us."

He laughed, let go of her, and walked inside.

⁓

Anna pulled the small blue paper from her old textbook, crumpled it, and threw it into the fire. The snow swirled outside the wall of windows but, so close to the flames, she felt only heat. This was how he'd made her believe they were together. By agreeing that people were crazy. By holding her hand and kissing her on her neck, her shoulder, the line of her clavicle. By pulling her in. Convincing her that he only wanted her and no one else. But the boy with illicit thermos and the almost too long hair who'd groped her in the BYU library was gone. He put on a tie. He sat on the stand. He played the good Mormon man so convincingly even she believed it. Telling her to calm down, to try and blend in for the sake of his job, his calling, their life together. Matt, that prick, who'd yelled her name whenever he came, who'd whispered there was no one like her, told her he loved her over and over and over. The same man who had looked their bishop in the eye, teary, repentant, and blamed her lack of faith for his infidelity in the same breath. The bullshit so thick on his tongue it covered every stinking word that spewed from his mouth. One by one she would destroy every object that still tied her to him. It had been three months since she'd answered her phone in the middle of the night, since they'd gotten each other off with words that left her breathless and feeling sick to her stomach. He'd finally stopped begging her to come back.

—

Anna pushed the double stroller up Fir stopping every so often to wipe the sweat from her forehead on her sleeve. It was too hot for early May. She walked passed the simple brick houses of various color and shape that were common to early 1960's architecture, the slanted roofs, the large front windows, mostly one-story ranches or cottage-style homes. The yards were well kept, with clusters of dandelions in a few of the lawns and a few bikes or red wagons discarded on sidewalks and in driveways. Elm was just down the hill from Oak, where she'd grown up and walkable to Kiwanis Park and the playground at Wasatch Elementary. Matt's TA had come to meet with him, and he said he was expecting some other students as well, so she took the girls to the park for a couple of hours. He could work in peace. By noon the girls had started fighting over one particular swing. It was Lula's nap time, and Honey had been up in the night with a croupy sounding cough.

She loaded them up a little early, hoping they would fall asleep in the stroller. It was a heavy push home. They were really getting too big for a stroller. Honey was almost five. Anna could see their little chests rise and fall in an even rhythm. Lula's head slumped forward slightly, the wispy dark curls partially hid her face. But other than her dark hair, she looked just like her daddy, full lips, the dimpled chin, long dark lashes resting on her flushed cheeks. Anna smiled and turned into the driveway. Weeds were beginning to reappear in the cracked concrete. She hadn't noticed the cluttered yard when she'd hurried the girls off to the park. The flat, grassy space was overrun with deserted tricycles, a few belonging to some neighbor girls who had been over to play earlier in the morning. There were broken pieces of sidewalk chalk scattered across the sidewalk leading to the porch and several naked Barbies stuck in the short bushes that lined the porch.

She gently guided Lula's head back against the seat, moving the soft hair out of her face. Honey's mouth was open, her eyes closed. The thought of carrying both of them in made her feel tired. She parked the stroller in the shade of their minivan and went to see if Matt was finished with his meeting. If he was, he could help her carry them in. On the way into the house, she stooped and picked up a few pieces of the stray sidewalk chalk. She gathered the dolls shoved in or hanging from the branches of the bushes and deposited them in a large basket on the front porch.

The entry was quiet. She brushed the chalk dust off of her hands and hung her keys on the hook. A pile of mail lay on the floor in front of the drop. She bent and picked it up, flipping through the stack as she walked down the hallway toward the bedroom. She stopped. There was something—voices—and for a moment she thought Matt might still be working. But the door to his office stood open, the room empty. She walked to the end of the hall and opened their bedroom door.

He was naked, kneeling behind a woman on their bed, one of his hands on her right hip, the other spilling over with the pale skin of her ample breast, his body moving eagerly.

Anna stood still, silent. He yelled the girl's name when he came, the same way he yelled hers. He kissed the girl on the back of her neck, ran his fingers down her spine, the same way he touched her, and turned.

"Anna! Shit!" He said.

She turned and ran down the hallway, grabbing the car keys off of the hook. She threw up all over the bushes, wiping her mouth on her bare arm as she stumbled toward the car. The acrid smell of vomit caught in the fine hairs. She couldn't breathe. She unbuckled Lula and then Honey and pulled them both from the stroller and laid them on the back seat without buckling them in. Matt ran toward the car, pulling on a t-shirt, his face at the car window, his hand flat on the glass. She put the car in reverse and pulled out.

"Shh, shh, Lula, it's OK, sweets. We're going to Nana's. Shall we go see Nana?"

It was no use. The scream of a child woken from an afternoon nap is loud, angry and impossible to quiet, to comfort. Anna drove up Ninth East past the temple, all the lights turning green, to meet her. She turned right on University Blvd toward the canyon, the sound of her daughters' tired screams like a transference of her own restrained impulse to howl. She wiped the tears that kept coming, her eyes blurry, her cheeks wet with them. She'd quieted her own sobs. The girls were whimpering, the movement of the car lulling them back into sleep. She kept her eyes fixed on the unvarying road, black, and followed the long-stretching double gold lines, until she turned onto the dirt drive kicking up dust. Her mom sat on the porch, as she often did in the afternoon, looked up, waved, and smiled. She stood and caught Anna in her arms.

"Anna, what on earth?"

"Matt—" the sobs choking her again.

"Is he all right?"

"He's fucking—"

"Anna!"

"His fucking teaching assistant. Mom—I don't think she's even twenty."

"What?"

"With the giant breasts and overdone eye makeup, big blond hair. God, what is happening?" Anna let go of her mother. She felt her head swirling and leaned forward, putting her hands on her knees.

"You're sure?"

"They were in OUR bedroom, mom, on MY bed." She wiped one arm across her cheek and smelled throw up. Felt her stomach lurch again.

Her mother held her hair back and then gathered her in. Anna shook. Several minutes passed before she remembered.

"Lula and Honey are in the car, can you—"

"I'm getting you to the couch first. Come on, sit down. I'll get the girls, don't worry about them."

—

Her mom had been there. She patched and mended the holes that opened up in the fabric of Anna's life. Helped her begin to make something new, with a worn kind of beauty, from the scraps. All the pieces were tearing again. All those boxes consuming her mom, one object at a time. What would she do now? Anna felt near panic rise up in her throat like a frantic butterfly. She couldn't ever go back to him. How was she supposed to do this alone? Anna thought,

Who will weave in the loose threads, mend the torn seams?

The dim white light of the storm filled the room. She felt desperation clutch at her stomach. She squinted and sat very still. If she could absorb and hold onto the warmth from the fire, absorb the sound of rustling papers, hold onto her sister's occasional voices, their shared breath creating the fog on the inside edges of the window, if she could hold onto them, she wouldn't be alone. Everything would be all right. And all those boxes reminded her that Jake would be at the store in the morning with her weekly delivery, so there was also the possibility of momentary relief, thirty minutes of forgetting.

Eve

Eve watched her mother's life crowd around the room, sorted into small piles: books on the floor, on the coffee table, photo albums open and stripped of memory. Brown cardboard boxes stood in precarious towers occupying the corners of the room, some full, some with their cardboard mouths spread wide, as if hungry to consume every piece of the past. A few books were piled unevenly on an emptied bookshelf to sort through later. She listened to the sound of the water running. Mary was in the shower. Eve looked and saw a thin stream of steam coming from beneath the bathroom door.

—

Eve walked into the humid room, the kelly-green vinyl floor, faded from years of wear, stained where other graduate students spilled and didn't pause their work to clean up. Rows of trays sat under glowing lights that hovered and hummed above the tiny plants like sleepy insects. She walked toward the long rectangular windows that repeated across the length of the wall. The sun came through as magnified heat, making the room sauna-like. Small beads of sweat formed along her hairline. Eve carefully gathered the tiny groups of roots she'd harvested from the various grasses, ferns, and bushes that made up the undergrowth of the local groves. Her dissertation would come from her research on the relationships between these plants and the aspens that grew between Frisco and Veil. She paid careful attention to each of the small dividers in front of her, mixing soils, feeling the difference in the textures, memorizing their subtle distinctions in scent: sweet, musky, or acrid earth. She pushed the tip of her pinky finger into the soil, making a small hole for each group of roots, placed them inside, and gently covered them over. With a long syringe, she watered the surface of the soil, waiting for the tiny pool to darken before squeezing one more time. Eve put her hand out toward the window, and held it in the sun until her palm was hot, testing the temperature on her own flesh. She arranged and labeled the plants, the fern lower, the grass in more direct light, the flowers inbetween. As she moved each box she smiled. It was time to see if she could grow a little life of her own. They'd been married for two years. Mo had recently accepted a tenure track position at CU, Boulder, and she was in the final stages of research for her dissertation. She examined the shelves one more time. Satisfied with her choreography, she trusted the light, air, and water to fill in the dance.

She closed the door behind her. The July grass looked as brittle as hay along the edges of the sidewalk. Drought restrictions limited watering to twice a week. Most summers

July meant afternoon thunderstorms, monsoon season in Colorado, sunshine blocked out by ominous thunderheads, the torrential downpour let loose until water filled the gutters and poured from the edges of rooftops and web-like lightning shot across a dark sky. The clouds still came often, dark as ever, but barren, ungenerous for all their show.

If Mo wasn't home she would strip down to her black camisole and underwear and wait for him. Eve had been through the temple. Alone, without him, with her mother and sisters, but she didn't wear her garments in heat like this. Mo didn't care one way or the other, so she was free to hold and practice her religion fluidly. The car behind her honked, the light had changed. She pulled forward into the intersection and made a left, driving beneath the welcome archway of maple trees that lined the road of their apartment building, four large square buildings of white brick, built in the late 1960's, complete with aluminum sliding windows and a small shared courtyard filled with more dead grass. Their apartment was on the ground floor at the back of a breezeway, number three, their main window in full shade of a large maple by afternoon. Eve opened the car door and heard the loud buzz, the swarm of window air conditioners turned to high. They hung from the six-story building like metal hives.

If he was home . . . she turned the key and opened the door. Mo sat on their secondhand futon, his legs too long to sit comfortably. He leaned forward, reading a book, his glasses slightly askew, his papers dumped on the floor beside him. She walked in and put her keys on the counter. Mormon or not, this was the only man she ever wanted to do this with. She took off her t-shirt. She unbuttoned her shorts and walked toward him.

"I'm ovulating."

He looked up from his book.

"Oh?"

Placing the book beside him he took his glasses off.

"Come with me," she said and held out her hand

"You're ready then?"

She nodded. He smiled. She pulled his shirt over his head. He pulled off his shorts. They sat facing each other. His eyes were dark brown, two red marks from his glasses on the bridge of his nose. He kissed her shoulder. She kissed his cheek, then the other. He traced the outline of her breasts, her flat stomach, the bones of her hips, running his hand around and between her thighs. This was how they began.

—

The fire had died down a little. Eve sighed and sunk deeper into the old comfortable chair. She pulled the blanket around her. The heat of memory did little to prevent the cold air from finding its way through the seams of the old cabin windows. She put her hand on her belly, and her throat tightened, so many years of trying, so many pills and procedures. The first time was the only time she had made the mistake of broadcasting her pregnancy too early.

Eve took several deep breaths before dialing her mom's number. "Hi, this is Sylvia. You've just missed me. Please leave your name and number at the tone, and I'll gladly return your call. Have a beautiful day!" Eve hung up. She didn't leave a message. One more answering machine at Anna's, Mary would be at work, she dialed Roxcy.

"Oh, Evie!" Roxcy said.

"It's still early, don't say anything. Ok?"

She didn't seem to hear her.

"When we had our first, I was so happy. There's nothing like holding your own precious baby in your arms. I worried you two were never going to get around to having a family and you'd just miss so much. It's the only thing that really matters. I know you have your Ph.D. and your plants, but I promise you this will make you forget all about that!"

"I don't have my Ph.D. yet—"

"Mom will come out when you deliver. She's amazing during the delivery, but she can be a little bossy once the baby comes. Even with Pete she was still telling me what I should and shouldn't do. She thinks the baby ought to stay in your room with you for the first few months. She handed me all these articles on the benefits of co-sleeping! She didn't co-sleep with any of us, and we're just fine. We used Ferber. Anyway, there are a few books that I thought were really helpful. I think I still have them."

"Rox, I'm only a couple of weeks along."

"I know, but you've waited so long, and it's never too early to make plans. Do you have names picked out?"

She lost Eleanor at nine weeks. Hazel at five, barely a bundle of cells. Ruby at nine weeks. Maude made it to ten. The last, the longest, she'd left unnamed. She only chose girl names because, in the recurring dream, it was always a little girl. It had been exciting at first, charting her body temperature, calling Mo, having him rush home. But over the course of a year-and-a-half, the sex became mechanical, like a chore to mark off of their "make a baby" checklist. It was a fall afternoon late in those early days when after sex, she lay with her legs up against the wall for 30 min. Mo had asked her to stop. Keeping her pelvis elevated, she reminded him that they both wanted a baby.

"I need a break. Just for a couple of months, Evie. When was the last time you enjoyed this?"

"It's been fine."

"It's been stressful. Will you please get your legs off the wall and look at me?"

"I only have 10 more minutes."

Mo pulled on his shirt, buttoned up his Levi's, and left. Eve heard the front door slam. She didn't move until the ten minutes passed. She walked out front, checking the sidewalk to see if he was coming back. At midnight she fell asleep. He still wasn't home. When she woke in the morning, he lay with his back turned toward her and a pillow pulled around his head. It was Sunday. She went to church alone.

Mo wasn't religious, but he came with her to the first hour of church—

Sacrament Meeting—for as long as they'd been together. He never asked her how she, as a scientist, could believe that angels, God, and Jesus appeared to a fourteen-year-old boy. He sat next to her. He held her hand. This was his gentleness. When she thought of the blessing of him, her body was full of gratefulness. He would be such a kind father. If only she could reach inside herself and pinch off the dead, broken bits that couldn't seem to sustain life.

For Eve, church was a beautiful web of connections that grew in a little ward where people took the time to know and care for each other. Like a root system that ran beneath Mormon soil. Even in the scriptures, the metaphors were plant-related: a mustard seed, a grafted olive tree, the exemplary lilies. Sometimes, like when her mom read aloud from Isaiah *all the trees of the field clap their hands,* or when a young woman spoke about moments of being held in God's love through her cancer treatment, or when the old men, who never cried, stood silent, gathering composure as they spoke about their grown children, she felt the same ineffable joy as seeing thin threads of green emerge from dark soil.

But today she felt oddly exposed sitting on the pew alone. She'd come in a few minutes late and sat down on the end of one of the center pews toward the back. A young mother sat next to her. Eve turned and smiled. She'd never had a conversation with her, but she'd seen her children follow her like baby ducks in a neat line. The two girls, who were older, wore their dark curly hair pulled back into submission by black headbands with large, off-white, silk roses attached. The toddler, a boy, had his hair cut short and wore a neatly pressed white shirt with a turquoise and navy striped necktie.

The oldest girl looked about six. The younger girl squirmed, swinging her legs and humming quietly. Eve smiled and remembered Anna swinging her feet that way when she was little. She saw the young mother whisper something unintelligible, then deliver a pointed little pinch to the back of the little girl's arm. The girl quickly refocused on her coloring book, which contained stories from the scriptures. Eve wanted to take her on her lap and run her hand over the little red mark on the back of the arm, to tell her she could hum quietly in her ear, that it was all right to swing her legs. The husband walked down the aisle toward the family. The young mother leaned over and picked up a brand-new baby from a car seat in the aisle and handed her to her husband. Eve hadn't seen the baby when she chose this pew. She closed her eyes. She tried to slow her breath, to stem the deep longing. The men formed a circle and blessed the new baby, Sophia Jane Warren, with a love of the gospel, with the constant guidance of her Heavenly Father, with a tender and loving heart. The circle opened, and the father held the tiny girl up to audible sounds of approval from the congregation. Eve smiled, silent, feeling the familiar ache pass through her body and finally settle on the left side of her rib cage where it fluttered, frantic and fearful as an injured bird.

The service ended. She walked quickly through the foyer filled with reproductions of paintings, scenes from the New Testament, Jesus talking to the rich young man, Jesus washing the feet of the disciples, Joseph Smith kneeling in the grove. Through the familiar halls of the Mormon meeting house. Past the bishop's office and the small wooden container on the wall held gray tithing envelopes and white donation slips. Past the bulletin board, with pictures of smiling families holding rakes, a recent service project cleaning the yards of widows in the ward, and a picture of beaming primary children with dripping popsicles, lined up under the climbing tree at the park where they held the annual summer picnic. The brown missionary plaques with smiling faces of several young men and one or two women, a scripture engraved in gold and a golden map, an outline of the country or state, showing where they were serving.

An older man with thinning white hair and a ruddy face grabbed her by the arm, Brother Sessions.

"Slow down there, sweetie. Where's that husband of yours today? When are you two going to get to work on multiplying and replenishing? The Warren's have already got four on you two, and you must be a few years older than that young lady!" He winked.

Eve smiled and looked toward the door. "Mo isn't feeling well. Excuse me, I have to—"

But Brother Sessions wasn't looking at her, though he still held her arm. He was waving at the bishop who was coming toward them, a quiet man, close to her same age. He'd never pushed with Mo. Why had she left Mo to come to church? Why hadn't she stayed and talked things through with him? She wished he were here. He would have, very quietly, asked Brother Sessions to remove his hand from Eve's arm and, very quietly, told this man that when a couple chose to have children was a private matter. Eve slipped her arm free.

"Hi," she said.

"Hello Eve, how are—"

"Bishop, don't you think this pretty little lady ought to start making some babies soon?" he said loudly.

The bishop's ears turned red first and then his whole face. "Well, Vern—"

"Excuse me," Eve said. "I have to use the restroom."

"Of course, of course. You tell that husband of yours we missed him today." Brother Sessions almost shouted.

Eve felt angry as she pushed open the women's bathroom door, tiny tan square tiles on the floor, two cramped stalls, one sink in front of a tall mirror. She didn't actually need to use the restroom and almost ran into Sister Christensen who was tucking in her white button down shirt.

"Oh, I'm so sorry. Excuse me."

"No, apology necessary. It's my fault." Eve turned to go.

"Wait, Eve, I've been wanting to talk to you."

"Oh?" All she wanted was to leave.

"Yes. I didn't imagine this conversation taking place in the bathroom. I suppose the Lord works in mysterious ways. I heard you and Mo are having problems. I'm only saying something because I've been through it, and I just wanted you to know if you ever need to talk."

"Oh," She said. She thought, *what is going on today?*

Eve tucked a loose piece of hair behind her ear and looked at the woman standing in front of her, late fifties, her middle well thickened, her arms a little too long. She'd said once in a lesson entitled "Sustaining the Prophets", that she believed polygamy had been a huge misunderstanding on Joseph Smith's part and probably had much more to do with his desires than the Lord's. Her frankness made others uncomfortable, but Eve genuinely liked her. She took a deep breath and smiled,

"Look, Sister Christiansen I'm a little tired today. I really need to get—"

"Fertility problems, I mean. Gosh, it sounded like I thought you and Mo are having problems in your marriage. That's not what I meant. He seems like a really fine person, kind, and I like you."

Eve's visiting teachers, two women assigned to each woman in an LDS ward who deliver a monthly spiritual message and offer any help that might be needed, had caught her at a bad moment several months ago. She had just had her second miscarriage. They'd nodded their heads furiously agreeing to say nothing to anyone, while Eve openly wept on her couch. Clearly, they'd broken their promise.

Eve said. "I actually need to get home. Mo isn't feeling well and—"

"Sister Smith from the Bible Park tried for three years, and Sister Lambert from Willow Creek, for ten, and me, well we tried for seven before anything worked. Lots of people struggle. But people don't talk about it. I don't know why? There's nothing to be ashamed of."

"Perhaps because it's private," Eve said.

Sister Christianson reached out and took one of Eve's hands in both of her own.

"I was young when we got married, nineteen, not like you, but I wanted a child so badly. I remember when I got my period the month after our honeymoon I just broke down crying."

"I'm sorry, I really have to go," Eve handed her a paper towel and reached for the door.

"I've made you uncomfortable. I seem to have a talent for it, but I just wanted you to know you're not alone. Maybe I shouldn't have said anything."

Eve stopped and turned. "How long did you try before you talked to someone about it?"

"About two years. Can I ask how long it's been for you and Mo?"

"Almost two. And I've had two miscarriages."

"Can I email you some names, Eve? Doctors . . ."

"Yes, thank you, sister—"

"Please call me Jenny."

"Thank you, Jenny."

"The church will be a much better place when we stop lying to each other. Life is damn hard, and we spend too much time pretending everything's perfect when nothing ever really is."

Eve laughed out loud, and Jenny stepped forward and gave her a firm hug that reminded her of her sister Mary who she'd never shared her losses with.

She was twenty-eight then and spent the next eight years of her life in an intimate relationship with various doctors, needles, and seemingly-endless tests. They put her on different combinations of hormones, discussing other options, more tests, new studies, new combinations of hormones, the statistical probabilities of In Vitro. Mo sat next to her at every appointment. He asked follow up questions. He reached for her hand, his warm, hers always cold. One doctor referred them to another. For the first few years, they went in hopeful they'd find the answer. They cut back spending to save enough money to fund their child in the making. She read book after book searching for some new insight that would allow them to conceive. She prayed almost constantly. All the tests and procedures, adjusting this or that about their lifestyle, the temperature on the dryer, their diet, their sexual positions. She dreaded sex. It had become about an outcome. The intimacy of their early marriage, feeling her way to his body, the reassuring pleasure of his touch, the intensity of the closeness she had never experienced with anyone else, was swallowed up by routine and constant disappointment.

She was only thirty-six. Most women, given the right set of variables, could still grow a baby at her age. Just like her plants; there were factors to consider and experiments to perform in order to determine why the seed refused to germinate. With her plants, she could adjust the sunlight, the moisture levels, adjust the temperature, add elements to the soil and take them away, loving the texture, the varied smell of the earth on her fingers. Eventually they would thrive.

"I'm done after this," Eve had said, just over a year ago, as they walked out of yet another office, this one a specialist in California.

"OK." Mo reached over and took her hand. The warmth of him a relief that spread through her like water. She looked at him, his dark face relieved and sad, his thick black hair like a mane. His full name was Mohsin, which meant helper, like hers.

Eve liked the way his hair curled around his ear lobe, holding on like a comma. He knelt close to her, showed her a plant he'd found in the grove. Held out the root, then turned it over and offered her the tiny flower held gently between his thumb and middle finger. She smiled and asked him where he'd grown up. In LA, he said, his mother was Iranian, non-religious, his father American, both Professors at UCLA. She thought,

You're beautiful.

She wanted to reach out and smooth his hair, to kiss his lowered eyelid above the mass of lashes, just beneath the brow. He spoke quietly and smiled at her. His eye teeth pointed inward, slightly overlapped the front teeth. She saw the thin line of dirt beneath his cleanly cut fingernails. Mo was a few years ahead of her completing a post-doc in soils. She was studying rhizomatic root systems and plant relationships in the undergrowth of aspen groves. Professor Hicks had suggested the partnership might be a good idea. They might find their data overlapped. Mo bent down next to her to point out another particular flower, unique to the floor beneath the Colorado Aspens. He used words without defining them, unlike the men in her undergraduate classes. He assumed that she understood.

They worked over the summer months, sitting in the quiet groves, sometimes close, sometimes far apart, always breathing in the same thin air. He'd observed the way she became absorbed in her work. The way she startled if he spoke without warning. When he walked up behind her, he had a habit of placing his large hand on her shoulder, softly, to let her know he was there. Neither one felt any need to fill the silence. They listened to the breeze pick up and watched the dark afternoon clouds roll in each day. Every afternoon an apocalypse. They'd worked together for three months this way, when the rain turned to hail. Tiny balls pelted Eve's legs as she ran toward the truck, Mo, just ahead of her, slid to the middle of the seat and stopped. She slammed the door behind her, laughing. She pushed her dripping hair back from her eyes. He kissed her when she turned to look at him, put his warm hand on her cheek as he pulled away, and looked at her.

Looking down she said, "I'm sorry. I like you. I really like you, Mo, but I'm Mormon."

"Alright," he said and laced his fingers through hers.

It took Eve time to let go of the story she thought her life would be: a nice Mormon girl meets a nice Mormon boy, they fall in love, they marry in the temple where they are sealed together for time and all eternity. They have lots of little Mormon children together. They attend church as a family every Sunday. This was the only marriage story she knew.

For the next month, she drove to Denver on Sundays to attend a different Mormon Singles Ward. She'd already dated everyone in the Boulder ward. She was twenty-six, working on a Ph.D. in the hard sciences. A little too career-focused, a little too old by standard Mormon marriage practices. Most of her girlfriends married right out of high school, and even her sister Anna, the least traditional of all of her sisters, had married early in undergrad. Eve accepted dates with every

Mormon man who asked her for the next eight weeks. Until she grew tired of fending off unwanted advances that only made her think of the hail, the small red splotches on her thigh, the taste of rain on Mo's lips.

When they started dating, he asked if he could attend church with her each Sunday. They sat in one of the shorter pews on the left side of the chapel for several weeks before the first Sunday rolled around. She sat nervously as one and then another ward member walked up to the pulpit to share their testimonies. God had helped them find their keys. God had brought them together with their one true love. Jesus was the Savior of all mankind. The boy prophet Joseph Smith saw him bright, hovering next to the God the Father in a green grove in upstate New York sometime in the late 1800's. She held her breath, praying that the weepy, red-haired sister would not bear her testimony about any current angelic visitations that seemed to be a frequent occurrence in her otherwise ordinary life, that no one would mention golden plates or miraculous healing blessings.

Where I see beauty, she thought, *he'll see delusion.*

She noticed the young Elders looking at him, dressed in their uniform of dark wool suits and white button-down shirts with a tie. The small clip on the pocket with their title "Elder" and last name. An irony that made her smile. She'd successfully avoided the missionaries for three weeks, by choosing a pew close to an exit. After a lengthy closing prayer, she pulled Mo from the pew and walked quickly toward the door. The missionaries waited outside the front door in the sunshine.

"Hello!" They said, extending their hands.

"We're actually on our way—" Eve smiled and tried to keep moving.

The boy didn't acknowledge her. He addressed Mo. "We'd really like to meet with you. Nothing formal, but if you have any questions or concerns about the Church." She flushed. They were nineteen-years-old. Mo was twenty-seven, a mature twenty-seven. Eve looked at him. He appeared nonplussed.

"I don't really believe in God, at least not as you define the term. I wouldn't want to waste your time."

The elder with white-freckled skin, red hair and very earnest blue eyes looked at him.

"But you've been here almost every week for over a month now."

"Yes, I have."

"Have you read The Book of Mormon?"

"Yes."

"You have?" Eve looked sideways at him.

He smiled and nodded.

"And have you prayed to see if it's true?" The missionary asked

"No, I don't pray. As I said, I don't believe in God. I read it because I want to know Eve better, and this is part of who she is. These are her traditions."

Eve slipped her arm through his.

She said. "You'll have to excuse us. We need to get going."

The other missionary who hadn't yet spoken also ignored her.

"If you don't believe, why do you come?"

"Because I love her, and this is where she is on Sunday."

They were married the next summer in the little aspen grove in front of the cabin. It wasn't a Mormon temple. The sunlight fell through the quaking leaves, the grove moving in celebration, his arm gentle around her waist, a small gathering of the people most important to them in their lives. The quiet, full of bird song and breeze, as holy and perfect as any temple she knew.

—

Outside, storm-white light illuminated the small snowy grove. The place that she kept returning to as a child, a wife, a woman of sorrow and acquainted with grief. She'd passed through the valley of the shadow of death beneath the same dappled light of late spring and early summer just over year ago—When she had been on the edge of losing everything, including Mo.

—

Eve spent the late winter stepping carefully across frozen patches on the sidewalk, hiding a sleeve of soda crackers in her bag, folding her exhaustion into comfortable sweaters and the down feathers of her coat. Seven years of infertility treatment, three miscarriages, and Eve had, finally, almost made it to twelve weeks. Safe. She'd told no one, not even Mo. She'd tell him at the end of the week over an ordinary dinner. The thought of his face at hearing the news made her smile. She pulled at the window, sliding it open. A swallow flew from the branches in a tiny rush of beating wings. Eve put her hand on the almost imperceptible round of her belly. Eight more weeks before she would feel a similar fluttering inside her body. The air smelled of melting snow, left over from a light spring storm. The blossom-covered branches had bent without breaking. The moisture left the grass soaked and green. The wooden floors felt smooth and cool on her bare feet. She wanted a cross breeze and crossed the room to open the door to the white-tiled bathroom. Her phone buzzed on the counter. She came down from tip toe, leaving the window closed and ran to back to the counter, thinking, if it was Mo. She wouldn't wait. She'd tell him.

"Evie? Hi, it's Rox."

"Oh hi, Rox. How are you?"

"I'm alright. I have a few minutes before I have to pick up Peter from school, so I thought I'd call. George is gone again. Some legal conference in San Diego this week. He's been busy with church stuff too. So am I. I feel like we haven't seen each other in forever. Good busy though—all good things. I shouldn't complain."

"You didn't want to go along with George?"

"To the conference? No, none of the wives were going on this one. He sent me flowers, roses again. I've never really liked roses. They're red. I don't love red. I've told him if it's roses, pink, even yellow, but you know George, he doesn't remember things like that." Roxcy sighed.

"You OK, Rox?"

"I . . ."

There was a pause on the line, and Eve took a breath. She couldn't tell Roxcy before she told Mo or her mom.

"I miss my kids, Evie. All of a sudden the house is so quiet and big. I know it's crazy, but I miss doing laundry, loads and loads of laundry, and folding it and putting it away. You know? And only Pete's left. He has so many friends, which is good, but it seems like he's never home. He's also started spending time with a girl I'm not thrilled about. She has a reputation. Probably nothing to worry about. And I have been playing a lot of tennis, so that's good."

"Oh, Rox." Eve breathed in.

"It's strange, I mean, I'm a happy person. I know I have so much to be grateful for. My beautiful home, my kids, they're good kids and the gospel of course. I'm very blessed. Anyway, I haven't talked to you in a while. What's going on with you?" Roxcy paused.

Eve felt the hard, deep twisting. She hung up the phone and put her hand on her stomach. A thin red trickle ran down her leg. She pushed the off button on her phone and walked toward the small bathroom, square white tiles on the floor, white grout, white sink, white toilet, white towels, white light.

Her underwear felt damp, a sickening tightening of her muscles again and the gush. A red flower bloomed in the middle of the tile and spread into a flood of little rivers running in the grooves of white grout. No. No. No. She doubled over, heard herself scream. Her body wrenched. She tried to take a breath, to think. This couldn't happen again. She was safe. Twelve weeks. She couldn't clean up the mess again, bleach the blood away. The tiles were slick with it. She pulled a pile of clean white hand towels from the shelf above the toilet and threw them down. She doubled over again. Her thoughts tore. She could not bear the warm, small hand, slipping away again. She reached for the medicine cabinet—her reflection as white, as everything around her, a ghost, unrecognizable in the small rectangle of the mirror. There was a bottle of dilaudid left over from Mo's recent bout with kidney stones. Her hand shook. She pressed down and twisted the lid open. She turned on the tap, cool water against her hand. She swallowed one, another, another. The red blur of the floor, the twisting, pain. She swallowed another, and another, the red kept coming, but the pain eased and stopped. She walked around the corner, to the couch in the dark little reading nook. Holding a blood-soaked towel between her legs, she laid down. The front door opened and closed. Someone called her name. She thought,

Is it 5:30 already?

She closed her eyes and drifted, her whole body giving in. It was Mo. He'd come home for lunch. He repeated her name over and over. Eve. Eve. Eve. She heard him open the bathroom door and thought,

It's such a mess in there. She disappeared.

—

Two months after that last goodbye, to the unnamed little one, Eve knelt next to her mom outside the cabin. She knelt on wet knees, carefully turning the soil to give the roots air, to allow the melted snow to penetrate more deeply. The crocuses were just beginning to sprout, pervasive through the new spring grass around the small cabin. Remnants of the garden from Oak Lane that her mom had chosen to recreate or dig up and take with her. They'd knelt there in silence for two weeks, working the earth. Her mom didn't look at her when she finally spoke, her voice soft.

"God is not punishing you, Evie."

"I know," Eve said.

"I don't think you do," she wiped her hand off on her jeans and looked at Eve. Eve closed her eyes.

"Maybe, if I would have started trying when I was younger," Eve said in a low, quiet voice.

"Open your eyes, dear."

She opened her eyes and looked, her mom's face blurred by her own tears.

"I know, mom. It's not rational. I just thought things would be different, my life, would be different. I would have . . . children . . . my work . . . a temple marriage." She laughed. "Mo won't ever come to the temple with me, and you named me Eve, the mother of all living." She laughed again, wiping tears from her cheeks. I thought I had made peace with all of it, but I—I don't know, everything feels so heavy, so empty, nothing has turned out . . . I'll probably never be a mother."

"There are so many beautiful stories, Evie. Not just one. So much life to grow beyond the human, and you are gifted in that respect. You understand things so many refuse to see."

"But I'm missing something that feels essential, mom."

Her mom began to dig with her fingers again, furiously working the soil. "The only essential experience for you is the one you're living."

Eve sat silent, surprised at the edge in her mother's voice.

"Look, I wouldn't trade you girls, you know that, but I gave things up that I shouldn't have. Didn't tend to my other gifts enough. This narrowness, the sacrifice of self on the altar of motherhood, isn't right or good or God. Being a mother is a wonderful thing, a beautiful piece of life, but it's not some pinnacle. And it is most certainly not the only way to learn love. Do you honestly think you'd be happier if you'd have given up on school and married one of those ridiculous boys you occasionally brought home?"

"No! No. I don't, really. I don't know. I just—I wish, I wish I could've had both, you know? And at church, there are all these women my age with their almost-teenage children and girls with babies. I have this deep longing mom, here—she shoved her fist between her ribs, this ache—"

Her mom put down her tools and gathered her in. "Oh, Evie, for that, I am sorry, so, so sorry."

Her mother's voice was quiet again, her arms wrapped tight around her. She could feel the strength of them, the same arms that picked her up when she was small. Eve let the weight of all the years, the hormones, the ensuing mood swings, the strained talks with Mo, the nights of mechanical sex, the Doctor's offices and needles, the hope, the cramping, the blood—so much blood—the emptiness, the small, warm dream hand slipping away again—fall into her mother's capable arms, into the earth beneath them and, she thought,

Jesus. This is too much. Take it. She thought. *Take it away.*

—

When she returned home, Eve's bishop had called, and she found herself sitting in his office. It looked nearly identical to every bishop's office she'd ever been in. There was a large wooden desk, a brown leather office chair, two lightly cushioned chairs facing the heavy rectangular desk. And she waited. She'd been back from the cabin for about a week. She promised her mom and Mo she would see someone to talk through all that had happened, to make sure the craving for her own disappearance didn't return to swallow her. The miracle of rest and time was already beginning to restore her to herself. She and Mo were finding their way back to each other.

Eve looked up at the picture of Jesus that hung on the wall behind the desk—a Salvador Dali painting of Jesus on the cross, a woman at his feet. It was a strange choice for an LDS bishop:no crosses on their meeting houses or temples, no crosses hung on gold chains around LDS necks, no paintings of the crucifixion in Mormon meeting houses. The given reason, she knew, was that it was better to focus on the joy of the resurrection, not the suffering of crucifixion, although she couldn't pinpoint exactly how she knew this. It was like an echo she'd heard coming back over and over across her years in the church. Eve looked at the picture intently. She stared at the folds in the woman's robes, the shadows in the gold.

Her bishop came into the room. He wore the expected dark wool suit, a blue tie, a white shirt. He shook her hand, said hello, and then sat next to her rather than behind the desk and leaned forward, his elbows on his knees. He rubbed his forehead.

Without looking at her, he said. "Your mom called me."

"Oh?"

"You're just back from a stay with her, yes?"

"Yes," Eve said, looking down at her hands.

"She, very kindly, and rightly, informed me I had failed in my pastoral duties."

"Oh, no—She shouldn't have—none of this has been your fault bishop."

"Wait, please, let me finish. I don't know what it feels like, Eve. I have no idea what it feels like to want a child and not have one, to face repeated loss the way you have. I didn't know the extent of what you and Mo were going through. Can I be honest with you?" He looked at the floor in front of him.

"Of course."

"I'm a private person, so I don't like to pry into other people's lives. I'm not sure why I was called as a bishop. I'm uncomfortable, don't really know what I'm doing. I'm not suited to this. I don't want to know about other people's lives, their suffering. I mean, I knew you'd been trying to have kids for a long time, but I assumed you were doing all right because it was easier for me to assume that. I see a person coming to church regularly, smiling pretty often, clearly thoughtful and intelligent. Mo is obviously a good man, and assuming you were doing fine required less of me, so please let me apologize."

"You couldn't have done anything. It probably would have felt intrusive if you'd asked. Really, when I swallowed those pills, I just wasn't myself," she said, turning toward him. "The hormones ... I'd lost a lot of blood very fast. I'm doing so much better now. I'm only here to ask for a referral because I told Mo and my mom that I would."

"My sister is a psychologist. I should have done this months ago, Eve. She doesn't work for LDS Social Services, so I don't refer folks to her very often. She's not active in the church anymore, but I trust her. You know, we mostly stick to the weather and church callings in my family, as far as conversation goes. I think it drives her a bit crazy, but she loves us. What I'm trying to say is that I'm so sorry I didn't think to recommend her sooner. Tell Mo and your mom, I'm sorry too please. And Eve?" He looked at her. "I really am sorry for everything you've been through. Please know that."

She felt her body relax into gratitude for the simple kindness of this man, his honesty, and vulnerability. For the few minutes of silence, for her own strange belief in Jesus—a mystical rabbi, an intuitive ecologist, a poet. And for her church, which was filled with these remarkable people. They sat looking at the painting together and then he asked if he could say a prayer, closing his eyes and bowing his head and folding his arms.

Eve didn't close her eyes as he prayed. She continued to look at the painting and let his words fade into the back of her consciousness like music. The muscles in His large legs, His head drooping to one side, so you couldn't see the face. This Jesus, male as he was, might know the pain, might understand emptiness. The woman looking up at him certainly did.

—

The fire had turned to dark gray ash. Eve looked, saw the snow swirl outside the window and then stood, the blanket still around her shoulders. She started slowly with a crumpled piece of newspaper and a match, blowing softly, until there were flickers of deep orange ember. She laid three pieces of wood on the grate, balancing them so they had room to breathe, so the flame touched each one. The absence of her mother's steady life-giving force felt palpable. Eve watched the flames rise and dance and thought,

If Mom was the first tree, the beginning. We're just shoots she sent out, the little grove. We're all one thing, really.

Simultaneously she felt the beginnings of warmth and smelled snow.

A single tree holds so many forms.

Mary

The heat in the room was thick with steam from the shower. Mary cracked the window and felt the relief of fresh, cold air. She smelled the snow. Using a towel, she wiped the steam from the mirror, the round circle of her reflection appearing like an apparition of her mother. Without trying, she'd morphed into a slightly different version of her: the same unruly hair, the slight unevenness of her smile, the same lines around her eyes and mouth. She blinked.

Every time someone she loved traveled anywhere, Mary fought premonitions of disaster. She dreamt of tornadoes, of lions, of flame-filled plane crashes. Her recurring nightmare usually followed—blew into her sleep like unsettled weather. A reminder of the first disaster, her failure to protect Roxcy, so long ago.

~

When their mom opened the front door, her little sisters stayed asleep. But the slap of cold woke her, so she counted them. *Me, one. Roxcy, two. Evie, three.* Roxcy laid her head in Mary's lap and Eve, on the seat next to them with her knees tucked beneath her belly and her diaper in the air,

Four, she thought. *The baby is coming.*

The drive over to her Aunt Violet's house took them up and over the winding Wild Mouse, a street that climbed the mountain like an s, straightened across, and rounded down into Indian Hills. She caught a glimpse of the round white temple blending into the storm, it's lighted steeple, like a tall golden fountain. They turned right, past the small, frozen reservoir, and into the unfamiliar neighborhood dotted with the giant houses sitting in yards the size of a small city park. Her aunt and uncle lived in one of the houses and had one of those yards complete with an outdoor pool, a trampoline, and tennis courts.

They'd been to the house before, a couple of times, with her parents. Mary knew the staircase had twenty steps. They had ten clocks and 207 books in the small library off of the family room. The swimming pool in the backyard was a large rectangle. She could walk six and a half steps before the shallow end dropped abruptly into deeper water. The drop frightened her, so she stayed close to the steps in the corner, watching over Roxcy and Evie. Except for the day, when her oldest cousin, Paul, had taken her into the deep end and slipped his finger inside of her. Mary blinked. She didn't like it. She didn't like to remember.

Inside the house, there were too many bedrooms-seven-and a maze of hallways that sprawled out like insect legs from the dropped living room, the library, and the kitchen at the center of the house. The master bedroom and bath were on the opposite side of the house from the other six bedrooms separated by a large family room. They'd played hide and seek the first time they visited, and Evie was lost for over an hour. Mary had imagined her tiny body at the bottom of the pool, had run there first. But the gate was locked, and the cover closed over. She walked the perimeter to see if there was any indication that Eve had somehow crawled in, felt her face wet with tears, her heart pounding with the fear that her little sister had drowned. She should've kept her close. They should've played as a team. But Eve was safe. She'd just curled up in one of the bedroom closets, behind a blanket and fallen asleep. They'd found her when she woke and started crying, disoriented in the strange place. Her parents had been with them that day and the day of the pool party. Mary had scrambled from the pool and done nothing when Roxcy jumped from the side into Paul's arms for her turn, for her ride to the deep end. She'd hoped her parents would know somehow, sense it wasn't safe. She had waited, silent, for them to stop him. They'd watched and laughed as Roxcy squealed when she hit the water, then turned back to their conversation. Mary felt terror that they wouldn't be there with them tonight, with her mother breathing hard and her father squinting into the storm. Her sisters were on their own. Not even a chance of help.

Mary counted her mother's breaths, which became short, fast, and heavy. It sounded like she couldn't get enough air. She saw her hand squeeze hard on the handle above the door and then release.

"God! Help me! Here comes another one. If this isn't a boy, that's it. This is the last time. I'm not doing this again, David."

"I know, Sylvia. Hang on."

Her mother would never swear, never take the name of God in vain. She decided it must be a sort of informal prayer. The intermittent street lights flashed past the window, and she counted them too: one, two, three, four, until they pulled into the driveway. Violet stood in the entryway, so thin, holding her robe against the cold air. Snow swirled in the light of the doorway. Her mom reached back and grabbed her hand.

"Take care of your sisters, Mary."

Light spilled over on to the marble floor. Aunt Violet's hair was rolled in large pink curlers, and she reassured Mary's father, her brother, that it was no problem, to take as long as they needed, to please give her best to Sylvia, poor thing. Her father looked down at Mary. She felt his hand, warm on her head.

"Be a good girl."

"I will."

She looked up into his eyes and leaned her cheek into his large hand.

"Everything will be fine, Mary," he said. "I'll be back to get you tomorrow, and you can meet your new little brother or sister."

He closed the large oak door behind him, unaware of his lie. Her stomach tightened.

Mary followed Aunt Violet down one of the hallways. It was wide and dark. Eve sat on Mary's hip. Roxcy's head lolled to one side on Aunt Violet's bony shoulder. She turned on a light, too bright. Mary saw her sisters squirm, felt Evie twist uncomfortably in her arms. The walls were covered with pictures of her cousins in button-down shirts, sports uniforms, or by the pool in their swimsuits. He was in the back row on the left, tall, square-shouldered, thin, his hair the color of straw. They were somewhere in the maze of hallways. Mary counted three turns but had already forgotten which directions. Evie kept wiggling. Aunt Violet spoke kindly, reassured her in a soft voice that her mom would be fine, that her dad would likely pick them up after breakfast in the morning. She tucked them in. Her hand felt cold on Mary's cheek.

"There's a bathroom just across the hall. I'll leave the light on." She said, closing the door softly behind her.

There were two full-sized beds, one on each wall with a space in between. Mary felt wide awake. She watched the door, the sliver of light beneath it. She heard Roxcy's breath become slow and even. Mary tried to keep her eyes open, vigilant in the darkness. She heard a creaking sound. She heard the wind whining around the corner of the house. The snow piled outside. Evie's small body snuggled into her, warm. Her breathing like quiet waves. She struggled to stay awake, felt herself drifting.

She woke up too late. *When had he come in? Where was he, whispering, over near Roxcy.* She stepped out of the bed, her bare feet on the plush carpet.

"STOP." Her voice sounded loud in the silent room.

"Mary, it's just me. I came into check on you. I think Roxcy had a nightmare. I heard her crying when I was walking to my room."

"GET OUT!"

Her eyes adjusted to the dark room. She was close to him now. He'd moved, and she could see the outline of his broad shoulders sitting on the edge of the bed.

"You can't talk to me that way. This is my house—"

"I'll tell my parents what you did to me in the pool. I'll tell them you were on Roxcy's bed. I'll—"

"Mary, you misunderstood." His voice low with threat.

"Get out." Her voice was low too. Sure. It didn't sound like her own. It sounded strong, but her whole body was shaking.

He reached out toward her, and she bit hard on his hand, tasted blood, sharp on her tongue, her heart pounding in her ears. Her parents had always taught her to be kind, even when others were not. She felt confused, as if she'd failed, but they also told her to keep her sister safe. He slapped her so hard her cheek burned. No one had ever hit her. The tears streamed down her cheek. He turned and walked to the door.

"Little bitch." He said. "They'll never believe you anyway. I'll tell them you're a liar. Everything I did is your fault. You let me touch you in the pool. You didn't stop me then. You let Roxcy come in next because you liked it."

He left the door open. His shadow a dark triangle across the beds. Then he was gone. A vase filled with fake flowers sat on the nightstand. Mary picked it up and walked to the door, closing it quietly. The tears tasted salty along the edge of her lips. She put the vase on the floor in front of the edge where the door opened and felt her way along the beds back to Evie, her cheek still burning, her body still shaking. She lifted her baby sister up and put her close to Roxcy in the other bed, tucking the covers around both of them. Mary climbed back to the other bed to open the curtains. Someone had left the back-porch light on. It looked like a night light. She checked the lock on the window, climbed down, and pulled the blanket off her bed. She curled herself at the bottom of their bed and placed her hand on Roxcy's calf.

She's not crying, Mary thought. *Maybe he didn't hurt her. Maybe I woke up in time. Or maybe, even if he did, Roxcy stayed asleep.* But she knew this was a lie she told herself to feel better. She'd woken up too late. She hadn't stopped Roxcy jumping in the pool. She'd said nothing to her parents. She didn't know why. He was a liar. She didn't like it. But, still why hadn't she said anything? Maybe it was her fault.

She whispered, "It's Okay Rox. He's gone. Dad will be here to get us as soon as the baby is out." Roxcy began to whimper like a puppy in the darkness. Mary wanted to slide up next to her and give her a hug, but she couldn't leave the bottom of the bed. She needed to guard the door. So she put her other hand on her sister's calf, so she knew she was not alone, and gently patted her leg. She said,

"Shhh, shhh," in the same way she'd heard her mother sooth baby Eve.

—

Mary felt herself shudder, the old feeling of helplessness moved through her body. Her young husband's untimely death was the second time a worry, this one mingled with a wish, had played out. These two fulfilled premonitions danced around each other like the swirling snow outside the window. Now a third irrevocable disaster had been realized: her mother turned to dust. All the memories created a storm that blew that first disaster to the surface of her mind, here in broad daylight, where she could look at the old images that still haunted her:

In the dream, she is an adult, but her sisters are all children. Anna is an infant, swaddled in her arms. Her tiny face looks just like Mary's son, Hank, did as an infant. Eve is behind her right leg. Roxcy is almost five, the age she was when Anna was born. Mary holds her hand and yells at him to get away. He stands there smiling, his chest bare, his heels on the edge of the pool. She carefully hands the tiny bundle to Rocxy, puts her hands on Roxcy's head, her lips move and deliver a blessing. Then she turns. She runs at him with the immense force of her grown body. His arms flail. She watches as he falls backward into the water. He struggles for a moment before sinking, arms and legs splayed, reaching upward. When she was younger in the dream, it was her cousin's face at the bottom of the pool. Now it is her dead husband, Fred.

~

It was Monday night at BYU, which meant singles ward "family night". Mary attended religiously. They were bowling at the Wilkinson Center. She was good at the game, regularly scoring over 200, and had been on many bowling dates here.

She quickly learned that most men didn't like to lose to a girl, which was also true in her math classes. Her scores were almost always the highest in her class. It made many, if not most of the men, uncomfortable. She'd seen Roxcy pretend not to know things with George. Noted the way George felt noticeably important when Roxcy asked for his help. But Mary had given up pretending around the time she turned nine-years-old. She'd just never been very good at it, even as a child. Instead, she tried offering to tutor her fellow male mathematicians. Sometimes they accepted her offer, but they rarely asked her out on dates. Mary wanted to marry and have children. She also wanted to be an accountant. God had given her an undeniable love and felicity with numbers, and she had faith that gift was not for nothing.

When she bowled, she always chose lane seven. Seven was her favorite number, the lines one long and one short, a clue to its uneven nature. She thanked the clerk and held her bowling shoes in one hand as she walked toward her lane. A boy stood in her lane, slipping his fingers in and out of a green ball, testing the fit. He was wide-shouldered, thin, and tall. She'd noticed him in church. His blond hair looked like cut straw. Mary walked over.

"Hi there," she said.

"Hello."

"My name's Mary. I don't think we've met." She smiled at him and offered her hand.

He shook it. His hand felt cold. "Hi, I'm Fred."

"You're new to the ward?"

"Yeah, I moved in between semesters. Just back from my mission." He said.

"Oh, where'd you serve?"

"Southern Spain."

"Warm then?"

"Yes, hot. It's freezing in here,"

"You'll warm up once we start the game. Any good at bowling?" She grinned at him.

"Not particularly." He returned the smile, the dimple in his right cheek like a tiny crescent moon. "I'm guessing you are?"

"I'll probably beat you."

"Thanks for the heads up," he said, laughing.

"Best to be prepared."

As they began, he continued to glance at her, now and then, a slightly amused expression on his lips. She made eye contact each time she caught him looking at her and smiled back, which seemed to surprise and delight him. Mary held the ball in both hands close to her chin, took three steps, a deep curtsy, and watched the ball follow the black and red arrows to the expected strike. Then she walked back toward him.

"Wow!"

"I warned you." She said.

"You did." He said.

She smiled.

"I've also noticed you seem to have all the answers in class too."

"What?"

"I'm in your advanced accounting class with Professor Hill. I sit in the back."

"Oh." Her heart fell. "You're up," she said.

Fred knocked down eight of the ten pins and returned to the scoring table. Mary watched him adjust the score. No pause for thought. No marks on the score sheet. That was a good sign. He asked her on their first date after she beat him by one hundred points. Another good sign. Four months later, they had set a date in June to be married in the Provo Temple, after they'd both graduated.

The black-gowned crowd swarmed the wide sidewalks, looking for the entrance to their school. The Marriott Center was a huge, square building with rounded corners where all the large campus events were held. Built from the sand-colored brick that was pervasive throughout the campus, it held 19,000 people who were currently making their way inside. Mary couldn't hear anything. Fred was talking. She shook her head.

"I can't hear you," she yelled. The background roar of people moving and talking, the mass of bumping bodies was too much. Nervousness always began in her stomach. There were so many possible disasters in large crowds.

Fred leaned in close and kissed Mary's cheek. He yelled in her ear, "I love you. Good luck."

When he pulled back into the bright sunlight, his straw-colored hair shining and his face in shadow, she felt sick. The broad shoulders, the thin frame, the tilt of his head—she saw her cousin, had a flash of a night she only remembered now in bad dreams. He moved away to find his parents, but the unsettling vision stayed with her, felt like a punch in the stomach. She couldn't find her breath; her balance wobbled.

Where were her mom and dad? She was supposed to meet them. She fidgeted with her fingers. She tried to get her eyes to focus on what seemed now to be unsteady ground.

She tried to slow her breath, in-one, two, three, out-one, two, three. Was it a sign?

"Mary!" Her mom was beside her. "Are you ok? You're pale." She put her hand on Mary's forehead.

"I don't know."

"Do you need me to take you home?"

"No. No. I'm going to get my diploma, but will you find Fred and tell him I needed to go lie down after. I don't feel up to lunch with you all. Is that ok?"

"Of course. Are you sick? Did something happen?"

"I think it's just all the people. It's too hot, too loud."

"Ok. We're walking you to your seat. David, take her other arm."

"Thanks, mom."

As soon as the ceremony was over Mary walked back toward her apartment across the winding white bridge. The people all around her seemed like only a blur of noise and color. She had to find a clear answer. She didn't understand why Fred's face had, for a moment, been her cousin's face. Mary followed the winding white bridge allowing the flow of people to pull her along. The bright sunlight felt harsh. She opened the door to the Harris Fine Arts Center, found an open piano room, and locked the door behind her. She knelt with her elbows on the hard, oak bench. Her hands pressed into her forehead. She could feel the pressure of them. She stayed in that position long enough that they made a mark. When Joseph Smith saw a bright light, it was Heavenly Father and Jesus saying that none of the churches were true. When the whole church witnessed Brigham Young's face transform into Joseph Smith, it had been a sign that he was the rightful prophet. Was this a sign? Did the transformation she saw mean that Fred wasn't true? Did it mean he was a pedophile? No answer. Just silence.

Two weeks passed. They sat on the old blue quilt in the patch of grass behind the cabin, the dew soaking through, quivering shade on the edge of the blanket.

"I think I need to slow things down, Fred," she said, holding his hand, looking down.

"You want to move our wedding date?"

"Yes."

"All right." He paused, "Can I ask if I did something wrong?"

"No, Fred, it's not you at all." Mary said, which was true and not true. "It's just fast. We've only known each other four months."

"I feel like I know you. I know you love the Church. I know you love numbers. And I know you love bowling. I think you love me. If I can hope that you love me as much as those three things, I'm happy to wait."

She laughed out loud and kissed him. "I do. I do love you, Fred. Not quite as much as bowling."

He kissed her again. "Well, we have the temple scheduled on June 5th. Things are already in motion, but we can put on the brakes if you need time. I don't leave for Officer's School until December. Promise me you'll marry me sometime before I have to go?"

His generosity, his willingness to wait, felt like an answer. Mary looked at her hand, the thin gold band, the tiny diamond. She looked at Fred, and he was just Fred, his hair slightly longer, a cowlick at the back of his part, his earnest blue eyes, the corners of his mouth turned up like he expected to laugh. Mary's knees were sore from pleading with God, but when she prayed, nothing happened. His transformation had happened only once in that flash of sunlight. She couldn't discern if it was a message or a phantom of her fearful mind. When she looked at him, then, in the shade, the feel of cool grass beneath her blanket, she felt sure of him again. That would have to be enough.

"October first. I promise." She said.

"October first sounds good." He said.

Fred kissed her again. Always respectful, careful not to cross lines. He kept his hands outside her clothes, on her back, her hip, in her hair. Fred was not her cousin. Mary repeated this to herself when he kissed her. She repeated it to herself as she looked at him across the altar. She repeated it despite his gentleness, tangible proof of his goodness, the first time he really touched her the night they were married. And continued silently reminding herself every time they were together in those few months leading up to his first deployment.

—

Looking at her reflection in the steam-fogged mirror, Mary felt the steam as the substantive expression of the fog of feeling that surrounded her short marriage. Fred, that good man, had ultimately left her free to raise their child without the worry that he would hurt him and she wouldn't know.

To raise their son Hank with only the help of her mother, whom she was able to trust without reservation. Mary never allowed herself to count the number of times she wished she could have felt differently. They'd both been there, her mom and Fred, to help bring the gift that would see her through the next twenty years of her life. She could blink, and there would be her tiny son, still diapered, his chubby arms reaching for her. She wanted to dive into the pool and pull Fred out. But she knew he wasn't at the bottom of any pool, nor was he back at her one-story condo. Fred had died in a flight exercise somewhere over Nevada a year after Hank was born. She'd had the dream the night she went into labor. It woke her with tearing pain. She was sure the baby was in danger. She was sure something horrible was going to happen.

—

Mary woke herself and Fred, her husband, with a scream. She smelled snow and looked to see it just beginning to fall. It swirled in the street light outside their bedroom window. She apologized to Fred between contractions.

"Mary, you have nothing to be sorry for. I'm calling your mom."

She knew he'd never seen her like this, after the dream she usually opened her eyes, reached for his hand and cried silently to herself while he slept undisturbed. He tried to tell her everything was okay. He laid his hands on her head and blessed her. He blessed her with calm. She couldn't locate this blessing in her churing body. She closed her eyes and saw gushing blood that was not there. Imagined a blue-lipped, lifeless infant emerging from her. She watched the gray light of dawn spread through their small kitchen window, everything becoming bright, and felt blank terror grip her. Fred went to the door.

"I've never seen her like this. I'm worried."

"You get the bag and keys. Everything will be just fine, Fred."

Her mom held a vase full of yellow daffodils, bringing her late March in early February.

"Oh dear, did I spill?" Her mom said, reaching for a towel to clean the puddle on the kitchen floor.

"No, mom. Help. Please. Help."

Fred looked at Mary and, without a word, walked down the hall to get the overnight bag. They'd talked it through a million times. He followed their plan.

"Right, I'll clean this up and grab a bath towel for you."

"All right, let's go!" Fred said. "Hold my hand, Mary. Squeeze as hard as you need to." He looked at her mother. Her mother smiled, nodded her head, and the three of them walked into the cold morning.

The drive wasn't long. The drive was excruciating. Mary could not manage. She forgot how to count. Numbers flew from her brain. Her body taking over, fast, painful waves coming on suddenly and breaking one on top of the next, leaving her gasping for breath.

Fred looked at her, reached for her hand. "Hold on. We'll be there in a minute." He ran a red light.

"Fred, slow down. She'll be fine if you don't kill us all by running red lights."

"Mama help, please!"

"Count your breath, Mary. Breathe in . . . two . . . three and out . . . two . . . three slow down and try to relax all your muscles. You're doing great."

She could do it when her mom reminded her, like she was a child again. Mary looked out of the car window and tried to count the snowflakes as they fell. When they arrived, the nurses apologized and complained, as they scrambled to find her a bed. They explained that labor and delivery was often crowded at Utah County Hospital but impossible when there was a storm. Babies dropped with the barometric pressure. Mary counted her breaths and wondered what science lay behind such a superstitious sounding phenomenon. Her mom rubbed her back, and Fred squeezed her hand. She saw other husbands grasping their wives' hands and felt uneasy, pausing down the hallways. Fred wouldn't always be here to hold her hand, which gave her an odd relief. He would often be deployed, far away, somewhere else. She would feed their baby, change him, and wash out his diapers, pick up his toys alone. Eventually she would take him to school, attend his recitals and sports events. Her mother did all those things with minimal involvement from their father, and she had had four children. Her father's callings in Church and his work at the university had left little free time to spend with his daughters. He insisted on and led 20 minutes of daily family scripture study and an evening family prayer. But she could easily manage that on her own. And her mom would be there when Mary needed help. She could hand their little one to her mom without worry. She could finish her Master's in Accounting and keep her job at the small firm. But what would she do when Fred was there? How would she smooth the prickly worry inside her that he might hurt their child?

It took seven hours and twelve pushes to set them both free. They wiped Hank off and handed him to her. Mary fumbled with her breast.

Her mother smiled. "The first is always the hardest."

"The first is all I'll have," Mary said.

Fred looked at her, dazed. He hadn't heard. She saw he couldn't speak, was overcome with emotion. Tears hung heavy on the edge of his eyes. He smiled down at her and their son, his hand on her shoulder.

"You never know." Her mom smoothed the loose hair from Mary's wet forehead and smiled reassuringly at Fred.

"I know," Mary said.

"Thank you for being here, Sylvia," Fred said finally. "Mary, you are amazing. Can I hold him?"

Mary fought the absurd reluctance inside her and carefully handed him to her husband. She turned to her mom and said, "Will you stay for a while?"

"As long as you need me," she said.

Mary watched the way Fred examined the small face, gently stroking the soft cheeks, his wonder at the small brow raised into pliant wrinkles. He held their baby boy easily, naturally cradling him in one arm. He counted his ten fingers, long, thin, reaching for a moment, then clenched in tiny fists. Mary felt a deep sense of contentment. She thought, *He is safe. He is nothing like that person. Something horrible will happen if I can't trust him. It will be my fault.*

For the next year, sleep eluded her in the midst of exhaustion, staring at Hank's tiny face and hands, breathing in the miracle of him. When they moved him down the hall into his own room after the first few weeks, she felt the distance was unreasonable. She would wake in a cold sweat dreaming of fire, wolves, or worse and feel her way along the walls, down the long dark hall to his small bedroom, just to put her hand on Hank's tiny back and feel his breaths in and out. Those baby breaths were her only sedative, so she'd curl up on the floor next to his crib and sleep deep. When Fred was deployed, Mary moved her baby boy back into her room and finally found rest.

A year and a half later two men sat in full uniform on her couch. They leaned forward, resting their elbows on their knees the way Fred had.

Mary heard their words like rushing water, like fulfilled prophecy.

"Mrs. Snyder? We're sorry."

She heard a date, "engine malfunction," "ambulance," and "too late." Mary felt immense sorrow and relief simultaneously. The tears ran down her chin and off her jawline onto Hank's little face. He'd toddled over to show her a block. The men in their uniforms looked sad or worried, deep crevices between their brows. One of them looked down and took the block Hank had offered. Her own visage remained calm, no quiver of the lip or crease of her forehead, just the steady tears. She couldn't think of questions to ask them but found herself praying silently.

Please take care of him and . . . thank you.

Mary felt horrified by her ambivalence, but somewhere, deep inside of her mind, she knew it would be easier. She would no longer have to make up a reason to interrupt when Fred was laying Hank down. Or pretend to want to listen to the book he was reading aloud on the sofa. The hyper-vigilance that never allowed her to rest when he was in the house left her exhausted. Always hesitant to leave her baby alone with his own father. But after the funeral, when she opened the door to her condo, the one she and Fred had bought with the money she'd saved from all her jobs since high school, she knew that Fred had set her free. He loved her that much. And she had loved him as much as she possibly could have. Little Hank would be theirs in the eternities, but hers here. In this small, quiet space, she could learn how to be his mother.

Mary took little Hank to the park frequently. She knew he needed to socialize with other kids, especially being an only child in a community made up almost entirely of large families. But it was pure duty. She dreaded the inevitable tears in any new women's eyes when they asked the inevitable question. "What does your husband do?"

Today the brunette with the fitted t-shirt, another brunette who only wore skirts, and the redhead who never wore makeup. These ladies all knew her story through the ward grapevine. She felt their pity as if it were something solid. They had no way of understanding how predictable and safe her life with little Hank felt. How much the rhythms of it felt more familiar without her late husband coming and going. They would have no way of understanding how hours of working with numbers calmed her mind. Or how sitting on the pews at church alone with her child, just as her mother had done, was not a problem. The long block of Sunday meetings a balm of repetition. How loss had created a new layer for her when she took the sacrament each Sunday, the way she felt palpable love and comfort in that bread and water. How the plan of salvation meant more because, eventually, she and Hank would be reunited with Fred, minus the worry she couldn't manage. What a relief and blessing that would be—the way it was a relief to spend time in her mom's yard instead of the park. Because when these same women who pitied her, got distracted by what color one or the other of them was going to paint their living room, they wouldn't see their children push Hank down, or pull his hair, or bite him. Mary saw everything—potential eye injuries, head wounds, and broken bones. By contrast, her mom's yard was familiar, enclosed, safe space where she could let him explore. Her attention could wander there, without fear that a small truck would leave a gash in his forehead that might scar him for life. When she gave him the rounded spade, he'd endlessly fill and empty planting pots with dirt, carry them from here to there, walk over to her to show off his talent, which she would generously praise. And her mom was there. She handed Hank a worm for his dirt, planting and replanting her perennial garden and asked,

"How's your energy these days, Mary?" She turned, blowing a loose piece of hair from in front her eye, pushing it toward her ear with the back of her hand.

"Good—only because of your help. I hope you know how much I appreciate it, mom. I don't worry about him when he's with you."

"Well, you inherited the worrying gene from your dad. He just can't turn his mind off. But, you know there's really nothing to worry about. I love having both of you here, keeps me busy. Hank is the busiest, sweetest, little guy. Look at him go!" She laughed, a sound that had always reminded Mary of a kaleidoscope of butterflies.

"He's gotten so big, so quickly," Mary said, holding her hand out to catch the pile of dirt he offered and pulling him in for a cuddle.

"Before you know it he'll be graduating from high school."

"Don't say that! I don't know what I'll do when he's gone. I love him so."

"Well, that never stops, my dear. It changes, but it never stops."

—

Mary thought, *That's it. That's the truth. Love never leaves, it just changes. Hank is gone. Mom is gone. And I have to take care of my sisters now. Everything has come full circle and I'm back where I began.*

Hank was now a grown man, a good man, like his father had been, thoughtful, responsible. He'd worried about leaving her to go off to school, but she encouraged him to go, reminded him she wouldn't be alone. She had her mom. She had her sisters. She had her work and church. She'd be alright.

She felt a gush of wind as snow blew in through the opened window and quickly stepped over and reached out to close it. The rush of cold air turned her cheeks pink. The mirror was completely clear of steam. She wondered how long she'd been standing hypnotized by the swirling snow.

Roxcy

Snow blew in under the gap between the floor and the front door. Roxcy set down the boxes labeled Deseret Industries and took her mom's wool coat from the wall of odd hooks, the antlers, the round porcelain, the bright jewels, Anna's eclectic touch again. She moved her fingers across the boiled wool, chartreuse, a color Roxcy usually avoided since it washed her out. The large buttons felt smooth, and she slid her hands into the deep pockets sewn on the front. Her mom had had it for as long as Roxcy could remember, the color of spring aspen leaves. She thought,

This storm is too early. September storms don't stay. The sun will come and melt it. It has to. I have to move the memorial outside. She'd want grass and sky not the white walls of the chapel. She liked flowers growing in the ground, not cut in an arrangement set up on the stand.

She didn't know why it hadn't occurred to her before, why she hadn't planned it that way in the first place. When she thought of her mom, it was usually outside in the garden or in the kitchen. She preferred being outdoors to being in, like her preference for Wayne to George. Her mom had loved Wayne, but had she?

Roxcy hadn't thought of him in years. His dark hair and hazel eyes. They'd been close in height and she used to examine them when he put his face close to hers, a swirl of blue, green, gold, and brown. He kept them open until their lips met, her last warm glimpse. Everything about him was warm and unhurried. Her body relaxed in the memory, the way he stood close behind her, his thumb through her belt loop, his breath in her hair. She'd thought she was going to marry him. He wanted to be a professor, work at a little liberal arts college, maybe in the Midwest somewhere where they could plant a nice garden, have a small house. She could open a little design business, and they would have as many or as few children as she wanted, whatever she wanted, he'd said. It was spring, and he'd been laying on the grass in their backyard, picked a purple crocus, and handed it to her.

Roxcy hung the coat back on the hook and put an old scarf at the bottom of the door to block the blowing snow. She walked back into the living room and sat down next to the pile of photo albums.

"What if we held mom's memorial outside? That grassy spot across the parking lot." She said.

Eve looked out the window and raised her eyebrows.

"I know, but it'll melt before Friday." Roxcy began thumbing through a pile of photos.

"I've been through those already. What are you looking for, Rox?" Eve said.

"Do you remember Wayne?"

"Wayne?"

"The boy I dated before I met George. I just wondered if she'd kept any pictures of him." Roxcy had been with Wayne for almost a year before George appeared and changed her whole life.

———

Roxcy paced the gray utility carpet of the small meeting area, occasionally sitting for a moment on one of the orange-vinyl-covered benches that ran along the edge of the atrium. Her eyes scanned the wide surrounding halls. Sheri was late for their study session. She heard the ding of the elevators moving up and down, the sound of the voices becoming echoes as they moved past out of the common area into closed hallways, or upstairs, hurried footfalls against the white stone floors. She could smell the greasy food from the Cougar Eat wafting through the double glass doors. She checked her watch as another elevator bell rang and looked up when she heard Sheri's laugh. Roxcy turned. He was standing there then, just inches from her, so tall it hurt her neck to look at him. An ache she found pleasant.

"Hi Rox, sorry I'm late," Sheri said, "This is George. George, this is my best friend, Roxcy."

"Nice to meet you, George." Roxcy smoothed her hair and smiled, offering her hand, looking up, up . . .

She thought, *He must be 6'4".* He smiled back at her. She'd never seen such perfect teeth.

"Hi," he said, taking her hand.

"I can't study with you, Rox."

"Oh?"

"George and I are going back to his apartment. He and his roommates have a big screen T.V., and we're all going to watch something, maybe *The Princess Bride* or *The Holy Grail*. You can come if you want, but I know you wanted to study for the test." Sheri said.

"You need to study too."

"You can study back in my room," George still held her hand. Sheri looked at him and then at Roxcy.

"Well, I don't know," Roxcy said.

"Roxcy's an honor code devotee, George. She doesn't break rules. She's a rule follower."

"I'll make sure my roommates don't come back while you're there. I promise, you'll be safe."

"I guess I could."

"Or I can come back and study with you after the movie. Or you can go to the library. I can meet you at the library after," Sheri's smile strained.

"No, no, I'll come."

Roxcy did like the honor code. She liked the long list of rules about, grooming and avoiding certain situations, rules that were created for her protection—no shorts or skirts above the knee, no sleevelessness in any form, absolutely no midriff tops. Men weren't allowed facial hair without a doctor's note. She wasn't sure why but trusted that there was a good reason. She didn't like beards anyway. They seemed unhygienic. No persons of the opposite sex were technically allowed in bedrooms, which made sense because no sort of sexual activity at all was allowed at the school, unless you were married, of course. No petting, no necking, she wasn't sure what those were exactly. Making out was fine if you were careful. No oral sex, which was gross anyway; no dry sex, commonly known as dry humping or levi lovin;' absolutely no actual sexual intercourse. You could be thrown out of school altogether if that happened to you. The modesty, hair length, and facial hair rules were small infractions, but they went on your record. Sheri got sent home to her apartment to change on a regular basis for wearing shorts and skirts that didn't quite hit the middle of her knee. She thought it was ridiculous, but Roxcy didn't mind so much. Why not leave a little to the imagination? She found shorts, skirts and tops that showed off her body without breaking any rules. And she liked clear lines. They made life less complicated.

As they walked across the sun-soaked parking lot toward Ninth East, he told her his full name was George Brigham Young, after the original Brigham Young, who was his great, great, grandfather. He'd recently returned from his mission to London, England. He loved Londoners. They were the best people in the world, he said. He'd enjoyed every minute of his mission, of bringing people to the true church of Jesus Christ. Best two years of his life, he said. He let slip that he served as Assistant to the President who had been the best mission president, Elder so and so. Did she know him? He was a seventy now, a general authority, like his dad. She listened and smiled while he talked.

She felt shocked when he walked her to the bedroom and opened the door. She'd never seen such blatant filth: piles of dirty clothes, unmade beds, the musty smell of sweat and men.

"Sorry, It's my roommate."

"I'll just clear a space," she said, smiling up at him.

While George, his roommates, and Sheri watched *The Princess Bride* out front, Roxcy put her books aside and cleaned. She picked up dirty clothes from the floor and put them in a large empty laundry bin in the closet. She made the two beds, dusted his dresser and reorganized his tie rack by color. When she turned to walk out after finishing the yellows, George stood blocking the door frame.

"Sorry! I didn't mean to scare you." he said, smiling, "I try to keep things clean, but it's pointless. You didn't have to do this, you know? It looks amazing, though."

"Oh, I don't mind. I couldn't concentrate anyway."

"Thank you, Roxcy, right?"

"Yes, Roxcy, after Eliza Roxcy Snow."

"Oh, I hope we're not related?"

"No." She laughed. "Eliza didn't have kids with Brigham or Joseph. She started the primary and youth programs though. I bet she wanted kids. I know I do. Oh, sorry."

"No, not at all. I want kids, too. That's why I'm majoring in PoliSci. I'm planning on law school. My father's a partner at Kirton McConkie."

"Sounds like you have it all planned out."

"I guess I do. I'll specialize once I get into practice. Most likely transactional. My dad's firm handles all the church's financial holdings."

"Well, shall we head out front?" She said, stepping toward him.

"You're not much like Sheri. She'll break a rule every chance she gets."

"I think it's just a phase. She's mad that her dad made her come to BYU. She wanted to go to the U, to get out of Provo." Roxcy laughed. "I don't know why. I love Provo."

George didn't move. "Sheri didn't mention you to me until today," he said.

"Oh?"

"We're just friends, Sheri and I, I mean."

"Oh, well—"

"Look, I'd like to take you out sometime."

"I'd like that too, but I'm actually dating someone right now—we should head back out, don't you think?"

George leaned in and kissed her full on the mouth. His lips were sure, urgent even, his hand on her low back. She didn't stop him. She returned it.

"Can we go out front now?" She said smiling up at him.

Sheri seemed irritated when the two of them walked back to the living room. Roxcy felt her cheeks flush again, guilty. On the walk home, she told her.

"Please don't be mad at me, Sheri."

"About what?"

"George asked me out."

"He asked you out?" Sheri looked straight ahead. "What about Wayne?"

"He swore you two are just friends. Are you just friends? I told him I was dating someone, and then he kissed me." Roxcy looked at her friend, trying to make eye contact. Sheri stopped and faced her smiling, angry.

"And I bet you kissed him back." Sheri turned and walked away. "I don't feel like talking to you right now."

"Sheri, wait. I honestly didn't know you liked him." Roxcy tried to catch up. Sheri waved her off.

"Just don't, Ok?"

Before she told Wayne, Roxcy wanted to make sure she liked George. Their first date was a hike to squaw peak. George kept a fast pace. Roxcy's legs ached when they reached the top. They hadn't paused once. He talked the whole way about his studies, his plans, his friends, his family. He would eventually be a partner at the firm, just like his father. It's what his dad wanted, and he thought he'd like the law well enough. She'd done the same hike with Wayne earlier in the season. He'd said almost nothing the entire way. He walked behind her, and occasionally, when they stopped for water or to look at a view, he kissed her on the back of her neck, making the tiny hairs rise. When he did talk, it was to point out the way the light hit a small patch of grass or the brilliance of a leaf or to tell her she was beautiful. She'd worked to keep up with George, she laughed at the funny parts of his steady monologue, no time to stop and breathe. No time to even think. She felt a small pang, but mostly she felt happy. Her last conversation with Wayne was not happy.

"You think you love him after two weeks?" Wayne said after a long silence, his eyes looking straight into hers.

She looked down.

"I don't know. I can see myself loving him."

"You said you loved me."

"I do, I do love you. But we're so different. We want different things."

"Oh? I thought we both wanted a home, a family."

She looked to her left, away from him. She couldn't say out loud that she wanted a big house full of nice things and an important husband, someone who would be a Stake President or a General Authority, in the church. She didn't want to worry about money, scrimp the way her parents had. She wanted someone who would have a lucrative career, not an English professor at some little Midwestern college. It felt shallow even thinking these things, but was it shallow to be honest? She wanted someone important in the church and community, someone successful. What she'd seen in Sheri's family with their large house up on the hill, a swimming pool, tennis courts, Sunday lunches at the club. Was it a sin to want material comforts? She didn't think so. Look at the twelve apostles, the leaders of their church. They were all wealthy and well-connected. Wayne hugged her for a long time, in his body she felt the relief of him and loss of him at once.

"Rox, I love you, that won't just go away. If you change your mind . . ."

"I won't, Wayne. I'm so sorry." She sobbed and he comforted her. Everything seemed backward, and she wished he'd gotten angry so it wouldn't be so hard.

"Give everyone a hug goodbye for me, will you?" He was talking about her family. Her mom, who loved him too. He pulled back and held her there, looking at her for a minute and then kissed her.

"I hope you're happy with him, Rox." He turned and walked out the door.

She panicked for a moment, her stomach dropped, and she felt a strong urge to run after him, but willed herself to stand still and wait for the feeling to pass.

Roxcy leaned over the bar end of the kitchen counter, her backpack still on one shoulder, her chin resting on her hands. Her mom worked in the kitchen, getting dinner ready. She couldn't stop thinking about George, it had only been three weeks, but she'd seen him nearly every day, and now he was coming for dinner, to meet her parents.

"He's a direct descendant of *the* Brigham Young. Great, great-grandson, or something."

"Oh? Which wife?"

"Mom!"

Her mother smiled at her. "Come here and slice these mushrooms, will you?"

Roxcy took the mushrooms and wetted a cloth to wipe them clean.

"Sheri introduced us. His dad was called as a Seventy a few years ago. That's how they met. I wouldn't be surprised if he ended up being one of the twelve apostles."

"How is Sheri? I haven't seen her around. Everything okay with you two?"

"I don't know. I think she liked George, but I didn't know she liked him, I swear." She didn't mention that Sheri had stopped returning her calls. "George's dad is going to get us tickets to General Conference, right up near the front."

"Pass me those peppers, please."

Roxcy passed her the peppers.

"Thank you, dear."

"I know you liked Wayne, mom, but at least give George a chance, ok? I need your opinion. I don't think I'd be happy in a little house, in a little town far away from here. I hate gardening. You know I hate gardening."

"I thought Wayne was the gardener."

"He is, and part of me still loves Wayne. Please don't make it harder. I didn't expect this to happen."

"I did like Wayne, but this is your life, not mine."

"Thank you, mom. Did I mention George's dad is a partner at Kirton McConkie. They represent the Church. And George is gorgeous and so tall. You'll see. You're going to love him."

Roxcy watched her mom dry the carrots. She handed them to her.

"These too, sliced into circles, please," she said, putting the carrots next to the cutting board. She looked at her for a moment, and Roxcy saw the familiar softness. Her mom leaned over and kissed her on her forehead. "You know yourself, Rox. I trust you'll choose your own happiness, and I'll love anyone who loves you."

Sheri had returned a few calls. But once Roxcy officially broke things off with Wayne, she disappeared from her life too. Roxcy left messages apologizing a hundred times. She'd tried to explain but had very little free time now. George wanted her at every Sunday dinner at his parent's house up in Salt Lake. He asked her to attend his singles ward with him, as along with all their activities. They studied for their separate classes at his kitchen table or in the library together. Sheri was hanging out with a new group of friends, anyway. Roxcy had seen them with her at lunch once and stopped to say hello. The boys let their hair grow over their ears, girls with braids or pixies and no make-up complaining about how stifling BYU was, the restrictive curriculum, the punitive rules, and on and on. They were so negative. When the semester ended Sheri transferred to University of Utah, and they completely lost touch. She felt a little sick and tried not to think about what Eliza had done to Emma. But she'd been so mortified when she learned that part of the story. This wasn't really the same, but it all made her feel uneasy.

"Is this my fault? Was there something going on between you?" She looked up at him.

"No, I've told you. I never liked Sheri that way."

"You swear you never did anything to make her think you had feelings for her?"

"It was all on her side, Rox. I loved you the first time I saw you."

"She was my best friend, George."

George pulled a small box from his pocket. "I was hoping you would marry me; then I would be your best friend. I think that's how it works."

Roxcy smiled, her eyes glassy with emotion, and he slipped a huge diamond ring on her left ring finger. They kissed for a long time on the wide slumping sofa in his living room, when he lightly stroked her breast, it was only a second before she stopped him. She kept him in check for two months, so they could both be worthy to marry in the Salt Lake Temple. She'd just turned twenty.

Roxcy wasn't prepared for how much it hurt when he pushed himself inside her—a slice, then like rubbing a raw sore. He was big. That was supposed to be a good thing. She closed her eyes tight, clenched, and held onto his back as he moved frenetically. She didn't mean to, but she thought of Wayne, the hairs raised on her neck, the gentleness of him, the way he took his time with everything. She tried and failed to stop her mind wondering how this might have been different with him. It only lasted a minute or so. She managed a bright smile when he asked her how it was for her. He stroked her cheek while she lied, and then he let himself roll off her and onto his side of the bed.

"Amazing! Amazing!" He said and fell asleep.

She reached for her dark blue silk robe and slipped out as quietly as she could. The marble tile on the bathroom floor of the hotel was so cold it hurt her feet. She locked the door behind her, turned on the light, and looked at herself in the full-length mirror. Her light hair looked stunning against the dark blue robe. Her cheeks were flushed. She choked back a sob. It was unclear to her why she felt desperate and terrified. She filled the large jetted tub in the corner of the room, hoping to drown the sense of some dark, unsettling deep inside of her, her body tense with unaccountable fright.

I trust you to choose your own happiness.

Sex didn't improve exactly, but it got easier to bare over the next year, never much foreplay, but she learned to relax. She thought she might have even had an orgasm once or at least come close. George never kissed her the way he had when they were engaged or brushed her breasts softly with his hand. He got more talkative as time went on and gripped her. She wasn't ever sure who he was talking to because it didn't feel like her, but he went on and on about how much he loved her breasts, her hips, her mouth. She quickly learned to put a pillow between the top of her head and the bedframe. With his whole weight on top of her, he moved in and out, like something was chasing him, and then came. Often, she went through her to-do list in her head. Then it would be over; he'd kiss her, ask her how it was. She'd lie and say "good," kissing him again. He'd roll off of her and go to sleep. Roxcy would always get in a warm bath and then find something to clean or study for one of her classes out in the living room.

There were a few times, if he'd been at the library late studying, that he woke her up in the night. His breathing sounded like a stranger, an animal. When that happened, she went very still. She would tell herself: this is my husband. this is my husband. this is my husband. Squeeze her eyes tight and will her body to relax, usually unsuccessfully, through flashes of terror. Like a waking nightmare, Mary yelling something and then curling up at her feet, putting her hand on her leg. When George finished, she'd go into the bathroom, lock the door, curl into the corner of the closet like a crazy person, and sob silently.

But he didn't wake her that way often, so she tried not to think too much about it. She succeeded in pushing the strange fear so deep that now she hardly thought of it at all. More and more, she didn't even have to pretend things were good, because they were good. Maybe not exactly what she'd imagined. She didn't know what she'd imagined. But she was really happy. George spent most of his time studying, coming home in the evening long enough for quick sex, food, sleep, and another kiss goodbye. This is what she'd wanted: ambition, focus, importance, and he adored her, brought her flowers every week, told her she was beautiful as he kissed her goodbye every day.

School was also going well for her. Roxcy's professors had started to single her out. She'd completed her redesign for a campus office space, found new ways of configuring the space to create both privacy and common areas. She'd turned one large workspace into four. Painted the walls an almost-white gray that illuminated the small spaces. Lined each room with simple bright white crown and foot moldings, airy filigreed light fixtures, white desks, filing cabinets to make the space seem larger than it was. They praised the ingenuity, the clean lines, the efficient and beautiful use of space, as well as the splash of greens she'd incorporated with tiny bonsais on each desk and a large close-up print of various tropical plants. The effect was so universally admired they had recommended her for a summer internship at a design firm in Salt Lake, unheard of for a sophomore.

Roxcy stared down at the plus sign on the pregnancy test. They'd been married four months. It would take her at least two more years to finish her degree. George had one year and then law school, probably out of state—probably Stanford, like his father. She held the test in her hand and sat down on the couch. They'd talked about this before they married, wanting a big family, Roxcy staying at home full time when they had kids, like her mom had, like George's mom had. George walked through the door a few minutes later.

"Rox? Why are you sitting here in the dark?" His hands were full of purple iris,

It's the season, she thought, *the baby will be here in spring.* She said, "Oh, I didn't notice."

George flipped the switch, and the overhead lights came on. "Here, these are for you." He kissed her cheek. "Everything OK?"

Roxcy squinted up at him. "Well, I have some news."

"Good or bad?" He walked toward their spacious apartment kitchen to set down his books.

"Good." Roxcy picked up the test and smiled. George came back in and sat next to her. He pulled her close, kissing her, laughing.

"I can't believe it! I'm so happy, Rox. We have to tell my parents."

His parents were thrilled and drove down to take them out to dinner at Sundance the next weekend in celebration. When Roxcy brought up her concerns about the timing of the internship, about finishing her schooling, George's mom said, "I finished my degree a few years ago."

"I didn't know that! What did you study?"

"Fine Arts," she chuckled, "I wanted to work in a museum when I was your age. Thank heavens I never did. I got pregnant right away, and I've never regretted the choice to stay home with my kids. It's such a blessing, so much more important than any silly job."

Roxcy knew this was true, felt it in every fiber of her being. Her mom had stayed home with them. She'd been the constant and present caretaker. Deep down, that is all she'd ever really wanted to be, a wife, a mother, to create a beautiful home, to care for her own children the way she'd been cared for.

"Well, I'll only be in my second trimester. I could do the internship. I could probably even finish up my degree slowly over the next few years."

"Why the rush?" His father said.

"What if we get one of our rental houses ready. There's a darling one coming up just south of campus in about a month. Plenty of time to get settled in before the baby comes. You'll have plenty of opportunities to use all the talent you have for design without ever having to work. You're going to be a wonderful mother, Roxcy. We are so happy for the two of you." She said.

Her mom's reaction was different. It hurt like an unexpected slap.

"A mother, well!" She said, stepping forward and taking Roxcy's face in both her hands, kissing her forehead. You'll love it, Rox."

"I have all sorts of plans. I think, instead of a bigger apartment, we might move into one of the little houses George's parents own. We can't move in, of course, until we fix it up. But it will be so nice to be in a house with a little yard. I have all sorts of ideas. His mom said she'd help me shop. They'll pay for everything. They're so generous."

"But you have almost a year before the baby comes. You should take that internship and finish up as much course work as you can in the fall. And I'm here. I can help with the baby. You can easily finish your degree."

"Dad's not well, mom. You already have your hands full. And I could, I guess, but I don't think I want to. I want to spend that time getting our home ready for a baby, and I'm already so tired. I don't really want to juggle both."

"Didn't you tell me that you were the first sophomore offered a spot like this? You seemed so excited about it."

"I was, but the timing just isn't good. Why are you pushing this? You never worked. You didn't even finish your degree, did you? I want to give my kids what I had growing up, and I'm not sacrificing anything if it's really what I want. And the prophets have been clear . . . "

"Oh, believe me, I'm familiar with the prophets' counsel on women working outside the home. I wanted to finish my degree, but it was a different time—more complicated and then with your father's health. What I'm trying to say is that I'm happy to help you so that you won't feel any regret. I can watch the baby; I can help with the house, whatever you need."

"I'm sorry you regret us."

"That's not not what I said, Roxcy. And it's not fair."

"Well, maybe we're not as much alike as I thought. I won't regret this decision. George thinks it's best if I take it easy. His parents think so too and I agree with them. Motherhood is more important to me than a silly degree."

Her mom smiled at her, her eyes resigned, and sad. For the first time in her life, Roxcy felt her mother's disappointment hover and split around her heart, strange and raw as a freshly scraped knee.

———

Roxcy looked at the old photograph. Her mom hadn't kept any other pictures of her and Wayne. Her younger self looked lit up in the honey-colored summer evening light gazed straight at the camera. The boy clearly adoring her, his face in profile. And now she could see why that possibility would have made sense to her mom. Now that she had children of her own, all she wanted was for them to find happiness, the right sort of friends, the perfect partners. But it had turned out that she was different from her mom, as painful as it was to admit. She slipped the picture back in the album. She picked up a picture of her own family, maybe ten years old. Her children were so small, so new to the world, and the idea that God had entrusted her with each of them, trusted her to care for and love them took her breath away. Her youngest, her Peter, still sitting easily on her lap.

Her other children had never touched alcohol or experimented with anything that went against the Mormon codes. They'd been obedient. It was this girl he'd been seeing, the tiny bright blue jewel in her nose. This was her fault. Roxcy's children didn't do this. She and George had taught them right from wrong. How many times had they read through Lehi's dream during Family Home Evening? How many times had they told them to hold to the rod of iron, which led to the Tree of Life, to safety, to God. Alcohol-tobacco-coffee-tea-pre-marital-sex-drugs-these were the mists of darkness. These could and often did lead to hellish dependency disconnection from God and family. Following the common-sense restrictions on alcohol, drugs, and even coffee and tea in the Word of Wisdom and guarding your moral virtue by keeping the Law of Chastity resulted in more freedom, not less. The other repeated lesson, Steadfast, a bronze bust of a horse's head that George inherited from his father, an ever-present object lesson on the mantel. The hard metal mane, swirling and lifted, the dark eyes wide, the blinders firm on each side. The title, engraved on a black plate in small gold letters read *Steadfast,* be Steadfast. Those blinders were protection from sin. And now her sweet Peter had taken them off and wandered into danger. It would be awful for George as the Stake President. His position as an admired leader in the community would be at risk—the things people would surely whisper—the judgments, the criticisms.

—

Roxcy paced back and forth. Was he lying on the side of the road somewhere? She'd tried his cell three times. Straight to voicemail.

"Hi, it's mom. Call me, please. It's well after midnight. I need to know you're ok. Please call me."

She walked to the window, opened the drape to look out onto the driveway, ten times? It was two a.m. Peter was two hours late. George was staying the night at a hotel in Salt Lake, thank goodness. There for a regional meeting of Stake Presidents. She was supposed to drive up to meet him after church, after checking in on her ward Relief Society where she served as a counselor in the presidency. She'd almost reached the point where she felt like she had to call him. Roxcy hated to bother him. He'd had so little rest the past few months between work and church. When she heard a car pull into the driveway, she looked out the window. A taxi in Provo? She opened the door, and Peter fell into her arms. He smelled like something rotten.

"Hi mom," he laughed and kissed her on the cheek—the awful smell on his breath.

"Pete, are you alright? Pete, look at me. Where have you been?"

"With Kristi and some friends."

"Where is the car?"

"At Kristi's."

He slurred his words. She felt the shock move through her like an earthquake.

"Peter?"

"I love you, mom." He kissed her on the cheek again.

"Are you drunk?" She covered her nose and felt the tears well in her eyes.

"I think I am." He laughed, hysterical laughter that turned into tears.

"I'm sorry, mom. Don't tell Dad, please? Don't tell Dad."

"Oh, Pete."

"Don't cry, Mom. I'm sorry. I'm so sorry."

She walked him upstairs, his arm around her shoulder, to the bathroom and turned on the shower. She turned the water on cold because that's what they did in the movies. She didn't have any black coffee, and wouldn't that just be adding bad to worse?

She tucked him into his bed, thought he was asleep, but he mumbled, "I love you, Mommy."

Roxcy had a flash of him at five, her beautiful boy, wandering the house looking for her just to hug her around the legs before he went back to building his Legos, or playing with his matchbox cars, his sweet little face, looking up at her. It had been difficult, painful, watching them all grow up and move away from her, preferring friends to time with her. It would hit her sometimes in the middle of lunch with her own friends, that in a few years they'd all be gone—and what would she do then? Her legs shook as she walked down the hall to her bedroom. She knelt by the bed and began to cry, couldn't even gather her thoughts to pray. She had no words. Her heart beat hard, tightened in her throat as though love, pain, and fear had some physical substance. That little face looking up at her with the straight blond hair falling just above those big blue eyes, saying, "I love you, Mommy." How could that small boy have grown into a teenager who would do this?

Just as the others, he had run his little hands over the hard edges of the horse's head, traced the mane, the eyes, the hard-square edge of the blinders with their small fingers, saying "Don't be tricked, keep your eyes straight ahead," His blue eyes earnestly examining the horse. She knew he believed, so why had he done it? The girl? He couldn't even look at her the next morning. He blessed the sacrament with bloodshot eyes, his head down the whole time.

—

Now she was stuck in this cabin and her baby boy was home in this snow storm without her. Her sweet Peter might become an alcoholic; there were those stories—all it took was one drink. He'd done this three times now. Was he already an alcoholic? She felt the panic and sorrow ripple through her again. And tried to reassure herself,

I've made a beautiful home with George. We have four faithful children who are almost grown. Peter may still be okay, or not, but our love has to count for something. And I just lost my

mother, when I feel like I desperately need her. Sadness is a reasonable reaction and, in time it will pass. It will pass. Everything will be alright.

She felt a tightness in her throat and breathed in deeply again, closing her eyes, holding the threatening eruption inside.

⁓

Mary chopped the onions. She watched Roxcy hover over the sauce, the steam rising around her face like a pretty, tired witch tending her cauldron. She watched her walk into the dining room and rearrange the table that Anna had just set, moving the spoons to the right, forks to the left, carefully refolding the napkins and placing them under the fork and knife.

Mary thought, *we're all here. Roxcy, one, Eve, two, Anna, three. All safe.* She pushed the thin slices of strong-smelling red onion off the cutting board into the salad bowl. Her eyes burned. She turned and looked over her shoulder. The light from the antler chandelier spilled over the table like a sunset.

Roxcy had pulled Anna's bright floral tablecloth off of the table. It had a practical protective coating that could easily be wiped clean, fine for everyday, but this was not everyday. She'd folded it carefully and replaced it with a white linen cloth finished with embroidery along the edge.

Eve placed the wooden salad bowl in the center of the table, feeling Mary's watchfulness, recognizing, for the first time, her sister's unobtrusive vigilance as another familiar repetition. She placed the large wooden spoon and fork on either side of the bowl. Anna sat and observed the rearranging. Eve looked at Anna.

Anna tore off a piece of Roxcy's homemade bread and dipped it in the béchamel, her hand not quick enough to catch a drip. It left a small cream-colored dot of grease on the pristine, white cloth. Roxcy sighed loudly as she wiped it away.

"I'm a slob," Anna shrugged her shoulders. "That's why I suggested just leaving my table cloth."

Their mother's absence a chasm again. She would've looked at Anna and shaken her head no, the signal to keep the peace. She would have said, "No harm done, this will come right out with a little baking soda and peroxide; let's just enjoy dinner."

Roxcy felt the sadness surge. She'd taken the time to plan and make this meal because she believed good food, prepared with care, made with the best ingredients: a strong Gruyere, the saltiness of good ham thinly sliced, and the smooth, rich flavor of a well-wrought béchamel, had power to mend, to soothe. Maybe also to distract her from the loss, from the worry over Peter, to make something beautiful in the midst of difficulty. It was her offering. She made herself smile as she walked back into the kitchen, putting on Anna's dirty oven mitts and pulling the crepes from the oven, the warm air hitting her face, everything would be fine.

"Shall we pray?" Said Mary, looking at Anna

"Sure."

Eve watched.

"It's your house, so your choice," Roxcy set the dish in the center of the table between the plates.

"Rock, paper, scissors for it?" said Anna, extending one flat and one fisted hand.

"I'll say it." Mary folded her arms, bowed her head, and closed her eyes. Her sisters followed.

"Dear Father in Heaven, we're grateful to be here together, safe from the storm. We're grateful for Anna, that she opened her home for us, and grateful to have Eve back here with us. We're grateful for the food Roxcy's prepared with so much care. We ask thee to bless it that it might nourish and strengthen our bodies. Most of all, we are grateful for our mom, the time we had with her. We are grateful for her guidance and example, and the way she loved each of us. We know she's with thee, and with dad again, but we're missing her. Please bless us to feel thy spirit, please offer us comfort. We say these things in the name of Jesus Christ, Amen."

Roxcy squeezed Mary's hand before pulling her neatly-folded cloth napkin onto her lap and smoothing it with her hands. Mary dished the salad, passing it to Roxcy while Eve served herself from the warmed crepe dish while passing it to Anna. Everything traveled in a circle, one sister to the next, each plate filled with food and each glass with clear water.

"The salad is all from our vegetable garden and our little greenhouse," Roxcy said, pushing the green leaves with her fork. "We have a wonderful Mexican man who grows it all for us, and cuts the lawn and keeps the flowerbeds too."

Anna grimaced. Eve, who had just taken a bite of salad, looked across the table at Roxcy to see if she'd noticed. Roxcy put down her fork

"Mom's dressing, right?" Eve said after she chewed and swallowed.

"There was some left in the fridge," Roxcy said. "Did I say something wrong, Anna?"

"The Mexican man? Does he have a name?" Anna said.

"George pays him cash. I don't write his name on a check, and I've only met him a couple of times, but he's a wonderful gardener. Jose? Jeffe? I should learn his name. I'm just not usually there when he is."

"Oh, at tennis? I wonder what Jesus would say about not knowing the name of your hired help?"

"This is about the tablecloth, isn't it? You're throwing a little fit because I wanted to use mine. I wanted to do this for you, for Eve and Mary. A nice dinner, my favorite dinner to make. I thought it might help."

"For God's sake, Roxcy, why does everything always have to be perfect? You come into my house and immediately start rearranging everything to suit you. You hide my coffee maker and make passive-aggressive comments about the clutter. Why can't you leave the tablecloth that's easy to clean? I'm doing fine, OK?!? You don't have to fix me."

"That wasn't—I wasn't trying—I just thought this was something I could do. We all lost mom, not just you." Roxcy began to shake visibly. "You aren't the only one having a hard time, Anna."

"What? George forget your flowers this week, or has perfect little Peter started smoking pot?"

Roxcy let out, a yelp, an intake of breath as if she'd been kicked. Anna looked at her. Had she ever seen Roxcy cry? Roxcy didn't cry. This was the second time today. Mary reached over and pulled her in. Eve moved quickly to Roxcy's other side. They both looked at Anna.

"Rox, I'm sorry. Really, I didn't mean—"

"I feel like I'm losing my mind," Roxcy grabbed Eve's hand and took a long deep stuttered breath, gathering control. "He brought me bunches of Daisies the day she died. The gardener, he had no idea, but they were all over the house, and I can't remember his name. I don't know his name."

"May in mom's garden. Daisie were everywhere." Eve said, rubbing her back.

"Do you remember the Iris?" Anna picked up the purple, knit silk, and handed it to her.

"May," said Eve smiling.

"I made these the other night when I was supposed to be changing the upstairs sheets."

"I noticed those this morning. They're so beautiful and the pictures," Roxcy said.

"I'm really sorry, OK? Why do we fight all the time?" Anna reached across the table and took her hand. Roxcy shook her head back and forth. "When the police called, I thought it was a mistake. It was just before three. I was sure I'd heard her come in as I was falling asleep. I ran to her bedroom to check, told them she was in her bed, but it was empty."

Everyone sat in the quiet that settled around the table, the sauce beginning to thicken with cold. Anna picked up the cube of pictures. She passed it to Roxcy. Roxcy saw her own grown-up reflection over the images of her sisters in their mother's lap, rubbing noses, in her arms laughing. Her mom was crouching down to meet her in the grass, the dew shiny in the morning light.

"It's ok to be sad, Rox. We're all sad," Eve said.

"Is anyone else dreading the memorial?" Mary said. They all looked up. "I mean public grieving is not really in my wheelhouse, you know?" They all laughed out loud. "How many people do you think will come?"

Roxcy took a long deep breath. "I sent the announcements to everyone in her contacts and in an old address book," she looked down. "I expect everyone who's local will be there." Roxcy looked sideways at Mary. "Aunt Violet might come. She was in dad's book." Eve caught a glimpse of panic flash and retreat.

"Who?" Anna said.

"Dad's younger sister," Mary said, leaning to pick up her napkin, which had dropped to the floor.

"I don't think I've ever met her," Anna said. She took a bite of her crepe and laid her fork on the plate. The food was cold.

"We didn't see them after they moved up to Salt Lake," Mary said.

Eve watched. Roxcy looked at the table, noticed the food was cold. She rose from the table and picked up her plate. She didn't look at Mary again.

"I'll put these in the oven, warm them up again" Roxcy began to gather the plates, balancing them on her arms like a waitress, another skill she'd learned as the mother of five.

"The address I used is probably old," she said, her back turned to them as she walked into the kitchen. "They probably won't come. I don't know if any of the addresses are current. I didn't have time to check. There wasn't any time."

She opened the oven door, felt the heat on her arms, her neck, her face. She slid one plate off her hand then the next, carefully maneuvering, two plates on the top rack, two plates in the middle.

"I bet they'll come," Anna said. "People stay in the same house here until they die. No one ever leaves. Were they at dad's funeral?"

"I don't know," Mary said, standing up. "Do you need any help, Roxcy?" She walked into the small kitchen. She put her arm around her sister and whispered something. Roxcy laid her head on Mary's shoulder for a minute and then looked back at Anna.

"I'll help you change the upstairs sheets after dinner, Anna."

Anna rolled her eyes at Eve.

Large flakes whirled in the illuminated space of the porch light, a slow, steady circular dance to the ground, piling layer upon layer. Each of the sisters periodically stopped in front of the wall of windows to watch the inches stack up one on top of another.

Mary tilted her head to one side and remembered the way the snowflakes fell on her cheeks as mom walked her to the car when Anna was born. The way he leaned forward into the steering wheel straining to make out the road ahead through the whiteness, the snowflakes filling the round circles of passing streetlights. The way her father kept repeating everything will be fine, while her mom groaned in the passenger seat. And Hank, too, came when the snow was a blinding swirl.

Roxcy pulled the quilt off of her bed and wrapped herself up. She layered memories, piling one on top of another, trying to bury the fragment of memory from that old storm, the flash of terror that still hid somewhere in her body. Replacing it with happy thoughts, her mother helping her with her gloves and boots kissing her cheek—safe. Elm covered in snow, too deep for cars, her mom holding baby Anna, watching them from inside the big window. Her breath on her forehead as she kissed her goodnight, the heaviness of her child eyelids and drifting, drifting. She needed a break from sadness. She did not think of Peter.

Eve watched the snow with relief at the cold, white stillness. Even here, where noise was minimal, the flakes cushioned the air, muffling sound, a thick quiet laid over everything. She closed her eyes and thought of her mother in the winter garden, just after an early spring snow, the branches outlined in frost. A blue jay flying from the bare branch. The force of take-off breaking the frozen twig open to reveal the green inside, the shock of life hidden inside the apparent death.

Anna tried to love each season. Her mom had. Pointing out the first crocus, running her fingers through the thick green grass, sitting on the porch with Honey on her lap, her arm around Lula, watching the light change. She called them all out to see the first yellow leaf in the grove. She lifted her face to the falling snow, catching the white lace in her eyelashes. Anna looked out the window, the drift growing beneath the porch light. The twisting white flakes circling and falling and turned toward the loft. Fatigue settled its weight in her bones.

One by one
    they walked
toward bed
    One by one
        they fell
            toward sleep
    dreaming
of snow

And there was the evening and the morning, the fourth day.

The wind blew all night, a mournful singing against the corners of the cabin. They woke to two-foot drifts leaning heavily against the low windows in the front room, the sky still white, as relentless as a blank page. The closets still held her clothes, untouched, her dresser full and the bathroom drawers. No one wanted to disrupt the day-to-day evidence of her.

It was Thursday morning, so Anna lied.

"I need to check on my shop."

"Can't you wait until this passes?" Eve looked up from her phone—no service. Her face pale framed by her short dark hair.

"I'm used to driving in snowstorms. Mountain living. I'll be back in time to help with lunch."

She slipped in and out of the truth like a soft pair of slippers. It was a habit, an easy way to avoid causing awkwardness or even pain. She excused it like this: *I do have to go to the store. It isn't exactly a lie. Jake is expecting me, and I need this. There's no way to explain to my sisters without upsetting them. How would Roxcy deal with the fact that I find the rough calluses on his hands deeply comforting, even necessary?*

"I'm making a run to Deseret Industries. Do you want to drive down together?" Roxcy said, standing with a hand on her hip.

"I'm not sure how long I'll be. I have to check on some inventory. If you want to wait?" Anna asked, sure of the answer.

"No, I want to get this done. I guess I'll just see you when you get back."

"I'll help you sort through the rest when I get back, Okay, Rox?" Anna said.

"Don't worry about it. Do what you need to do. I need to keep busy anyway."

Anna grabbed her keys from the blue and green ceramic bowl on the counter. She pulled her long bright pink parka off of one of the antler hooks.

"I wish you'd wait," Eve said and thought, *she's hiding something.*

"I'll be fine. See you soon."

As she opened the door, the blast of cold air stole Anna's breath. She moved through the thick, white swirl to her car, climbed in, and closed the door. She turned on the engine, which sluggishly caught, then turned the heat and the fan up to high. When she adjusted the rearview mirror, she saw her cheeks were pink from the cold.

—

Anna examined her reflection in the long, straight mirror that hung next to the bathrooms in the shop. There were small changes in her face. When she smiled and then relaxed her eyes, the creases softened into thin rivulets. They didn't disappear. There were tiny smile lines, like parentheses, barely visible on each side of her mouth, a thin, barely perceptible crease between her eyes on her forehead. Her face was aging into a map of her life. She thought, *That line starting between my eyebrows is his fault. The prick.*

She turned sideways, examining her body. Her small breasts pendulous, resting just on the top of her rib cage, even with the bra. She hated under-wires, the way they rubbed against the bone. She was still lithe, her muscles supple from near-daily yoga practice, from hiking, from skiing, but her breasts. . . . She cupped them in her hands, elevating them to their former youthful position, letting go and watching them fall back into the discouraging droop. She thought *I shouldn't have criticized Roxcy for her implants or the Botox. I'll look like a hypocrite if I ask her for the doctor's name now. I don't have the money for it anyway.*

She didn't hear him come in, the jingle of the door opening. His reflection appeared behind her in the mirror. She smiled and quickly pretended to smooth her shirt, her cheeks noticeably flushed. He looked the way she'd imagined Jesus looking when she was a child, long thick hair, warm brown eyes, a beard. She noticed his hands, large and slightly dirty, holding the edge of the boxes. She thought of them moving over her body. He smiled.

"They're nice," Jake said.

"What?"

"Your breasts. Nothin' to worry about." His tone matter-of-fact.

"Uh—"

"I have a few more boxes to unload."

"O-kay?" She said, a half-smile pulling her mouth off balance. "Thanks, Jake."

Jake had been delivering her inventory since she opened the shop eight months ago. He brought her boxes filled with bolts of fabric, yarn, notions, knitting, and sewing patterns. She hadn't really looked at him before. He was too young for her. Sometimes he asked how her business was going or complimented a new display she had in the window. She always thanked him and smiled. Their interactions were cordial, professional.

Today, because he finished unloading the regular delivery as she answered the phone, he'd walked around to her side of the counter. She held the phone with her chin and signed the electronic signature pad, leaning in toward him. He held it steady for her. She breathed in and thought, *He smells like soap.* She felt the warmth off of his body. She looked at his hands again and then up to his face as she handed him the stylus and hung up the phone.

"Thank you," she said, smiling at him.

"No problem."

"So, it's been a rough year, personally, I mean and I still sort of blame my breasts."

"Oh?" He chuckled

"Business is great, though. I love my shop."

"It's a nice shop."

"Would you mind, I mean, if you have time, could you help me put these in the storage room?"

"I have time."

She picked up two of the smaller boxes, and he followed her with one large box.

"How long have you been doing deliveries?"

"Since I dropped out of college. . . . About five years now."

"Ah."

Anna put the boxes down and reached for the thin blue ribbon she wore around her neck that held the key. She pulled it off and the ribbon caught in her hair. She felt his fingers gently work it free.

"Thanks," she said.

"Sure."

The key slid into the knob, and she turned it to the right, holding the door open with her knee. It was dark, no windows. She flipped the switch, and the fluorescent bulbs flickered. Rows of shelves filled with bolts of popular fabric, labeled bins with zippers, buttons, elastic and other sewing notions, filled the small room. Other bins held the most popular yarn brands in dizzying colorful variety and still others toilet paper and paper towels. It reminded her of a deserted street market, an image that felt pleasurable.

"Right here is fine," she said.

He set the boxes down and turned toward her and barley paused before he stepped close and kissed her, his mouth slightly open, his breath warm. She moved into him, wrapping her arms under his. That was the first time.

Three months passed. Three months of waiting for Thursday, waiting to lay her body down into the softness of the sofa. Waiting for the thirty minutes of someone touching her, taking care of her first. Waiting to forget sleeping alone every night for those few minutes each week. Shutting her eyes tight when the image of Matt and the girl flashed across her mind. Anna knew very little about Jake, other than he spent winter skiing and summers rock climbing, that he brought her boxes full of texture and color each week, that his hands were large and generous. When they explored the curve of her, when his mouth came to her breast, she remembered she was enough. For those few minutes each week, she believed she had always been enough. It felt like a miracle.

—

Anna took off her boots and shook the snow from her hair. No one else would be out in this storm. She locked the front door behind them anyway. There were only three or four cars in the parking lot, besides their trucks, most buried in snow. She unlocked the storage room. She'd reupholstered the couch herself, choosing a geometric print that hadn't sold well but felt as soft as new grass.

"I didn't know if you'd make it."

"I'm here." She brushed the snow off her hat.

"I'm glad."

He kicked off his shoes, unbuttoned his jeans, and climbed out of them. Pulled off his t-shirt. She smiled as he kissed her neck, his arm wrapped behind her, pulling her in beneath him, their hands working together to slip off her sweatpants and underwear. His free hand worked with the rhythm of her body. She smelled the snow in his hair, her face damp with its melting. She didn't know or care how he understood where and how to touch her, what she needed. Why he so easily tuned to her resonance, so easily found the current of her body, fluent, the ache building, traveling the length of her, electric to her toes. Anna closed her eyes, her mouth open, and felt him lift her shirt his tongue on her raised nipple. As he pushed himself inside her, the resounding crash of metal against metal. Two car alarms blared.

"Shit!" She said, slapping the sofa with a flat hand, her brow furrowed

"Ignore it. Someone else will go out." He continued to kiss her neck, her ear.

She eased him away and sat up.

"I can't, sorry. I'm too distracted. My sisters are going through my mom's things right now. I shouldn't even be here. I told you she died, right? Did I tell you?"

"I came up to your cabin, remember?" It was the first time she had seen him look hurt.

"I'm so sorry." She put her hand on his cheek. "I'm actually having a hard time remembering anything." She kissed him. "I can probably get away again tomorrow? Oh—no. It's the memorial."

"What time?" He buttoned his jeans.

"Ten, I think. At our old chapel. The big one on Ninth East, in Provo."

"Isn't that for BYU married wards?"

"My sister got special permission. She has connections—her husband has connections."

"Can I come?" He brushed the hair off his forehead and met her eye.

"If you want to, I guess," she shrugged. "It wouldn't be weird?"

"No." He leaned in and kissed her again. "I'd like to come."

"Okay. 10 a.m. Saturday. It might be a baptism by fire. All my sisters will be there. Matt will be there," she said.

"I've had the water kind. It didn't kill me. I'm going to see what happened out there."

When he hugged her, it felt familiar, as if they actually knew each other, as if he might walk in the door at dinnertime. She slipped one foot and then another into her sweats and shimmied them up her legs. He went out and closed the door behind him. She heard the bell ring on the outside door and felt a small draft of cold air. She grabbed her sweater off the floor and pulled it over her head. As she came out of the room, rewinding her hair into a loose bun, she looked out the large picture window. Anna stared at the mangled front of the white Mercedes SUV.

"Fuck!" She said under her breath. She pulled her coat off of the rack by the door and frantically searched for her keys.

Roxcy

Eve begged her to wait out the storm, but Roxcy couldn't sit still. She had to keep moving before the sadness wandered in again. She pulled on a pair of her mom's heavy snow boots, zipped up her parka, and found some heavy gloves in a little brown basket on the closet shelf. When she opened the door, the wind pushed against her body. She ignored it, pulling the door closed and pushing back. George had bought her an industrial scraper, and she easily cleared the windshield. When she slid into her seat, it was warm. He had insisted on leather with seat warmers. She felt a small swell of gratitude for all the little ways he took care of her. The view through the windshield looked straight in on Eve sitting in one of the large chairs, pulled close to the fire. Her eyes were closed, her face in profile. One of her hands rested on her stomach. Something about the posture made Roxcy's heart ache. She remembered her own hand, just that way, on her own belly when she was pregnant, the pleasure of her roundness, the hope growing inside her. She looked over her shoulder and backed the car up to the porch and hopped out. Roxcy opened and closed the front door each time she moved boxes from the entry to the back of her car, trying, for Eve's sake, to keep the cold out of the cabin. Trying, for Eve's sake, not to disturb what little warmth the fire provided. She wondered how many miscarriages there had been and felt guilty that she had no idea, that she'd never asked her.

—

Roxcy wore one of her mom's old bandannas on her hair to keep the dust off, but her eyes still itched. She hung the last crystal on the chandelier, her biannual deep cleaning of the house almost complete. She'd saved the chandelier for the morning, when the sun would come through and the light passing through the crystals would dance across the wall. Maria had taken care of the basics, the sheets, the bathrooms the floor boards and floors. It left time for Roxcy to organize every cupboard, clean out and box up old clothes, and go through the files, all of which she'd done. All that was left was the storage room downstairs.

Their year's supply of food storage and water took up half of the storage room. There were rows of favorite dry cereal boxes, grouped in yellows, greens and whites, boxed mac & cheese, bags of donuts, treats for when Peter's friends came. The rest consisted of various canned goods, number tens, full of rice, oatmeal, wheat, flour, and pasta they'd canned themselves at the bishop's storehouse. Some of it was good for up to 40 years if stored properly. The shelves facing the food storage were deep and full of large plastic bins grouped by color. Holidays were on the top shelf, green for Christmas, pink for valentines, light green for Easter, navy for the Fourth of July, orange for Halloween, and brown for Thanksgiving. The light blue bins held extra linens, the light green office supplies. One large, velvet black box protruded uneasily from the edge of the shelf in the right- hand corner of the room, the large black print, FOR EVE on its side.

How long has it been? She thought.

Roxcy stood on the stepladder and carefully pulled the box off the shelf. She kept her weight forward over the box, which was heavy and awkward. She walked into the carpeted hallway and gently set it on the ground. Kneeling, she opened it up and removed the large black trash bag she'd laid across for extra protection. She pulled out one item at a time: a crib-sized flannel blanket, pink with tiny white daisies, and edged with pink grosgrain ribbon. She rubbed the soft fabric between her fingers and thumb. There was that afternoon in the meadow, years ago, eating strawberries and watching the late afternoon sunlight drift through the aspens. Her kids had been small. It was summer. She and Eve had taken them to the cabin to visit Nana and have a picnic. They sat there together and watched the kids chase each other in and out of the trees, laughing, out of breath. Eve had said,

"I'd like a little girl of my own someday. A boy would be wonderful too."

She remembered her mom had picked a wild iris and handed it to Evie. She never picked wild iris, insisting they were more beautiful left to grow in the earth. It was a remarkable gesture. All of it was remarkable, vivid, the taste of the strawberries, the look of hazy, golden light, the sound of her children laughing, all mingled into sharp, bright joy: Eves's sadness, a dim line of blue barely visible at the edge that she could only see looking back. When Eve told her she was pregnant, that first time, Roxcy remembered what she had said about a little girl and immediately called Anna to help her. They had sewn the edges of this soft pink rectangle together and hand-stitched swirls of thread over the body of the blanket to keep the two sides together. She and Anna had worked together as peacefully as she ever remembered. She was uncomfortable with the word grace, which seemed to strip away the necessity of effort, but, she thought, the whole sequence of events had been just that, full of grace. So where was Eve's baby girl?

Roxcy placed the blanket, still folded, in her lap. Just below the quilt, she found her favorite books on pregnancy, Sears & Sears, *What to Expect*, the Ferber book on sleep. She flipped through the neatly outlined pages, the little notes in the margins about each of her pregnancies, the highlighted sections, a different color for each of her children. Beneath the books, she found seven white, long-sleeved fortune cookie onesies. She ran her finger over the double-stitched bright red seams and smiled at the funny little sayings printed on the front in Asian looking script *you will find a surprise in my pants*. One for each day of the week. She refolded them and laid them carefully on the blanket. Next, a small mountain of zippered sleepers, so Evie wouldn't have to fuss with snaps in the middle of the night, and at the bottom of the box, an eclectic collection of picture frames in various sizes. She'd picked them up here and there, anytime she saw a frame with carved flowers or vines curling over the edges, black, off-white, slightly distressed, a new thing made to look old. They were empty. Roxcy saw her face reflected in the glass, her furrowed brow, sadness, or anger in her eyes. She did not like to feel sad and angry. She carefully repacked everything in the order she'd found it, as the familiar thought darted into her mind. Was it some sort of punishment for Eve choosing to wait so long, choosing a Ph.D. over early motherhood? She shook her head, treating her thoughts like sand she could erase like an etch-a-sketch, by shaking.

Roxcy knelt there on the soft carpet, bowed her head, folded her arms and began. It was almost a memorized prayer she'd repeated it so many times, her eyes shut tight. She pleaded with Him to please reconsider, to see Eve's patience, her kindness, gentleness, her generosity. She would be such a beautiful mother. This time she added that it seemed very unfair. Then she prayed, at the very least, that Eve might be filled with comfort and peace. She stayed there kneeling, with her arms folded for a long time after she'd finished praying. She waited, like that, for the whisper of a still small voice, some reassurance that her prayer had been heard. Her heart beat, her breath moved in and out, but nothing else. She opened her eyes, closed the box, walked back into her storage room, and replaced it high in the corner.

⁓

The storm was worse than she thought. Snow came down as thick as white feathers. Roxcy slowed and leaned forward in her seat. What was the trajectory of choice? Eve chose her work. Anna chose Matt. Peter chose that girl. Would she lead him to some irreparable harm? It seemed impossible to map the dizzying possibility of consequence that resulted from one choice. The fear came like choking—a fluttering panic caught in her throat. This storm was ridiculous for September. It needed to stop before tomorrow. The snow needed to melt so they could hold the memorial outside, although it might be only flurries in the valley. She would see soon enough. If the Sundance Store was open, she could stop on her way back and pick up some new earrings or a bracelet to wear to the memorial. Amethyst maybe, to go with the purple brocade shirtdress she'd found at Nordstrom's. It looked like one of the dresses her mom wore in an old picture. Maybe she'd find something sweet for Anna's girls as well—little bracelets, perhaps. There was plenty she could do. She could dust and sweep and mop. She could wipe off floorboards, which probably hadn't been cleaned in months. She could get all the things cleared out of the cabin so Honey and Lula didn't come home to stacks of boxes. She could do that for Anna and her girls. She could buy all of her sisters a new piece of jewelry. At least Mary hadn't come along to look at price tags and blurt out words like ridiculous or unbelievable. Mary could easily afford nice things as a partner at her accounting firm. She really ran that place, had run it for years, even before they gave her the title. But Mary was frugal, just like their father, about money.

Before she divorced, Anna had shopped with her. Anna knew her taste and found the most lovely things. For those few years when their lives had oddly synced. Matt worked

224

toward tenure and served in the bishopric, so he was gone a lot like George. Like George, he also came from a wealthy family who were generous with Anna, and he'd come into his trust money when he'd graduated from Stanford with his Ph.D. They both had cash to spare, leisure time, and cleaning ladies. Of course, Anna was Anna, so she had still complained about Matt's service in the bishopric, the time it meant away from her and the girls. Roxcy had tried to listen, but she understood that supporting a husband in his church leadership was a worthy sacrifice. It meant people looked at you a certain way, that they admired and listened to you. She was content and fulfilled in her role as wife and mother. She didn't really understand. If a person wanted a nice house, a cleaning lady, a man to keep the gardens and lawn, and money to spend, they shouldn't complain about long hours at the office. George was doing his job so that she had resources and time to make a beautiful home and to be there for their kids. Where was the tension? What was the problem?

Any temporary connection snapped after Anna's divorce. Now, on the rare occasions they went out together, Anna bristled visibly if Roxcy offered to buy her something. The old quick defensiveness of their childhood and adolescence exploded into offensive attacks. She rolled her eyes if Roxcy talked about her church calling, she ordered coffee at Starbucks and swore. Once, she had even yelled "Jesus!" when a van had almost sideswiped them. The anger radiated off of Anna, and it made Roxcy feel defensive and tired. So much so that she found it harder and harder to spend time with her. Everything was coming apart. She needed her mom. They all needed her.

The road curved. Something bolted in front of her car. Roxcy swerved to miss. A deer? She couldn't see. The car lurched over the steep embankment. It slid down the rocky slope into the Sundance parking lot. She thought, *I'm going to die.*

Both of her feet pressed hard against the brake. The front of her Mercedes slammed into the side of a black Cadillac, knocking the snow from its roof and windows. Alarms on both cars screamed. Roxcy pushed the airbag away from her body. She tried to catch her breath, only peripherally aware of a person running toward her car. In her mind she repeated calmly, *no, no, no.* A young man stood outside and knocked on her window.

Roxcy thought, *He needs a haircut.*

She unpried her hands from the wheel and pushed a black button. The window rolled down.

"Are you all right, ma'am?"

She looked past him.

"I think so," she said, trying to smooth her hair with her shaking hands. "Do you know whose car I hit?"

"No, it doesn't matter. Does anything hurt? Can you move all right? I'd like to get you in out of the cold." He said.

Her entire body felt like an exposed nerve, but she smiled.

"Yes. I'm fine, really, a little shaken up. Do you work here? I need to find out whose car I've hit."

"I don't work here. I deliver inventory to some of the shops. I'm sure we'll find the owner. I want to make sure you're all right first."

"Thank you. I think I need to sit here for a minute if you don't mind."

She rolled up the window and left him standing in the snow. He waited. There were only four cars in the parking lot. Hers, the one she'd hit, a delivery truck, and Anna's truck lightly covered in snow. He had his phone to his ear. Was he calling 911? Her hands shook. The ski lift sat quiet, the runs covered in at least a foot of white, the pine branches heavy up the mountainside. It looked like midwinter. She'd seen Robert Redford once, when she was a teenager skiing here. He came straight down the slope and skied right past her at the bottom. He was shorter than she expected. She'd heard he wasn't a tall man. Still, the proof had disappointed her. She wondered how she managed to hit anything given the breadth of space in the parking lot. Would there be sirens, and police officers, in this weather? Would a paramedic appear to look her over? That would probably be a good idea, to let a paramedic confirm that she was alive. She let go of the steering wheel and brushed her hair out of her eyes. She pulled down the visor mirror. Her face looked unusually pale. She ran her finger just under her eye beneath her lashes to wipe away the smudged mascara. She must have been crying; her cheeks were still wet. When she looked at her hands, they continued to quake, as if she were cold. She thought of bare aspen branches in a strong wind. She looked at the snow-covered lot, the small rock wall on the edge. She stared at the series of steps that led through a little wood, a mix of aspen and spruce trees that hid the storefront, the restaurants, and remembered Anna's shop. She could see the corner of the window through a gap. The young man knocked at her window again. She guessed he was about thirty, maybe a little younger. He looked like he spent a lot of time outdoors, which aged a person. He'd put on gloves. She rolled down the window.

"I called 911, but the road up is pretty bad. I want to get you inside if you're sure you're okay to move."

"My sister's shop is just behind there," Roxcy pointed.

"You're Anna's sister?" He said.

"Yes, one of them. You know her?"

"I deliver to her shop," he looked away.

"Oh, that's your truck."

Of course, she thought, *the blue jacket.*

Roxcy opened the door and climbed down out of her car, her legs almost gave way, but he caught her arm. He wasn't too tall and wasn't short. He reminded her of someone. Was it Wayne? She looked at him and said quickly

"I guess I'm not OK. I mean, I'm not hurt or anything. But I feel—"

"I'll walk you in. I'm not going anywhere."

Roxcy was shocked by the volume of the wail that came from her. She immediately tried to slow her breathing, to look up at the sky, but the snowflakes were thick and cold. They stuck in her lashes and stung her cheeks. The young man put his arms around her, gathered her in as if they knew each other, and she let him hold her for a minute.

He said, "Shh," in her ear. His breath was warm and smelled of mint.

Nothing was ok, but she sunk into the warmth of him before pulling back a little horrified at herself, insisting again she was fine, thanking him, apologizing. She felt so tired.

She looked at her crumpled SUV and saw her mom flying off the empty freeway in the darkness. She squeezed her eyes shut. The image kept repeating. She'd crossed a frontage road before she hit the electrical pole. It must have been rough, bouncy. Roxcy hoped her mother had slept through it, but if she woke up too late to stop it, seeing her mother's eyes open, aware of her own death. She kept wiping the streaming tears from her face, now that the sobbing was under control. She kept seeing flashes of Peter, when he was a small and blond boy, looking up at her, —hearing his little boy voice.

"Mommy, I love you."

And the dark room when she'd been about that same age, the snow swirling outside the window in the circle of light. Evie, so small, warm, next to her. Mary curled at her feet. The terror. The sadness and fear twirled together inside her.

The young man stood quietly, waiting for her to calm, gently holding her arm. She blinked hard, tried to make her mind pause. He watched her with genuine concern. It wasn't Wayne he reminded her of; it was Jesus. He looked like the picture that had hung in the hallway on Oak Lane, the same, warm brown eyes, the neatly trimmed beard.

"I think you should sit down. Can I walk you to the shop now?" He said.

"Yes, thank you. I'm sorry. I lost my mom three days ago. She died in a car crash,"

she said, as though this explained everything.

"Anna mentioned it. I'm so sorry."

They walked slowly and carefully across the snow. George would have been spouting reassurances about the car, about

229

eternity, about her mom being with her dad again. But this young man was quiet.

"What's your name?" she said.

"Jake."

"Thank you, Jake."

"It's hard to lose someone."

"Yes, it is. Thank you for saying that. I'm not a sad person, you know? It's frustrating because I can't seem to snap out of it. I can't even really talk to my friends or George, George is my husband, about it without the reassurances. But they just don't help. I mean, it doesn't feel like what I need, doesn't seem to give me any comfort. I know I'll see her again, but she's gone right now, you know. I'm LDS, so . . . Are you LDS?"

"Lapsed," he smiled a little. "Sorry."

"Oh. Well, I'm very active. George is the Stake President, actually. He always says this is not a gospel of sadness. If you're not happy, you're doing something wrong. And he's right. But this is different, isn't it? I mean, I still need her. I need her here, not there. And I thought, I thought I had years, you know?"

He squeezed her hand and opened the shop door. The bell jingled.

"Rox! Are you okay? I saw—I can't find my damn keys."

"Anna, please, stop swearing."

"Sorry," Anna hugged her. Roxcy pulled back and looked into her eyes.

"I'm not okay. Mom is gone. And you're divorced. We can't even go shopping together anymore." She turned to Jake. "It wasn't her fault. Her husband, who we all trusted and loved, is a complete liar. He cheated on her. He's a horrible person. He has his trust fund and didn't even lose his job at BYU. Can you believe that? It's insane. Meanwhile, Anna has to leave her girls to work, and she's stopped going to church. She drinks coffee now."

"Rox! Shut up, all right? Wow, you need to sit down," Anna turned to Jake, her eyes wide. "Sorry, thank you for your help. You can go. You probably have deliveries."

"I don't actually . . . the snow."

"Oh, right." Anna blushed.

"She's just a pile of ashes now. And my kids are growing up and leaving, and my youngest, my youngest is struggling. Just when I needed her the most." She looked up at Anna. "I'm sorry. I don't know what's wrong with me. Truly."

"It's ok, Rox. What's wrong with Peter? What happened?"

Roxcy began crying again. "Mom's dead. She's gone."

"I know," Anna said, sitting her down and rubbing her back. Anna glanced at Jake. Roxcy leaned into her, her body curled, embracing herself, one hand clinging to her own shoulder, the other clinging to her opposite elbow.

"I totaled my car. I swerved to miss a deer. I think it was a deer. I couldn't see very well. I went over the edge of that embankment."

"Oh my God, Roxcy!"

"Please don't take the Lord's name in vain, OK? I know you've given up on God, but please, when you're around me . . ."

Anna stroked her hair.

"Just the Mormon one. I'm sorry. I've been overwhelmed and thoughtless lately. I'll try harder. I'll try harder"

"I love you. Everything's just wrong right now."

"I love you too."

Roxcy noticed that Jake stood close to Anna, his leg almost touching her shoulder. He held a box of tissues in his hand like an offering. She took one and blew her nose.

"How do you two know each other?" She said, brushing the tears from her cheeks.

"Jake and I? He delivers almost all my supplies, "and he's a good friend."

"That's right," Jake said, smiling reassuringly at Roxcy.

Roxcy watched closely as Anna turned and said, "You can go. We'll be all right, really."

"Ok, if you're sure," he said and handed her the tissues. Anna quickly grabbed his hand. "Jake?"

"Yeah?"

"Thank you. Really. Thank you, for everything."

"You're welcome, Anna."

"Yes, thank you so much for your help, Jake. I'm not usually like this, I promise."

He lifted his eyebrows. "You just lost your mom and crashed your car. There'd be something wrong with you if you weren't a little unhinged." He looked at Anna. "I can drive you back to your cabin. The truck is good in the snow."

"No need, but thanks."

"See you Saturday then." He turned and walked out.

"Saturday? He's coming to the memorial?"

"He is."

"Are you two seeing each other or something?"

"We see each other when he brings the delivery. And I called him when mom died. He cleaned the cabin while I slept. Jake's really kind—no performing. But he's just a friend like I said." Anna spoke carefully.

"He needs a haircut, but you're right. He is kind. . . . I should do something to thank him. Do you know what he likes, any hobbies, interests? Does he golf, do you think?" Roxcy said.

Mary

The flakes fell abundant and restless. It was impossible to get an accurate count. Anna and Roxcy weren't home. The storm seemed to be getting worse. Mary paced back and forth between the living room and her bedroom, pausing to check the driveway each time, still empty. One bar of service appeared in front of the window in the loft upstairs. Neither were answering their phones. She left voicemails. She tried to send texts, but nothing would go through.

ARE YOU ALL RIGHT?

PLEASE TEXT ME AND LET ME KNOW THAT YOU'RE ALL RIGHT!

ANNA?!? ROXCY?!?

She pictured cars flying off roads into the river. The doors stuck, the freezing water seeping in. She saw blue faces, glazed over eyes.

Eve slept on the living room couch with one of their mom's books open on the floor beside her. Mary stoked the fire and adjusted the blanket to better cover her sister, who looked cold and pale in the white light. Was Eve coming down with something? Did she have cancer and was just waiting to tell them?

As she fell back into her old habit of keeping track of them, counting them, the panic rose. She kept coming up two short. She looked for a distraction from their absence, a distraction, from the remnants of her mother stacked in the corners of the room. Some of those boxes held their mom's financial records. Mary would take those to her office. She would sort through everything, settle debts, close accounts, and divide any remaining assets according to the will. But not now. She had to distract herself from the absences with something manageable, concrete.

She walked back into her bedroom and opened the drapes. The window looked out onto the grove of trees. The branches bent under the weight of the too-early snow. She could see the road. She would see the old truck when it came. She would see the white Mercedes SUV. Predictable numbers would calm her worry, the emotional distance of a stranger's life organized into neat columns and decimals. She sat down at the small table against the wall. The wooden legs carved in a swirl like thick rope. She remembered this surface in her mother's room always stacked with books. When she was small, she opened the pages to find the pressed fern between protective sheets of parchment, tiny white daisies, Queen Anne's Lace . . . all the wildflowers that grew around the cabin, except Iris. Her mother never picked the wild Iris. Now the surface of the desk was bare, except for her laptop, the blue power light pulsing. The books had been moved to the living room shelves or placed in boxes.

She opened up a file on her computer. It was a relatively new account, a young couple had just had their second child. This couple would likely have three to five children. But the second child meant there would be no more room on the mother's lap for the first. The second child meant the end of childhood for the first.

～

Mary looked up. Her mama's round belly blocked her view. It cast a shadow across Mary's small upturned face. She thought, *Baby* and reached out her hand to touch.

"Sit here, Maryberry." Her mama's voice was warm. She felt the softness of her arm around her. The book balanced on her belly. No more room on her mama's lap at storytime.

As she grew, Mary watched her mother's body change again. She felt shadows of the same trepidation, another small loss with each blooming. But she quickly discovered that baby Roxcy also belonged to her. She would hold on tight to Mary's finger when they walked together. She would look up at Mary and smile. She loved her baby sister. As Mary got older, she began to keep track of her, attached herself, as if she were her little sister's shadow. Her mama smiled and told her she was a good big sister to take such good care, but Roxcy was safe, Mary didn't have to worry so much. When Eve came, it got harder. If they went in different directions,

Mary couldn't split herself in two. She would pick up Eve and carry her on her hip, just like her mama did to keep them together. By the third time, and last time, her mom was pregnant, Mary had grown tall enough that the belly did not block her view of her mother's face. She noted the way her mom's arms had softened. Thought the fullness and light in her face beautiful. Like paintings of the Virgin Mary, her namesake, her mama had shown her in books, in the long blue robe with golden light around her head. She waited all year for Christmas time when they would tell about Mary's story in church.

When she was pregnant, her mama sat down more often, and Mary could lean against her. She could help by holding Evie in her lap while she read them stories. Sometimes, she stood in front of the oval mirror that hung on wooden hinges. Mary shoved a pillow up her own shirt and wrestled the long lump, as best she could, into the shape of a ball. She wanted to be a mother, to have that softness, to feel everything slow down. She wanted the glow around her face. Each Sunday, she learned this was the most important thing a woman could be. But the pillow stuck out the top of her shirt, it looked malformed and worrisome, and who would take care of her sisters if she had a baby of her own? Additionally, her arms and legs were still too long for her body, bony at the elbows and knees. She pulled back her thick, wild hair into a low pony-tail like her mom's, the pillow slipped lower and lost all shape. With her hair pulled away from her face all she saw were her unreasonably large, round eyes and big mouth. She looked like her father. She pulled the pillow loose and quickly removed the ponytail holder. Everyone said she was just like him because she loved numbers. She also worried the way he did. She didn't want to worry or be like her father, a person who was there and not there. Who sat on the stand during church. Who gathered them for scripture reading in the evening and then disappeared. He left before she woke. He said little at dinner and spent most of his time at home in his office or leaving to attend important church meetings. On occasion, when he had one of his math books out and was sitting in his large chair in the corner of the living room, Mary would walk up quietly and look over his shoulder at the pages. She stared at the strange symbols coupled with the numbers. When he noticed her there he would reach back and smile at her, say, "Hello, there Miss Mary!" and muss her hair.

It was her mom that tucked the covers beneath her chin and whispered her story in her ear. It was her mom that left the scent of citrus on her comforter to breathe in. She fed her and washed her clothes and made a place for her to snuggle into the crook of her arm when they read scriptures. When Mary worried about getting to school on time, about her sisters being in different classes, it was her mom that suggested Mary count things, the pictures in the hallway, the books on the shelves, the blooms in her garden. She wasn't sure whether she started counting everything because of the bedtime story or if her mom had seen a need and created a solution. Mary had been counting things for as long as she could remember. If she mentioned her habit, people misunderstood. It wasn't compulsion. It was pleasure. It was calm. She believed God lived in numbers, maybe more than in all the stories. It was the order of them, the predictability. And all the scriptures about sheep.

Like a shepherd He will tend His flock, In His arm He will gather the lambs And carry them in His bosom; He will gently lead the nursing ewes.

If one went astray, he would leave the ninety-nine.

Not one hair of the head is not counted.

He counted and kept track of every living thing.

"Mom?"

"Mmmhmm." Her mom was down to her wrist, planting something in the garden.

"It's Tuesday."

"Shoot! What time is it, Mary?" She said, turning to look at her.

"Four. Primary started already."

"Well, I guess you could go as you are. Do you want to go late?"

"I could take the girls to Grow's Flats, so you can work in the garden."

"You'll make sure to keep them safe?"

"I'll have them back before the sun starts to go down. That'll be about dinner time."

"Of course, you will. Go ahead. Thank you for your help, sweetie. I can always depend on you."

"You're welcome," Mary said, feeling very grown-up for twelve.

So, instead of washing up, combing their hair and walking down Elm, around Fir and to the church for two hours of sitting and listening to lessons on Joseph Smith or Jesus, instead of singing about popcorn on apricot trees and the shushing of chapel doors, they ran across the asphalt path, onto the dirt path that ran behind the Olson's house. They ran wearing jeans with grass-stained knees, their hair set free from barrettes and elastic bands. The houses hid the gradual effect the plateaus might have had. They made the gray mountains look as if they shot straight into the sky. But the old pasture hid behind the houses along Oak Lane. The flats were wild grasses mostly, interrupted by patches of scrub oak and the odd boulder, which served as a perfect perch for Mary to watch over her little sisters. The barn swallows chirped and swooped above their heads. They mingled their song with the sound of the breeze.

Her sisters spent most of the day pretending, but Mary had lost her ability to suspend reality. She stood at the edge of the rock, keeping watch. And counting things: the tufts of grass, from the edge of the path to the rock, from the Grow's fence to the scrub oak, the number of robin calls, the swallows swirling above her head. She counted the clouds in the sky. She counted the large rocks on the hillside before scaling one and then another. She looked down and counted her sisters, one, two, three. She counted the number of windows in the houses above the flats. She counted the number of roofs on the houses below. She counted her sisters again, always returning to her responsibility.

～

They still hadn't come back to the cabin. It was going on four hours, much longer than it should have taken for Anna to check in at her store, and for Roxcy to drop boxes off at D.I., even in the snow. If you tripled the normal drive times of approximately ten minutes for Anna, and fifty minutes for Roxcy, accounting for weather, they should have been home hours ago. Mary walked up the narrow stairs to the loft again, to the corner where her phone now had two bars. Her messages dinged, one, two, three, four.

Everything has changed, and nothing has changed, Mary thought.

Eve

Eve heard bells ringing and walked into the warm light. She felt the small hand slip into hers and looked down. The little girl had dark hair, eyes and hair like Mo, those impossibly thick lashes. Eve crouched down and kissed the soft cheek, and the child smiled at her, put her small free hand on Eve's cheek. She stood up again, still holding her hand, and they walked slowly down the path between the aspen trees. The dream child set the pace, pulling her along.

"Do you see their eyes watching us?" Eve said.

The small face smiled up at her. The grass thick and green, beneath the flicker of light and shadow. Eve tried to slow her down, took smaller steps, but she couldn't slow down time. When they reached the meadow, as always, she let go of her hand. The child looked back over her shoulder, laughing as she ran, stepped off the path, and dissipated into light.

Eve opened her eyes and saw white. The minimal daylight through the storm had already begun to wane. Anna's truck pulled into the driveway. She heard Mary behind her running down the stairs.

"Oh Evie, I didn't want to wake you. You looked so tired, but they're home now. And safe. Thank goodness, they're safe."

Eve smiled up at Mary, not hearing her. She felt red longing in her heartbeat. Slowly, she opened and closed her left hand.

Anna and Eve

Anna lay with, her hands behind her head watching the moonlight spread across the wooden beams of the ceiling. Her hair spread in a dark halo on her pillow.

"I see the moon and the moon sees me. God bless the moon and God bless me. That's what mom used to say when she laid the girls down. I'd hear them repeat it back to her," she said turning to look at Eve.

"She was good at bedtime. She was good at everything." Eve paused. "It looks like the storm is finally clearing,"

"It does. Mary almost broke my ribs with that hug. I guess she was worried."

"She worries all the time. It's part of the way she loves. I'm so glad Roxcy's all right."

"We couldn't take another loss right now. I miss her, Evie . . . it hurts." Anna said, her eyes welling. "She knew all my secrets and loved me anyway."

"Me too."

"What are your secrets, Evie?" Anna said.

It was quiet for a minute. The moonlight spread across the room. It illuminated both of their faces in soft blue light.

"I had another miscarriage last spring. I've had five in all."

"Oh, Eve." Anna stood up and stepped across to her sister's bed. She laydown next to her and hugged her.

"With the last one, I was twelve weeks along. When the bleeding started, I swallowed a lot of pain killers. Mo found me losing consciousness on the couch. Lucky he came home. Otherwise, I wouldn't be here. Anyway, he couldn't sleep after that. I'd wake up and find him watching me. I came and stayed with mom for a couple of months. It was right before things fell apart for you."

"God, Evie! How did I have no idea? I should have—"

"You should have read my mind? You should have somehow known I went crazy for a minute? I told mom not to tell you all. I didn't want to be a burden to you. The sadness was so heavy, crushing. But now, I feel like someone else needs to know. Just in case it comes back, but I think we're done trying. I can't take those hormones again. They turn me into someone I don't know."

Anna hugged her and said, "I'm sleeping with a twenty-eight-year-old delivery man who brings beautiful fabric to my store."

Eve wiped the tears from her cheek with the back of her hand and laughed out loud.

"Oh?"

"Shhh. I can't tell Roxcy and Mary. Not yet. Maybe not ever. Every Thursday at 8:00 a.m. On the couch in my storage room. It sounds like a porno."

"I wouldn't know." Eve was shaking her head, still quietly laughing.

"Matt liked to watch together every once and a while. I guess he was watching a lot on his own too." She paused. "You know the girl?"

"The one he—"

"Yes, her breasts were the size of bread loaves, and Matt was kneading them. Have you seen what's left of my breasts? They look like those tiny half-filled water balloons. Twenty-years-old, big-breasted, blond. She was my opposite in every way."

"You know what he did had nothing to do with you!"

"My brain knows that, but tell my sad little breasts. They don't believe you."

"Did mom know about—"

"Yeah, I told her. She said I should do whatever I needed to. What do you make of that?"

"It sounds like mom. She was . . ." Eve searched for the right word, "unorthodox."

"But she went to church every Sunday! And, I mean, by Mormon standards, I'm a sinner. No question. But I don't think she ever thought of me in those terms. I just don't know how being an active church member and being okay with fornication go together."

"Nothing was black and white for her. I think she held it all loosely."

"Like our stories. The way she shaped them to fit us."

"Or us into them. I think I've spent my whole life with some part of me believing I was the Eve in my story."

"Huh. Me too, I guess. I can recite it from memory still."

Eve paused and turned on her side toward Anna. "So, what's your delivery man's name?"

"Jake. He's not mine and just barely a man. I don't really even know him. Except, I think he's a good guy. I mean, what you see is what you get, which is a relief after Matt. You should've seen him with Roxcy today."

"What?!?"

"We were at the shop together when she flew off the road. She interrupted my orgasm. Typical," Anna laughed.

"I knew you were hiding something! You drove down to the store in a blizzard for—"

"For sex, yes. I've taken desperation and loneliness to a new level. But Roxcy was a mess, Evie, a complete disaster. Have you ever seen her fall apart like this?"

"No, she's always in perfect control. But losing mom—"

"You're right. She said something about Peter too. I wonder what's going on there? Has she said anything to you?"

"No. Poor Roxcy. You need to take it easy on her, Anna."

"I know I do. I just wish she'd stop worrying over my eternal soul and acting so superior all the time. It's exhausting. But I'll try harder."

Anna looked at her sister, the moonlight throwing shadows into the hollows of her cheeks and lighting Eve's closed eyelids. She reached for her hand and held it tightly for a minute.

"Everything's going to be all right, isn't it?"

"It already is," Eve said.

"Have I ever told you that you remind me of an aspen tree, Evie. You always have, even before you started studying them."

Eve opened her eyes and saw the familiar shadows flicker on the white-washed wood. "They're all connected? The root systems, I mean, a grove is really just one tree."

"I think mom told me that."

"I remember when Roxcy was pregnant with her first, with Hannah, putting my hand on her belly and feeling her little body sort of nuzzle into it. It wasn't a thought; it wasn't even a feeling, it was like a need. I needed to feel that in my own body."

Eve felt the familiar emptiness spread through her. The two sisters sat in the silence. Anna lay her head on Eve's shoulder.

"Please stay, Evie. Don't go."

Eve understood she was not talking about going back to Colorado. She stroked her sister's hair.

"I'm trying to stay, making friends with the sadness rather than treating it like an enemy. Strangely, I find it visits less frequently. But I am tired. I need to sleep."

Anna stepped back across to her own bed. She laid down on her side facing Eve, saw that her sister was already adrift somewhere in the dancing shadows. Anna scooted carefully out of the bed and tucked the covers over Eve. When she lay back down and closed her eyes, she felt like it was swaying. Over the course of a year, she had lost her husband, her religion, and her mother. Anna opened her eyes to steady herself. She followed the slope of the ceiling to the intersection, the place where the two opposing slants met and held each other, her eyes ran along the beam supporting the center, supporting everything.

Anna listened as the cabin settled around her. The swaying feeling in her exhausted body, the creaking of the cabin, made her think of an old ship, Christ's apostles caught in the tempest, turgid water, and rebirth. *Except a man be born of the water and the spirit, he cannot enter the kingdom of God.* Anna repeated the verse in her mind, like the rhythm of ocean waves. Why did she find the image and the words comforting? Her thoughts moved to the story of Christ calming the tempest, of him walking across the water, his disciple sinking in the effort to reach him. They taught that agency began at eight, that an eight-year-old knew right from wrong, a child could make the choice between salvation or damnation. Before eight, a child was innocent, unaccountable. That baptism, the act of being immersed in a small tiled font in front of your family and friends meant you had entered the gate. Supposedly, only Mormon baptism qualified you for entrance back into the presence of God.

Anna thought, *We are all born of the water and the spirit in that final push, in that first breath of air. We are all children, we are all innocent, we are all sinking and reaching out for help. We are all, already, saved.*

It was like her mom's voice was in her mind reframing things to fit the world she perceived. She could stop fighting so hard if she could remember, if she could listen. Anna remained aware of her sister's breath and her own breath syncing, felt the warm wave rise and fall. Her breath became breeze; the light changed into a dance. She floated into the small grove of aspens in front of the cabin. Water falling in the midst of sunshine, like a mist. Her mother, alive, stood next to Mary in the whisper of air. They all lifted their faces into the moving light, toward the new green leaves and the sunshine. Mary melted into her mother. Eve was there too, witness to the miracle. Roxcy, grown, looked down at her, took her small hand, and they stepped forward into the grove together.

Mary and Roxcy

Roxcy waited until the pipes in the house went quiet. She listened for the sound of running water, for footsteps, for the whispered voices of Anna and Eve to dissipate into the air. With the thinning quilt around her shoulders, Roxcy walked quietly to the door. She carefully turned the knob, opening the door slowly and without sound. Always listening, the careful movement a vestigal of habit formed in the years when her children were babies. She knocked quietly on Mary's door before pulled it open and peeked in.

"Can I come in?" She whispered

Mary nodded. The drapes were pulled wide, and the moonlight cast everything in a blue glow. Mary sat in a halo of yellow light from the small bedside lamp. Her laptop was open and a file next to her on the bed.

"Of course. Come on in," she said putting the file on the nightstand.

"Anna and Evie get a sleepover and I could use some company. Did you hear them laughing?" She climbed into the bed next to Mary searched for her hand. It was warm, and Roxcy held on as though they were still children.

"You ok?" Mary looked at her over the rim of her reading glasses, set low on the bridge of her nose.

"I think so, a little sore."

Mary squeezed her hand. "You gave me a scare today."

"I shouldn't have gone out in that weather. I just can't sit still. My brain won't stop."

"A blessing and a curse, I guess. You got us all here together, and that's a good thing."

"It was nothing," Roxcy said, smoothing her bright hair.

"It was a lot of work." Mary said, "Especially on such a hard day, but you did it."

"I don't miss her as much if I'm moving, if I'm busy. I don't think as much."

"I totally get that," she smiled and tapped the folder.

Roxcy smiled, and neither one said anything for a few minutes. They sat together in the moonlight feeling comfortable closeness in their silence.

"Anna and I are no picnic, huh?" Roxcy finally said.

"Anna's . . . Anna. She's had a hard time lately and let herself get too defensive."

"She was really kind today after the accident. I totally lost it."

"Well, she loves you, and she's had a really hard year."

"I know. Honestly, I can't imagine." Roxcy paused. "These last few months I've had my own challenges." Her throat tightened. She closed her eyes and breathed in and out. Sometimes she choked like this when she bore her testimony in church, overcome with emotion, and gratitude, but this feeling wasn't grateful. This feeling that kept welling up inside her like it wanted to devour, to destroy. It didn't warm her. It felt like something hiding in the closet, something cold, that preferred the dark. She felt the unnamable thing in the shadows, afraid that, if she swallowed, fear might spread and dissolve her from the inside out. Roxcy looked around to see the room, to reassure herself that 30-plus years had passed, that they weren't little girls anymore. Roxcy never told anyone. Her eyes were shut the whole time. She only heard and felt the things that her body remembered sometimes. The day and the night and the day that Anna was born, a lifetime ago. She was a grown woman now, had had her whole, full life to crush that tiny moment. Since the trouble with Peter and now the loss of her mom, every bad thing had been untethered. The feeling dissipated, her throat relaxing. She swallowed and felt grateful for Mary, her big sister.

"Did you want to talk about it?" Mary said.

"That night? I can't remember exactly, but it's like my body reacts. And I'm terrified sometimes for no reason. Most of the time, ninety-nine percent of the time, I'm absolutely fine. I haven't had anything for years. Since early in my marriage. But it's all stirred up now, and I'm worried that he'll come with Aunt Violet to the memorial. And, Mary, what would I do? It would be unbearable."

Mary sat quiet for a long time.

"I never told you how sorry I am that I didn't take better care of you, Rox. I'm so sorry, so, so sorry."

"What are you talking about? You saved me. I mean, I do remember you yelling at him. I remember that." She paused, "Mary?"

"Yeah?"

"Pete has come home drunk five times in the past two months."

"What? Oh, Rox. That's hard. I'm sorry."

"I haven't told George. I was going to talk to Mom, but—" Roxcy began to cry again. She felt tired of crying. It was not her habit and felt foreign, but she could not seem to stop herself.

Mary looked at her sister. She pushed away the image of her nephew passed out under a street light, an addict, homeless, and alone. She took a deep breath and repeated what her mom had said to her.

"Listen to me, Roxcy. You're a good mom. You've given Peter everything he needs to make good choices. Kids have to learn for themselves sometimes. That's not on you."

"But what do I do?"

"You love him, and you tell him to stop, that it's hurting you. It feels worse than it is because Mom's gone, but it's not the end of the world. I had the same thing happen with Hank."

"Hank? He's such a good boy, I never thought—"

"He did, a few times. He's a good boy, a good man now. He puts his mission papers in next summer. Mom told me to do what I just told you, and it worked. It will work for Peter too."

"You really think so? I suddenly feel so much better. Like a weight lifted." She sighed

Mary hugged her tight and said, "I want to switch sides, Okay, Rox?"

"Okay."

The moon spilled over them, and the shadows of aspen trees reached into the room. The night air felt like winter more than fall, but the storm was over. Mary stood, and

Roxcy shifted herself beneath the blanket to the side of the bed closest to the window.

"That moon must be big."

"I think it's almost full. Shall I close the drapes?"

"It reminds me of sleeping out in the meadow. I love the shadows of our aspens. If you're ok with it, I think I'd like the light tonight."

"I am."

Mary looked over at Roxcy, a round lump curled beneath the covers, her knees tucked up to her chest like a snail. When she smiled, and Mary noticed the fine wrinkles around her sister's eyes.

"Do you want to read a little bit together?" Mary said. "My ward is doing the Book of Mormon challenge this year. I still have to read my four and a half pages today. Might help calm our minds."

"Mine is too! We're in 2 Nephi, Isaiah." Roxcy groaned, and Mary laughed.

"I've found if I just let the words sort of wash over me and don't try too hard to understand them, it's sort of beautiful. Like poetry."

"I hate poetry." Roxcy said and sat up.

Mary picked up her scriptures, the thick book with a black leather cover she'd gotten as a gift at her baptism when she was eight, Mary Taylor engraved on the bottom right-hand corner in gold script. The thin pages beneath the worn leather were an intricate part of the equation that balanced her life. These stories about God and love and beauty that she'd learned as a child, rediscovered on her own as an adult, and passed on to her own child, their familiar rhythms a balm. She passed the book to Roxcy.

"You start."

"All right. Where are you?"

"Chapter 8."

"Oh, I think I'm a little ahead of you, but that's all right. Let's see.

Hearken unto me, ye that follow after righteousness. Look unto the rock from whence ye are hewn, and to the hole of the pit from whence ye are digged. Look unto Abraham your father, and unto Sarah, she that bare you; for I called him alone and blessed him. For the Lord shall comfort Zion, he will comfort all her waste places; and he will make her wilderness like Eden and her desert like the garden of the Lord. Joy and gladness shall be found therein, thanksgiving and the voice of melody . . .

The rise and fall of Roxcy's voice speaking the old verses became ebb and flow in Mary's mind. She counted back the years that had produced the fine lines next to her little sister's eye, moving away from the present death of their mother to her earliest memory of birth. When they brought Roxcy home, she was two and a half. She thought she remembered the warmth of the tiny body on her lap and her parent's soft, whispered instruction

She is small
Be gentle
She is small
Be kind
She is small
Take care
Take care

Take care . . .

Mary usually knelt to pray, followed the proper form of thanks first, followed by request, but tonight Mary simply closed her eyes and thought.

Dear Heavenly Father, please give her comfort, please. Take care of all my sisters. Please help me know how I can be of help to them.

She took three deep breaths. Felt her breath slow, and her worries ease. The air around them was cold, and she scooted in toward Roxcy for warmth.

And there was the evening and the morning of the fifth day.

The double wooden doors that lead to the cultural hall are propped open. Sounds of clicking dress shoes move across the lacquered floor of the basketball court painted with black, red, and, blue lines. Thick, heavy velvet curtains hang above cupboards which are open wide, filled with rows and rows of tables and chairs pulled out from the large storage cupboards beneath the stage. There is a line of people, mostly young men, waiting to help carry.

Mary walks out, holding two folding chairs in each arm. The ease of her regular movement hampered by a straight black skirt, the slit an insufficient allowance for her naturally long stride. She's careful of her white button-down shirt, ironed, with the large cuffs.

Roxcy stands outside, holding the door open in the tall glass-enclosed entry. She directs the traffic, in her three-inch black pumps and deep-purple shirt dress, the collar turned up, a string of creamy pearls at her neck. She points across the parking lot to a small grassy area, smiling, thanking those carrying chairs and tables as they pass. The young men smile back, tell her it's no problem, they're happy to help. George called them all this morning, last minute, once she was sure the snow had melted and the ground was dry enough to move the whole thing outside. She simply explained that her mother preferred the sky to ceilings, that the setting mattered to her, as he always does, George made the necessary calls. They laid out rows of chairs on the grass where, as a teenager, she'd played touch football at Wednesday night youth activities. When her mom had dropped her and Mary, wearing their tight jeans, rolled into a peg at the ankle. Roxcy smiles and points.

"Do you see? There—yes, by the woman with short, dark hair. That's Eve, one of my sisters."

Eve stands in the grass, the sun hot against her bare legs, as though it forgot the storm completely, as though it's summer again. She bears silent witness to this beautiful act, this coming together to acknowledge their mother's life. Still, she is more at ease in intimate spaces than in large groups, even friendly ones. This public grieving will lead to a time when she's allowed to sit quietly, surrounded only by her family. Already she wants to be back at the cabin, to have time with Mo and her sisters, her nieces and nephews. She craves the feel of soil on her fingertips too, longs to be back in her own garden and groves—one more day and night and day. As people arrive, Eve searches the crowd for the reassurance of her sisters.

Anna holds one end of a long rectangular table. A young male missionary the other.

"Stop for a minute, OK? I'm losing the table cloth," she bends low to set the table down, readjusts the white table cloth that slips from her forearm, slips off her black pumps to let her toes stretch out from the point. Her dress is a semi-sheer cream linen, fully lined, sleeveless, that comes to a low v at her sternum. As she bends down and forwards, the pale skin of her small breasts swells slightly at the seam.

"Ah, thank you. Much better!" She stands up.

The young man looks fixedly at the deep, green, grass which is beginning to dry in the morning sunshine. Anna rolls her eyes and pulls her hair into a haphazard bun at the base of her long neck. She wonders how her tiny, thirty-four-year old breasts that have nursed two children could cause such havoc in this ruddy-cheeked boy.

She thinks, *He probably grew up on a farm in Idaho for Godsakes! Milked cows, birthed calves.* "Ready?" She says.

"Me, sure, fine." His gaze still down.

"Elder? Look at me for a minute, ok?" Anna smiles wide, her bright red lips exaggerating the whiteness of her teeth. "Listen, don't feel guilty. It's completely unnatural for a boy to spend two of his most virile years as a celibate, but I promise I'm not trying to seduce you. You're a little young for me." She winks at him.

The boy's ears turn red, and the color travels to his cheeks.

"Let's get moving, Elder."

Roxcy looks concerned.

"What's Anna doing?" she says aloud before turning back as the next round of chairs comes through the doors. "Just through here, yes, on the grass, you see?" She smiles. "Right where Anna is with the other table. You know you boys are saving us here."

They walk on, moving the long table across the paved lot toward the grass.

"You're very good at this, Rox," Mary says as she walks through the glass doors again carrying four more folding chairs, two in each hand.

"I'm in my element, I guess."

"It was a good idea to move it outside. It's perfect." Mary stands next to her sister and rests the chairs against her hips. She shades her eyes with one hand.

"Look at that poor boy's face. It's so red you can see it across the parking lot. What has Anna said to him?"

"Heaven knows!"

Roxcy sighs, "Oh well, I think mom would like this, right?"

"She'll love it," Mary kisses Roxcy on the cheek. "Onward and upward." She lifts the chairs and starts back across the parking lot.

Roxcy thinks, *She always walked us to church when the sun was shining, even if it meant we'd be late.*

She catches her reflection in the glass and remembers looking up at her mother standing in this same spot, holding the door for her to pass through.

Her sons begin to file past chairs in hand. She blows each of them a kiss and stops Pete to give him a hug, which he can't return because his hands are full.

"I love you, mom."

"I love you too, Petie." She moves his hair off his forehead and out of his eyes. "Time for a haircut?" She pulls him back in and whispers, "You're breaking my heart. No more, okay?"

Pete sets the chairs down to hug her, his voice in her ear.

"I'm really sorry, mom, really. I won't do it again."

"Thank you. Now get those chairs over to Aunt Evie."

Tears threaten, but she stops them, runs her finger beneath her eye just to be sure, and widens her smile. She watches him walk away, her baby, notices that his pants are getting short again. She can't seem to keep up with how fast he's growing. She watches the line of men, old and young carrying the chairs across to the grass.

How many now? Twenty good souls moving back and forth in a line?

She'll call The Brick Oven once things are set up, make sure there's a table ready at for them at lunchtime, pay for the pizza and pasta bar as a thank you.

Like busy ants, she thinks and remembers a Sunday when they were all still small and paused on their walk to church to watch a line of the tiny black insects building their hill on the seam where the Pierce's driveway met the sidewalk. The smiles of her sisters' faces around her. Their voices mingling together. What an odd thing the way an old memory flashes and falls into focus. They'd been late to church that day. She must have still been six or seven. She remembers the heads turning as they scooted in near the back—the smiling faces of the Daltons, the Calls, the Mechams. And a few disapproving looks from faces that have faded into only a feeling or sense, the specific visages gone. She remembers the reassuring weight of Mary's arm around her shoulder. Evie sitting close and quiet, and Anna swinging her legs on the edge of the bench.

She watches the stream of chairs move across the parking lot and take shape, a lovely, rounded curve of rows. These good, large, male hands, capable and willing, placing them on the grass and flow back across the parking lot for more. Suddenly the nagging anxiousness evaporates.

He won't come. He only exists in small dark spaces behind closed doors, years ago. This is happening outside, now, in the light. The women will make it beautiful. The men will do the heavy lifting.

These almost-men who could be home playing video games and the grown men working in their yards or watching a football game, but these boys, many of them strangers, are here lifting folding chairs for her mother's memorial service. They're easing the weight of loss. It's beautiful, her eyes well. Beautiful. This is what her church is. This is what it means to be a Mormon. She feels a swell of tribal pride and a deep sense of gratitude.

Eve closes her eyes and tilts her face upward toward the warmth of the sun. In the orange glow of her closed eyelids, she sees her mother's face, turned toward a flower, laughing, tilting toward the sun.

Her ashes, she thinks, *will be next year's grass.*

She opens her eyes. Images float into the haze of morning light.

Mom is the grove.

She remembers her there, always at the edge of things. Eve and her sisters in the center, hands joined, spinning in a circle until the dizziness took over and they were a laughing pile in the grass.

She's still here everywhere, she thinks. *We're still there too. All our past and present and future selves.*

This is not the correct story of eternity, but Eve feels it move through her like a dream through the trees, this stillness beneath the sorrow is where some unnamable truth hides. She turns back to the task of adjusting chairs, making sure they'll meet with Roxcy's approval. Then arms around her waist. Mo is here. She turns around, breathes in his familiar smell, feels the rough stubble on his cheek against hers.

"How are you?"

She answers him by leaning her whole weight into him.

Mary walks over, then Anna, then Roxcy. They pass him around smiling, crying, greeting him, embracing him, all thankful for his steadying presence.

Mary steps back and watches her sisters laughing. Anna stands next to her barefoot. Eve and Roxcy in front, leaning in toward each other. In their thirties and forties and simultaneously, the memory of them, small, long-limbed rolling wildly down the hill at Kiwanis. Mary at the top of the hill clapping, watching, counting them down.

When they managed to stand from the tumbled pile at the bottom of the hill, she knew their hair and clothes would be strung with bits of grass, their bare knees smeared green, but she had forgotten to worry. They had all kicked off their flip-flops. She remembered that the blades felt cool against her bare feet. She was aware of the millions of tiny white roots that anchored the grass into the soil beneath.

"Come on, Mary, come on!"

She smiled, lay down, and rolled. The hill turned her over and over. She felt her body bump, a pleasant pain in her elbow, and then her knee. She saw her sisters' faces mixing, blurring shapes of warm light. The ground leveled, and she stopped by knocking them back over until she was surrounded, her head still spinning, their smiling red-cheeked faces coming into focus. Anna grabbed her with a small hand. Her hair in pigtails gone askew and pulled her back to the top of the hill.

"You OK there, Mary?" Anna reaches for her hand.

Mary's been crying off and on, all morning, never making an effort to hold back the emotion she feels. Anna doesn't know anyone else who cries in such calm streams.

"I was just thinking that everything will be all right, you know, even though mom is gone." Mary squeezes Anna's hand with her free one. "You call me when you need help with the girls, okay? I want to help."

"Okay, Mary. I will." Anna laughs, a little taken aback by the urgency in her sister's voice. She turns and hugs her, feels the surety of her strong arms. And has flashes of being very small, propped on Mary's hip. Mary giving her a piggy-back when her legs got tired. Evie sitting close and reading her books on the moss-colored couch. Roxcy cleaning up her scraped knee, letting her peel the paper off the bandaid. Her mom, there too, somewhere in another room or in her garden. Anna leans her head on Mary's shoulder and reaches for Evie's hand.

"Mom! Mom!" Honey and Lula hugged her legs. "Hi, Auntie Mary! Hi, Auntie Evie, Hi, Auntie Roxcy. Look! Look!"

Her sisters bend down to kiss their foreheads, hold their small hands as they twirl in the new dresses their daddy bought them. Mary steps forward before Matthew can join the circle. She takes his arm and turns him. Anna squats down and smiles at Honey and Lula, but her eyes burn. She gathers her little girls in and listens to their chatter like a welcome blessing. She hopes he won't stay for the service and knows he will. Anna watches Mary move him out of the way; she sees her kind smile at odds with the firmness in her eyes. An expression she knows from her mother's face and thinks,

My daughters will always have each other.

Anna feels gratitude weave itself through her. Her mother was always there, but so were her sisters. She leaves Matt to Mary, trusting that she'll take care of it and turns away with relief.

It is nearly 10:00 am. The parking lot fills quickly with cars parked at a slant between the bright yellow lines. The Taylor sisters sit in the first four rows. Roxcy and George's family of six look neatly pressed, as if they are dressed for a family portrait. The men in white shirts with navy blue ties and dark blue suit coats. George in dark gray wool suit, white shirt, and purple necktie that matches Roxcy's dress. Her girls and daughters-in-law all in dark navy or purple, hair long and curled, lashes long and thick with mascara, all wearing high, sharp, heels. They could be Roxcy's own daughters, both physically and in style. They sit next to Eve and Mo who looks informal without suit jacket or tie. His black shirt matches his hair, the top button undone. He laces his fingers through Eve's. She leans her head on his shoulder. Across the aisle, Mary sits on the other end of Anna's girls whose ruffled silk dresses almost cover her lap. They swing their legs over the edge of their chairs.

Mary's boy, Hank, offers the opening prayer, his voice deep and full of emotion. He sits down next to his mom when he finishes and puts his arm around the back of her chair. She pats his hand. Their mother's bishop-who none of them know at all-stands next. He begins listing true things that are wrong. They shift in their seats.

"Sylvia Taylor was a stellar example of what it meant to be a Mormon wife and mother." Without looking at her George takes Roxcy's hand and squeezes it.

"I knew her husband very well from work and church callings. He was a humble man who served as a ward clerk in a bishopric for years, never complaining, never missing a meeting." Mary raises an eyebrow.

"She sacrificed her own ambitions to support her husband, a renowned and much-missed professor of mathematics. I remember him telling me once that Sylvia kept the house sparkling and that she liked to garden a little."

Eve lifts her head from Mo's shoulder and stares.

"She raised these four beautiful women you see right here and loved her grandchildren. She'll be dearly missed, but she's with her husband and her Savior now. God must need her for some important work. We must trust His judgment and take comfort in our knowledge that we have binding, ordinances that will allow us to be with our loved ones again."

Anna rubs her temples.

Roxcy looks pleadingly at George, who stands to shake the hand of this well-meaning man, thanking him for his wonderful words, his words of comfort. There's an audible breath when the bishop joins those sitting down. George stands silent for a moment before he begins.

"Jesus is the resurrection and the life. Sylvia Taylor believed in her Savior. She's with him now, reunited with Jim, her parents and his, enfolded in the arms of unfathomable peace and love. As her bishop reminded us, we know that when a couple is sealed in the temple, they're bound, not just for this life. This is a fact that can give us some comfort in this difficult time. Sylvia was remarkable. I feel it a great privilege to have been part of her family, to still be part of her family. We will see her again, our mother, our grandma, our friend. We will see her again."

Eve thinks, *In the spring.*

Roxcy's children, who each play a different string instrument, come to the front and play *For the Beauty of the Earth,* and something clicks into place.

It's their turn now to lay a memory at the feet of this community of people who have loved their mother and come here to share in the joy of her life and sadness of her passing.

Mary looks out across the crowd, her gaze met by the familiar and kind eyes of her childhood, Brother and Sister Call, even some of their kids in the third row, and the Clarks. There were the Anderson kids, even with all the tumult they'd faced growing up, some were still active in church, and even those who weren't, sat in the rows tattooed and pierced. And dear, sister Byer alone now, her hair neatly curled as always, but full white. Mary smiles back at all of them and feels the blessed weight of the years of being taught by these good people, being loved and supported by them. They brought casseroles at the birth of each of her sisters. Threw her a wedding and baby shower. Brought her accounting work and generally cheered on her life. They had loved her like she belonged to them. Their presence, the comforting pressure of ongoing care.

"Thank you for being here. I can't properly express what it means to me." She paused and began. "My mother knew I loved to count, so I used to count her plants for her. I kept a tally sheet that she hung on the shed door. She had the gift of knowing who people were and trying to help them become themselves." She looked into the crowd and faltered

267

as her eyes stumbled across the thin face of a neatly dressed older woman in the back row. She had to look at her note card before she continued. "She named me after Mary in the scriptures and found a way to put me in that story. She used to look at me working at my math homework and say, *but Mary kept all these things and pondered them in her heart.* Hank, my son, who is sitting right there, was mostly raised by two women, my dad here and there too, but mostly me and her. He turned out all right, I think, and I'm grateful to her for that every day. I will, I do, miss her, but I'm so grateful she raised me in this church, so grateful for my sisters, who are still right here. And I will keep all the things she taught me and ponder them in my heart. I say these things in the name of Jesus Christ. Amen."

Roxcy stops and holds onto Mary for a minute before proceeding to the front. She has two or three notecards in her hand and flips through them quickly and then looks up smiling.

"My mom named me after a woman who knew how to get things done, and then she taught me how to do. She taught me that soaking the dishes for a few minutes before you wash them makes the washing more thorough and efficient." A chuckle runs through the group.

"She taught me how to fold a fitted sheet by sliding the corners into each other. She taught me that the scriptures were worth reading by reading them with us every day. She was there to help me down the stairs when I went into labor with my first beautiful baby, so I could learn how to be there for my daughters when they had babies of their own. She spent the next twenty-plus years helping me learn how to be a mother who does. My mom, my mom, Roxcy raises her pointer finger, knew how to take care. I know she's with the Savior and probably talking with all our foremothers, exchanging gardening tips." More Laughter. "I am so grateful for her, everything she did for me, and I know that she'll be with us still, helping us along from the other side of the veil, until we meet again. I say these things in the name of Jesus Christ, ever grateful for all he did for me, amen."

Her voice never shook. Not a drop had fallen from her eye. She walks, satisfied back to her seat and takes George's hand, which he offers to help her sit down.

Eve recites:

"In the beginning, God created the heaven and earth. And the earth was without form, and void; and darkness was upon the face of the deep. And the Spirit of God moved upon the face of the waters. And God said, Let there be light; and there was light. And God saw the light that it was good. Genesis 1:1–4

This is the beginning of the story from which my Mom took my name. She loved a good story. She cared for metaphor as if it were one of her ferns or flowers and was a gifted gardener who knew how to plant, tend, and grow. In the story of my real life, my mom was a steady light. For me, the world feels a little dimmer with her absence. However, I know she isn't really gone. I can see her in the faces of my sisters, and I will feel her joy every spring when all the flowers she left behind bloom again. She taught me to love with my hands in the earth. She taught me to love And so, in many ways, she's always part of me too. I remember once, in the middle of a dry winter, when everything seemed dead, she told me to look up. There was a blue jay sitting upon a bare tree branch.

She taught me to look up, to see beauty, to live. I say these things in the name of Jesus Christ, amen."

Anna hugs Eve as they pass. She looks out and sees that Mary sat Matt strategically behind the Clark boys, who were all well over six feet tall. She smiles, places her right hand close to her collar bone as if its weight might slow her racing heart.

"I loved my mom more than I've ever loved anyone, except my girls and myself. You see, I'm the baby and, as such, have assumed the world should endlessly revolve around me. Also, my mom named me after a prophetess—further inflating my ego." Laughter. "Unfortunately, my life did not follow the pre-scribed plan. I was recently divorced, and she helped me begin the work of rebuilding. While I worked to start a business that will support us, she read to my girls every night, cooked us dinner, and did the dishes. So, she was a good mother and grandmother. She was also an interesting and interested person. She was finally getting a chance to finish her botany courses to complete her B.S. in botany and go on for her M.S. in Ecology. It was a goal that I know was really important to her, and she didn't give up. She never gave up on anything, including me. I'm grateful for her big, open heart. Regardless of my tendency toward self-centeredness, even selfishness, she taught me to look outside of myself and see the beauty around me. She taught me to see God in the fabric of being in every human face and in the rich texture of this world." Anna paused. "That was my mom. I'll miss her every day."

When she looks up, Jake smiles at her, standing behind the last row, his arms folded.

She smiles back and says,

"I guess we're going sing 'Give Said the Little Stream' one of mom's favorite primary songs, and my daughter Honey will say the closing prayer?"

Roxcy nods. As soon as the prayer ends, Mary's on her feet. Aunt Violet is in the back row. She turns and steps into the aisle but all the kind people block her way. All those familiar faces their hands stretched toward her in attempts to offer comfort. She sees her aunt move toward the table, *maybe she'll stay.* Maybe. She tries to get Roxcy's attention, but Roxcy has her back turned. She's talking to Elder Holland, a member of the twelve apostles who served, for a time, as the bishop of their ward.

George would start name dropping, and Roxcy would try to distract Elder Holland by telling a charming story.

"Excuse me, just for a minute," Mary says, trying to get Eve's attention.

"Evie!"

Eve looks at her over her shoulder and Mary motions for her to come.

"Everything okay?"

"Aunt Violet, I think she was on the back row. Short gray hair and a black dress. Can you see? I mean, see if you can find her."

"I'll try."

"Thank you. Thank you, Eve. I'm so sorry, Brother Weist, you were saying . . ."

Eve makes her way through the crowd back toward the hedges, around the crowd. There's an older woman in a black dress suit. Her back slightly curves, as if her body has begun to fold in on itself. She has very short white hair.

"Excuse me!" Eve yells. She waves her arm, and the woman turns.

While trying to listen to Brother Weist explain the intricacies of the afterlife as he understands them, Mary's attention wanders to Anna, Matthew, a younger man with brown hair. She sees Matthew putting on his regular show. Who was he still trying to fool here where everyone knows what he did? The other man stands close to Anna, looking at her now and then. He seems completely uninterested in what Matthew is saying. Eve smiles.

"Well, it was nice of you to come," Anna says. She turns and looks at Jake, slightly unshaven. He's combed his hair. "Are you hungry, Jake? There are sandwiches."

"Sure," he holds out a hand to Matthew. "Nice to meet you. Good luck with your writing."

Matthew flashes a wide smile and opens his mouth to say something, but Anna turns away. She calls, "Come on Honey and Lula. Say goodbye to your dad, and let's get a little food in you."

Roxcy taps Mary on the shoulder. "Can I borrow her for one minute? Excuse us, just for a minute."

"I didn't see him. He wasn't here, was he?"

"Who?"

"The cousin."

"No, no, he didn't come. But I think Aunt Violet did."

"What?!? Did you talk to her?"

"No, too many people. I sent Eve to see—come on, Eve's right there."

As they approach her, Eve turns toward them.

"What a strange day. Beautiful and strange." The light is behind her, and her sisters have to shield their eyes to see her face.

"What?" they say together.

"Strange," she repeats. "Aunt Violet doesn't like crowds. She sends her condolences and her love. She said she came because she loved mom and never understood why mom stopped talking to her."

Mary and Roxcy glance at each other.

"Do you know?"

"Yes, I don't want to go into it right now."

"Okay. I got her number. She wants to have us all up for dinner soon. Her children are all grown and have big families. I guess they all go to their house for dinner on Sundays. She mentioned her oldest was just called as a bishop."

"Oh." Roxcy says.

Mary puts her hand to her stomach

"Are you all right?" Eve says.

"Maybe we should start cleaning up?" Mary turns.

Roxcy quickly changes the subject.

"People haven't even started leaving yet, Mary. Although I wish Matt would leave. I wish he wouldn't have come. He's unbelievable, isn't he? I hope Anna's bringing the girls home to the cabin. Have you two seen the Torontos yet? They're as cute as ever, completely white hair, but cute as ever. He's still calling her his sweetheart. Go sit down someplace where people can find you. I'll get sandwiches. Go! Sit! Save me a seat."

They watch Roxcy walk over smiling, gathering plates. Anna talks to a young man neither of them knows. Roxcy sees him and stops. She walks over and says hello, hugs him looking at Anna, then back to him. Anna walks over to her girls.

"Who is that with Anna?" Mary says.

"You should ask her, but I think his name is Jake."

"The one who helped Roxcy?" Mary lifts her eyebrows.

"Yes," Eve laughs and lets the silence settle back between them. The sun moves across the midpoint of the clear September sky, a deep settling blue. The warm light like something solid and sure. She feels the warmth on her arm and closes her eyes.

"Are you really doing OK?" She says.

Mary sighs, "Oh, I will be fine. How about you, Evie?"

Eve leans her head on Mary's shoulder.

"I am."

And there was the evening and the morning, the sixth day.

The melted snow leaves behind the smell of leaves, wet and decomposing. Leaves still clinging to the aspens changed from light yellow to a deep gold. The men have come and gone. George brought their mother's ashes, set them on the mantel above the fireplace and they took all the boxes away. Now the cabin belongs only to Anna and her girls. Mo stayed behind to take Honey, Lula, and Fred, out for a walk. Eve knows how Mo will stop and squat close to the ground to name whatever fading flowers he finds. She thinks of the way, when one aspen seems to die, new shoots take its place. She's told her sisters about the miscarriages, loss after loss, the breakdown and the end of their trying for a baby. As they eat the ham sandwiches on Roxcy's homemade bread, the room seems to hold the weight of what might have been and relief of what is: the four of them here, the grace of having shared all they have, and missing her together.

Mary chews her sandwich slowly, counting each time her teeth come together. When she reaches forty, she swallows. She glances at Anna and smiles. She let her know that she will come each week and take her girls to church. They can sit on the same row they sat on with Grandma. She will bring snacks and something to color. She will whisper to them about the bread and water, how it is a symbol of the deep, wide love Christ personified, and how the sacrament is like a new start every week. They can all have lunch together after. She feels grateful to have thought of it, to have found a way to help her baby sister. She likes that Anna will have a break, and she will fill a gap in some small way for her nieces. Satisfying, like balancing an uneven equation.

Anna's still a little weepy after Mary's generous offer. And confused by the relief that she feels mostly okay about her girls going to church. She had resisted that part of the divorce agreement, but with Mary, who looks so much like their mom, it's not so bad. And they won't be outsiders. Of course, she'll have to unwind a lot of the nonsense they learn after get home each week, but she smiles back at Mary, grateful.

The room is spacious with the boxes gone, and Roxcy feels an odd relief, almost joy, at the transformation. It is right that the space is Anna's now. Her sister has enough to juggle without worrying about a mortgage. And maybe she and Pete can cook her and her girls one warm dinner each week, something easy to reheat. It would be a way she could reconnect with him and help out. She might buy her some new dishes for the kitchen too. The ones she saw on their last trip to Mexico bright blue with yellow hens. Anna will love them.

Eve says, "Look."

And they follow her gaze out the window. The sunlight permeates the grove and falls through the windows, bright and trembling. Eve pushes her chair back. She walks to the entry and pulls a thick, cabled sweater from one of the hooks, finds her mother's green rubber boots in the closet and slips them on her feet. She walks to the mantel and carefully lifts the smooth container that holds their mother's ashes, walks back, and opens the front door. She turns.

"Are you coming?"

Eve steps out into bright haze. They leave their half-eaten sandwiches and bowls of soup on the table. Without thinking they follow her down the familiar path, feel the sun, warm on the back of their necks. The light plays around the edges of their hair in misty halos. The aspen trees still watch. Their vertically-stacked black eyes note the increased length of their legs, witness the strands of gray in their hair, see the parenthetical lines around the edges of their smiles. It takes ten minutes of walking, of listening to each other's breath mix with the breath of the breeze that makes the light flutter. Light and shadow move across their backs. Their feet slosh through mud puddles. The grove opens into the small meadow. Their mother's untended garden. Her ferns on the floor of the groves turn to rust along the edges of their green leaves. The bodies of wildflowers lay smashed and wilted to the ground. But they know in the spring the meadow will blossom again, fill with Queen Anne's lace, golden yarrow, wild rose, and iris. They stand in the midst of memory. Their eyes, past and present, see the outcropping of rock where they spent summers playing pirates and keeping watch for bears and mountain lions that never appeared. Where mom sat just below on the blanket, her hair held back by the blue bandanna, large round black sunglasses shading her eyes, always a book in her hand: a field guide about local birds or flowers, a small worn book of poetry, or a small set of scriptures. Her voice reading aloud about the western meadowlark, hushing them to listen for its clear song. Her voice talking about the way a fallen tree trunk becomes a home for chipmunks, moss and ants. A poem about grass being a prayer, another about wandering roadsides and fields, another about the sky, scriptures where trees clapped their hands, everything melting into everything else. Those midsummer nights, when the air still turned cold, when they lay on their backs, their sleeping bags on top of a tarp, and attempted to count the stars. She showed them the swan and the eagle and taught them to close their eyes and feel the moonlight on their eyelids. When she said, "you see? when that light touches your skin, you know you're made of stardust." and their eyes grew too heavy to hold open, and they floated into sleep, full of heaven.

The image and echo of shared memory moves between them as thick as the gold afternoon light. Eve stops at the edge where grove meets the meadow lit with red-tipped flames of dying grass. She walks in a slow circle, spilling her mother's ashes onto the familiar earth. The circle closes, and she steps outside. Eve silently passes the box to Anna, who begins to walk her own circle linking her lines to Eve's. The pattern continues with Roxcy and,bfinally, Mary. Like an unlearned sacred rite, they create a round repetition, edges that overlap, their mother, themselves, the grove of trees, a new constellation.

The box is empty, and they stand still for a minute, together. Mary wipes the tears from her cheek and jaw. She replaces the lid. Roxcy comes close, puts an arm around her. Anna holds onto Eve's hand and slips her other into Roxcy's. Without urgency, they turn and walk into the sway of shadow and light along the narrow path through the grove that is all one tree underneath.

[S]he blessed the seventh day and hallowed it, because on it she rested from all the work of [her] creation.

Acknowledgments

Writing never happens in a vacuum, at least not for me. There are too many people to name who helped me write this story, including all the books I've read and loved. But there are a few people I want to thank out loud, my teacher Bobbie Louise Hawkins, who passed away before I got the chance to thank her, but gave me the tools of writing in snapshots and collage. Thanks to my first editor, Phyllis Barber, who provided invaluable editorial suggestions on a first draft of this book. In addition, Amanda Waterhouse, Mary Smith, Andrea Bobotis, Roberta Payne, and Natalee Tucker who read later versions and, likewise, provided generous and important feedback. To Lighthouse Workshop in Denver where I workshopped portions of this story and met Ainsley, Julie, Paulette, and Windy, who are my prose writing group along with Andrea, Roberta and Natalie. You all have been an ongoing source of inspiration and support in this final stretch. My thanks to BCC Press and especially Michael Austin who has championed this story, told exclusively in the voices and through the perspective of Mormon women, and has given his time and his fine editorial eye to *Sylvia*. Thank you to Olivia Pendergast for the beautiful cover painting, and to Christian Harrison for his elegant and striking cover design. There are countless other friends and family who have supported me through this process that I simply don't have room to name, but you know who you are and how you each mean to me. Finally, and most essentially, my family. My mother, Janice Dyer Newey, imperfect as she was, who cared for me and instilled a deep love of literature and language. And my own sisters, Von Schwen, Jeanie Baker, Melody Newey Johnson, and Syl Carson, who are not the sisters in this book, but to whom I owe my life, my healing, and so much love over my entire lifetime. I dedicate this book to you, the women in my immediate family. Thank you to my kids for understanding when I closed the door and yelled for them to go ask dad, for loving books, and loving me. I love you too. You have been and are my best teachers. Finally, Jonathan Warner, there are no words. You've read and reread every version of this story over the years. You've offered endless edits, encouragement, and support. For short periods, you've willingly taken on all of childcare and housework to create space and time for me to write and in the long run you've been my partner, my love, and my dearest friend.

TWILA NEWEY holds a B.A. in English from Brigham Young University and an M.F.A. in Writing and Poetics from The Jack Kerouac School of Disembodied Poetics at Naropa University. Writing *Sylvia* led her from fiction to poetry. In 2019 she was a finalist for the Coniston Prize at Radar Poetry and won honorable mention in the JuxtaProse Poetry Contest. Her poems also appear in many journals including *Summerset Review*, *Rust & Moth*, and *After the Pause*. She also reads poetry for *Psaltry & Lyre*. Twila was raised Mormon and spent her childhood wandering the Wasatch Mountains near Provo, UT. She now lives in the San Francisco Bay Area with her husband, Jonathan Warner, and their four children.

Made in the USA
Middletown, DE
04 December 2020